A SIN LIKE FIRE
KINGDOM OF BETRAYAL 2

EVERLY FROST

Frost, Everly
A Sin Like Fire

Cover design by Claire Holt with Luminescence Covers
www.luminescencecovers.com

For information on reproducing sections of this book or sales of this book,
go to
www.everlyfrost.com
everlyfrost@gmail.com

In the moments between choices, darkness waits.

CHAPTER 1

My heartbeats are heavy with grief. A furious sorrow threatens to destroy me.

Crimson rain has soaked the white ash at my feet, turning the ground to blood. Droplets cling to my silver hair, mingling with the tears streaking down my cheeks.

The Vandawolf lies dying at my feet.

The unruly strands of his dark-gray hair fall across his face, mingling with his sweat. His eyes are closed, concealing the permanently-amber iris of his left eye that reflects his wolfish soul, while the tip of his single, sharp canine tooth is visible between his lips.

Blood bubbles up around the tooth, slipping down his chin.

His strong legs are folded beneath him, his broad chest tipped to his left so that he's facing me. The crossbow bolt that tore through his right shoulder protrudes from his torso while its tip is angled back into the ash beneath him, propping him up.

His inky-black armor is mangled, bone-deep gashes visible between the broken plates.

Seconds ago, his breathing was ragged.

Now he's so quiet, I fear he will soon stop breathing altogether.

I stand between him and the humans who betrayed him.

High up on the ramparts of the wall that protects the human city from the wasteland surrounding it, metalworkers and carpenters gleam down at me. Their leaders have proclaimed their victory.

Nero, the leader of the metalworkers' guild, and Vincent, the leader of the carpenters' guild, raise their hands to their men in triumph.

Braddock, my former guard, laughs down at me. "Throw down your tools, Asha!" he cries, his ruddy face flushed with victory. "We'll treat you with mercy. I promise!"

His laughter sickens me, but some of my rage is turned inward.

I created the deadly weapons they used against the Vandawolf.

With my own hands, I fashioned the giant crossbow from which they fired the bolt that impales his chest; I forged the harpoon, the net, and the weighted chains, each powerful enough to fire in a flash and take down a monster within seconds. All of which are now aimed at me.

I have a choice to make and only moments to make it: Destroy the humans or save the Vandawolf.

I've vowed to do both, but one must come first.

No matter which path I choose, it will cost me dearly.

I grit my teeth and set my intentions.

Whatever the consequences, no matter the pain my choice brings me, I will not allow the Vandawolf to die.

Raising my hands and spreading my fingers, not once taking my eyes off the men on the ramparts, I take a slow step back, quietly positioning myself in line with the Vandawolf's head.

I lower myself to my knees, as if I intend to surrender, my hands remaining upraised.

"Your tools!" Nero shouts, the men controlling the weapons relaxing a little. "Remove them."

My hammer rests in the belt at my waist. I have two black medallions, one currently curved around my right bicep with the other wrapped neatly around my left palm.

Each medallion is a band of titanium alloy an inch wide and five inches long. Each must be struck with the hammer to awaken its power. Once awakened, the medallions can be turned into any weapon of my choosing.

My medallions are already awake.

I am most dangerous with a medallion pressed to my left palm. In this state, I can transform living matter. It's a skill I discovered by accident.

I've turned monsters to dust and to stone—but only when I was close enough to touch their skin.

I'm deadly to any living thing right now.

Including the Vandawolf.

And now comes the choice that will cost me.

With exaggerated movements, I move my left hand toward my right bicep, as if I'm about to press the medallion from my hand onto my arm and command it to become an armband once more. After that, I would only have to lever

3

both medallions off my right arm, allow them to drop to the earth and, once they're no longer in contact with my body, they will sleep once more.

But that is not my intention.

My weight is toward the Vandawolf. I'm already positioned at his head. In reaching for my bicep, my right arm has lowered near to his left shoulder—the one that's dug into the muck.

Up on the wall, the men behind the harpoon, net, and chains are watching me closely, but they've leaned back a little, visibly relaxing. Not completely, but enough.

I suppose they're so accustomed to seeing me obey commands that they don't even consider that I might be feigning compliance.

It will take them seconds to realign their weapons, which will give me the time I need.

My right hand snakes out and snaps around the Vandawolf's shoulder, my fingernails scraping through the blood and ash on his skin as I wrench him upward and to the left with all my strength. I'm in danger of dislocating his shoulder, but I can't worry about that right now.

The muscles in my legs were already bunched, giving me the momentum I need to heave him up and out of the muck. I lift him high enough off the ground that the bolt's tip comes unstuck, although the bolt itself remains embedded in his chest.

Within seconds, I'm dragging him as fast as I can, plowing backward, more than aware that gravity could push the bolt further down through him, but I don't intend to keep him raised that long.

My destination is the stone monolith five paces to my

left: a giant wolf that rose from the ash in the wasteland only a short time ago this morning, and now rests, chest to the ground, facing outward from the wall.

The Vandawolf and I fought it while it was still alive and I turned it to stone.

There's safety and shelter in front of it.

Up on the wall, the men have snapped to attention, their weapons jolting as they attempt to follow my movements.

Braddock, Nero, and Vincent are all shouting at once, their commands a jumble of sound.

"Stop her!"

"Kill her!"

"Shoot the bitch!"

I want to scream out my rage at them, but I don't make a sound, channeling all of my energy into pulling the Vandawolf with one hand across the sludge, desperately keeping my left fist safely clenched at my side.

I can't touch him with it. Not while the medallion is wrapped around it. It was with this hand that I turned the giant wolf from living flesh to a stone monolith. I did it with a single thought, and I can't risk the damage I could do to the Vandawolf.

If I had more time, I would remove the medallion, but I'm conscious that it's my greatest defense against the weapons that will split the air and cleave and crush me when they fire.

The monolith is so close. The brightness of the sunlight shining around it is a bitter sight since I might not reach it in time.

The Vandawolf is tall and heavily muscled, and even

with the enhanced strength that my tools give me, I'm struggling.

Three paces. Two—

Crack!

The sound of the harpoon's firing mechanism chills my blood.

The shrieking whistle of air around the barbed spear is amplified in my ears.

In that second, my instincts tell me that the men have shot wide of me, but not wide of the Vandawolf.

If the harpoon hits him, it will end him.

No!

My left hand flies out into the path of the oncoming harpoon and my right knee slips beneath the Vandawolf's left shoulder so he doesn't drop to the ground.

My palm is raised to meet the harpoon's barbed tip, a defensive move that is pure instinct and defies the weapon's deadly nature.

The harpoon will tear through my hand before it rips apart my upper body and spears through the Vandawolf's chest, binding us together before it plants its barb into the rain-soaked earth.

I count my remaining time in this world in the space of a heartbeat, but I can't regret my actions.

The Vandawolf and I were bound from the moment we first met. Our end should be the same.

The harpoon's tip hits my hand.

Power blasts from my palm, through the medallion resting against it, and outward into the harpoon.

I sense the rush of energy through my body, down my arm, and into the oncoming metal.

The melodic *clang* of metal meeting metal rings in my ears as clearly as the sound of my hammer when I forged the iron that made this harpoon and bent it to my will.

It happens so fast that the command I mentally scream doesn't register within my thoughts until the harpoon transforms in an explosion of movement.

Shield.

The harpoon's tip wraps around my hand, a wide band folding over the top of the medallion, taking the shape of a handle. At the same time, the harpoon's shaft bursts outward, as if the metal is water and I stomped my foot into a puddle of it.

Within a blink, it evens out and extends into a shield that stretches all the way up past my face and all the way down to the ground where I kneel. It's wide enough to cover my width, along with part of the Vandawolf's body where the metal curves outward.

The impact of the movement jolts me backward through the muck, but my right hand tightens reflexively around the Vandawolf's shoulder and my leg digs into the ground beneath him, keeping him elevated.

I'm now on one knee in the ash, the metal shield held upward in my left hand.

I gasp for breath, my eyes wide, my heartbeat erratic.

Relief courses through me—along with disbelief—but when I close my eyes for the briefest moment, I sense the tingle of magic within the metal handle I'm now gripping.

I forged the harpoon. I heated the iron in crimson coal and spent hours hammering my power into it before fashioning it into the shaft and barb.

My only explanation is that the metal remembered me.

Another Blacksmith may well have been more successful at setting the metal's final form into the harpoon's shape, but it was my first time forging anything.

It seems my inexperience has saved my life.

I don't second-guess it.

Ramming the shield into the open ground so hard that the metal twangs, I use it to cover my final steps to the monolith, hurriedly catching hold of the Vandawolf's left shoulder once more and wrenching him behind the stone barrier before the men can get another shot off.

They still have another crossbow bolt, along with the net and chains, but it seems they're smart enough not to waste them on our disappearing forms. Once fired, they have to come down here to retrieve them.

The giant wolf came to rest in such a position that its front legs and paws are curved in front of it, leaving a wide gap between them, but also forming two thigh-high barriers on each side. Anyone who comes after us will have to travel around the wolf and its front legs to get to us.

In the distance, Braddock gives a frustrated roar, which mingles with the shouts from Nero, Vincent, and the other men.

Pulling the Vandawolf the final steps into the shelter provided by the wolf's body, I maneuver him carefully onto his right side to keep the bolt from doing any further damage. It's a difficult task one-handed and I only achieve it by using my knees to keep him elevated.

Finally crouching at his back, I position myself facing outward, just as he is, so I can see any threats coming our way.

If only that meant we were safe.

I've bought myself time, but not certainty.

We may be shielded from the humans for the immediate future, but they won't remain idle indefinitely. I have no doubt they'll be debating the merits of sending men down to hunt us. Or they could simply wait for when I'm forced to step beyond the safety of the wolf's body.

Meanwhile, the Vandawolf is bleeding out with every passing second.

His armor is made of interlocking plates, and I had already pulled some of them away, leaving his injuries plain to see. The crossbow bolt would have killed him if it had impaled his left shoulder closer to his heart. The other gashes had been inflicted by the giant wolf before I turned it to stone, and on their own, those wounds were already life-threatening.

My left fist presses to my heart as I face the horror of his injuries. I try to stifle the rage and fear that's rising within me, but the medallion only magnifies it. Again, I consider removing the black band from my hand, but again, I dismiss the thought. I can't afford any delay in my ability to defend myself.

If I die, the Vandawolf dies.

My hand rests on his upper shoulder and I can't stop myself from shaking.

My medallions allow me to see the flame of the wolf's soul that burns within him. It's a beautiful predator that appears to me like a silhouette within his body, taking the shape of the amber-eyed wolf that was merged with his body ten years ago.

The wolf's energy usually writhes and burns, but now

it's far too faint. Too subdued. It exudes a terrible sense of acceptance that threatens to break me.

I want it to rage at me, to thrash like it usually does—even to hate me. I want to sense its snarling mouth and slashing claws. I would take its anger because it would mean that it's alive. That the Vandawolf is fighting to live, but instead...

It appears ready for death.

Which means the Vandawolf is, too.

The energy around him is fading, so muted now that it's almost imperceptible. Just as his breathing has become far too quiet.

I swallow my sob, trying to choke back my grief, trying to stop my hot, angry tears.

He told me to leave. He told me to go with my family and take my freedom.

I asked him why he would give us our freedom after all this time, and he told me what I'd already known in my heart to be true:

"Love is more powerful than hate and fear combined."

Now, he needs help that I have no skill to give.

Even the human healers wouldn't be able to save him from this.

My sister, Tamra, is his only chance, but she will be hours away by now, traveling east with our brother, her twin, Gallium, and the human man, Thaden Kane, who was transformed against his will by a Blacksmith, just as the Vandawolf was.

How can I keep the Vandawolf alive long enough to reach Tamra?

Even if I keep him alive, how can I get him across this wasteland without being killed by the men on the wall?

I have nothing with which to bind his wounds, other than the shirt beneath my armor, and that would barely make it around his broad chest.

"I'm sorry," I whisper, reaching for his face, my left hand coming close to brushing his cheek before I jolt backward, reminding myself how much I could hurt him.

With these medallions—

My thoughts stop, my expression falling blank, as I focus on the metal wrapped around my left hand where it hovers so close to his pale cheek.

It's metal that I can command into any shape I need.

A cold chill passes through me.

I've never dared to touch the Vandawolf while I was carrying my awakened medallions; I've always fought the impulses that tempted me to breach the gap between us and explore what could happen.

My tools—my hammer and medallions—once belonged to the Blacksmith, Malak, who enslaved the humans in this city for thirty years.

Like Malak, I'm left-handed.

No other tools ever worked for me.

But Malak's cold malice lives within these tools, an insidious force that creeps within my mind and threatens to take root within my heart, tainting my thoughts and my intentions.

It was Malak who created the Vandawolf. When he merged the Vandawolf's human body with the soul of a wolf, some of Malak's Blacksmith magic also transferred to the Vandawolf.

Blacksmith magic is drawn to itself.

Fiercely and irrevocably.

Just as I'm drawn to the Vandawolf now, fighting not to lower my left hand to his face, wrap my fingers around his jaw, and close the gap between us.

The humans might wish to kill the Vandawolf, but I could do much more harm to him than to give him death.

I'm on a knife's edge as I fight the cruelty that surges through my mind and body, fight the terrible thrill, the awful impulses that I've struggled so hard to deny.

Mold him to your will.

Make him yours.

The battle within me is harder now because those terrible thoughts bring hope.

I can use this power to save him.

I have no other choice.

It's this or let him die.

If this is yet another choice that costs me, so be it.

But first, I need to remove the bolt from his body.

I clamp my right hand on his upper shoulder, repositioning my current kneeling position so that the left side of my left leg supports his back and I can lean over him to reach with my left hand for the crossbow's shaft where it enters his body. The tip, where it is at his back, now extends across the air in front of my knees, protruding by a whole foot.

I have to break the shaft near the entry or exit wound so that I only have to pull it a short way to remove it. Otherwise, I'll have to push the entire length of the bolt through his body.

Wrapping my left hand around the bolt, just in front of the entry wound, I close my eyes and focus on my power.

I mentally reach for the same surge of energy that rushed through me when the harpoon came into contact with my hand.

Then I clench my fist as far as I can around the bolt and send a command through the medallion, ordering the bolt's metal to soften and pull apart.

The metal groans, a low, creaking sound in the near-silence that has fallen around me.

Otherwise, the bolt doesn't react.

My forehead creases in confusion. The harpoon changed in an instant. I created this bolt in the same way I made the harpoon. Surely, it should respond to my commands.

I press my hand harder around it, willing it to obey me.

Break!

It resists, creaking and groaning in the quiet.

Frustration billows within me because I can sense the thread of magic still alive within this metal. It's enough that I should be able to command it one last—

My heart sinks and my eyes widen with realization.

Oh, no.

Thaden helped me create these weapons. When his human body was merged with the soul of a dragon, he was left with bronze scales across his right shoulder, up the side of his neck, and down to his waist. The scales covered his right arm and hand. Because of that, he is able to safely handle my medallions with that hand.

Not only that, but the Blacksmith magic that was left within him when he was transformed provided a well of power he could access.

By wrapping one of my medallions around his right palm, he was able to use an ordinary hammer to transfer the power from his body, through the medallion, and into the metal he forged.

I made the first crossbow bolt, but he made the second one.

This is the one he made.

It's *his* energy I sense within it.

I will never forget the moment Thaden accidentally touched me when the medallion was wrapped around his hand. A blast of heat, of dragon's fire, lashed through me and I sensed the dragon's pain and rage in its final moments. Its light had turned dark. *That* is the energy I sense in this bolt.

Which would explain why it isn't answering my commands. This metal doesn't recognize my power. It may as well be any other lump of iron that requires forging in crimson coal and hammering until it obeys me. If it were organic material, living matter, it would be a different story.

Damn! Hot tears burn behind my eyes as I accept the fact that I'll have to push the bolt all the way through the Vandawolf's body.

Again, I have no choice.

I steady my breathing and count myself lucky that the Vandawolf is unconscious.

Reaching as far left along the shaft of the bolt as I can, I grip it tightly on that side, preparing to push with my left hand while I steady it on this side with my right.

I harden my heart and clench my stomach muscles, while forcing myself to breathe evenly as I push the bolt slowly and carefully. Along the way, I stop and reposition my hand until I can reach the base of the shaft, wrapping my palm flat against it.

My breathing grows more rapid with every bit of progress, but it's not because of the awful process.

The closer the end of the bolt gets to the entry wound, the closer my left palm draws to the Vandawolf's chest.

The closer reality comes.

Finally, I'm half an inch away from pressing my powered hand to the Vandawolf's skin.

It's at that moment that I pick up the commotion in the distance; the creaking of the portcullis on the far side of the gate in the wall.

The humans must have decided to come out to hunt me.

Even if I thought the Vandawolf would survive longer, my time for choosing is at an end.

Thaden himself said to me: *You have to fight cruelty with cruelty.*

With that thought, I stop fighting the malice in my tools and allow it to cloak my heart and shield me from my choices. Oh, my guilt and fears will rage back at me when I have the chance to remove my tools again—assuming that time ever comes. But for now, my path is set.

Pulling the bolt through with my right hand, I allow my left palm to connect with the Vandawolf's chest.

Power surges through me, so much power from both his body and mine, striking and clashing so hard that my head spins.

If the Vandawolf were at his full energy, I'm sure I wouldn't be able to breathe right now.

But it's the wolf's confusion that hits me the hardest, the

question I sense from it, breaking through the cold shield I've welcomed around my heart.

Why would I do this when I know it's the last thing he would want?

To keep him alive but wrapped in metal that may as well be barbs against his skin?

Far better to allow him to die than to inflict this torture on him.

I remember the first time the Vandawolf held me on Malak's enormous anvil—a titanium alloy table that had soaked up all of Malak's brutality, all the screams and all the horror he'd inflicted. I remember the agony I'd felt when I was exposed to so much pain, but the Vandawolf roared at me: *"Do you think it hurts you more than it hurts me? Do you think I don't feel everything?"*

Hot tears leak from my eyes because my resolve is complete.

To save him, I will become the monster.

My battle now is to control the commands, to cut through the mess of desire and guilt, and focus on what I need to achieve.

Cover the entry wound.

Spread out across his chest and fill the gashes like streams.

The medallion obeys me far too easily, liquifying and spreading across his skin from the point of origin on my palm. The metal in the medallion is capable of expanding in size exponentially, this single band forming daggers, spears, and swords, although I've never fully tested how far it can stretch.

As far as it needs to, it seems.

All too willingly.

As soon as it covers the wounds on his chest, filling the gaps and halting the bleeding, I continue pulling the bolt through the rest of his body. Again, slowly. Ignoring the distant sounds of marching boots that are muffled behind the still-closed outer gate. Commanding the medallion as I continue to work.

Spill through his body.

Attach to his organs.

Fill the spaces.

"Become him," I whisper. "Become new muscle, new sinew, new bone."

I sense the metal fusing and bonding, becoming hard where it needs to be hard and flexible where it needs to be flexible, mimicking and replicating the broken parts of his shoulder and chest.

Finally, I pull the bolt clear at his back, sending a quick command to the remaining unused metal in my medallion.

Cover the exit wound!

The titanium responds, pouring out across his skin so quickly that only a single drop of blood slides down the Vandawolf's back before the metal hardens and the exit wound is plugged.

The flow of blood has stopped.

The black metal solidifies once more, taking on the outline of a splash of liquid across the back of his shoulder.

I lift my left hand from his chest, my palm now bare.

The medallion is now part of him.

Rivulets of molten metal have adhered to his chest, a film of titanium filling all of his wounds, mimicking flesh and muscle and skin. Metallic streams that glisten in the morning sunlight.

He is a patchwork of cold metal, and it is my doing.

I leave him on his side, not wanting to upset the sealing process in case it's ongoing, but I carefully slip my arms across his chest and back, my cheek pressing to his upper shoulder.

His heartbeats are weak at my ear. Sweat bathes his brow. Shivers are coursing through him, little ones, although I'm certain they'll only get worse.

But he's breathing more deeply, and the blood loss has stopped.

He's alive. For now.

It's a consolation I repeat to myself.

My mind and heart are no longer as protected from my emotions as they were only moments ago, because the medallion on my right bicep is nowhere near as powerful in that location as it would be if I pressed it to my left hand.

I can't stop the groan of regret rising within me as my face brushes the edge of the black metal now fused to the Vandawolf.

It is cruel and unkind, and it stings and aches and punishes.

And now I have forced it on him.

The consequences will be mine to face.

CHAPTER 2

I've barely raised my head when the sound of the outer gate opening reaches me.

The humans are coming out.

I take quick stock of my weapons. My hammer is clipped to my belt and I have one medallion currently positioned around my right bicep. I can choose to wrap that medallion around my left palm, but that will only benefit me if I can get up close to the humans and make physical contact.

Otherwise, I can transform it into any weapon I want.

The Vandawolf has two daggers, both of which are sheathed at his waist. I can't transform those, but I can certainly use them.

Of course, I also need to think past the fight—assuming I survive it. I need to get the Vandawolf out of here, but he's too big for me to carry over my shoulders. Even with my enhanced strength, I don't have the size to support him.

My focus flashes to the landscape around me. The wasteland stretches for at least another three hundred feet until it reaches the edge of the Sunken Bog, which sits on the eastern side of the city and extends all the way to the mountains. The ashen ground of the wasteland is dotted with skeletal trees, their branches splattered with blood-rain, while the bog is wet and marshy, filled with large, rotted trees and insects. Even without rain, the ground within the bog sucks at everything that touches it, trying to sink and pull it all down.

Somehow, I need to get the Vandawolf to the edge of the bog and then through it to reach the mountain pass, where my family and Thaden will be waiting.

The squelching sounds of boots in the distance tells me that the humans are only now stepping through the gate. The front of the monolith where we shelter is a solid hundred paces from the wall.

They may try to muffle their whispers, but their footfalls will give their location away. Unlike me, they won't be accustomed to moving through this sodden earth. I've trained myself to run through it and I've built up the muscles needed to keep myself from sinking with every step.

The mud will slow them down considerably.

I judge I have at most five minutes before they reach me.

I need to use that time to its fullest extent.

My focus flashes to the shield wedged into the earth just beyond the monolith—to the large surface it provides.

Then upward to the stone wolf's face.

Protruding from either side of its nose are two tusks that are shiny and smooth and appear as if they're made from black onyx. They're sharp at their pointed ends, but they're also long, thin, and only gently curved—and most importantly, they're unbreakable. Not even my magic could shatter them.

If I can attach the tusks to each side of the shield, they can act as poles.

If I can turn the shield into a stretcher, I can transport the Vandawolf on it.

I don't have a moment to waste.

Leaning back from the Vandawolf and putting space between us, I press my left hand to my right bicep and cause my last medallion to wrap around my left palm. Then I take hold of my hammer in my left hand too.

I shudder at the immense power now raging through me. Holding both the hammer and the medallion in one hand is like clutching fire.

I can't use this power on the tusks, but I need the extra physical strength it will give me.

Taking a few steps back, while remaining within the shelter of the wolf's chest, I prepare to make the jump up to the tusks high above me.

If I had a longer run-up, I could reach them in a single bound, but not from this close.

I inhale, exhale, and then I leap forward, sprinting the few steps it takes me to reach the monolith's right front leg. Landing neatly on it, I use it to spring higher, stretching for the nearest tusk, my fingers reaching... *reaching*...

My right hand closes around the tusk.

For the briefest moment, I consider using my momentum to swing myself up onto the beast's head, but that position will only expose me to the humans on the wall, so as soon as my hand closes around the tusk, I swing the hammer as hard as I can.

My hammer smashes against the beast's face, right where the tusk joins its nose.

Cracks shatter through the stone, chunks dropping across my head and shoulders. I had hoped that my body weight would help, but the tusk doesn't immediately break off.

Twice more, I hit it, swinging each time for momentum, before the stone finally gives an ear-splitting *crack!*

My weight does the rest.

Right before the tusk snaps off, I swing myself forward again so my downward trajectory takes me clear of the Vandawolf's vulnerable body on the ground.

Landing smoothly with the long tusk gripped in my right hand, I drop the onyx bone into the ash and immediately go back for the second one.

I leap for the second tusk, springing off the wolf's other leg. My right hand closes around the bone and my hammer strikes at the base of the tusk in two hard, rapid hits. My muscles strain, but I put everything into it.

This time, the tusk snaps off immediately.

I plummet to the ground again, this time landing beside the Vandawolf, my boots sinking into the muck with the force of my landing.

Above me, the wolf's face now bears cracks and is gouged inward on both sides of its nose where its tusks once were. I suppose I'm lucky the tusks weren't part of its skull or I never would have been able to break them off. But these monsters are a grisly mix of all the animals that were killed on this land over the course of decades: boars, deer, bears, wolves—even mice and lizards.

Dropping the second bone to the ground next to the

Vandawolf and latching my hammer to the belt around my waist again, I quickly check his breathing.

He's still stable.

Proceeding more carefully now, I prowl around the front of the monolith's left leg in the direction of the shield I left in the ash.

It's close enough that I will be able to crouch and grab it without risking being hit by the second crossbow bolt. I may even get a look at the men in the distance, although retrieving the shield will certainly get their attention.

I'll need to move fast.

Crouching low, I dive behind the shield, wrench it up out of the drying ash, and launch myself back behind the monolith.

In that split second before I reach safety again, I assess the humans coming toward me.

There are eight of them. All men I recognize but never interacted with directly before. Five are metalworkers, three are carpenters. They're still fifty paces away.

I didn't spot Braddock, Nero, or Vincent among them and I'm not surprised. They won't risk their lives facing me.

The men shouted when they saw me, but I've moved at a flash, and I'm already well behind the monolith.

Resting against the stone wolf's leg, I take a moment to process what I saw.

Those men may not be experts at moving through the wasteland, but they've been smart.

They aren't wearing heavy armor that would weigh them down, and they're spread out so they won't get in each other's way.

What's more, in the moment that I glimpsed them, it

looked like four of them were in the process of splitting off and heading around the other side of the monolith.

They must plan to converge on me from both sides.

But it's the weapons they're carrying that really give me pause. Each man had a metal crossbow already loaded with a bolt.

The shaft of each bolt looked like it was made of iron, but the tips glistened with some sort of crimson substance.

I don't know what it is, but it gleamed in the sunlight as darkly as the titanium now crisscrossing the Vandawolf's chest.

The hairs on the back of my neck are standing up, my instincts telling me that the substance on their weapons is dangerous, although I can't pinpoint why.

Along with a bundle of crimson-tipped bolts I saw across each man's shoulder, they're also carrying short-handled axes, the kind used to chop wood at close range.

I may be uncertain about the nature of the bolts, but I know exactly what the axes are for.

They're to cut off my hand.

That's all it takes to render a Blacksmith powerless. Without my left hand, I will never be able to access my power again.

The Vandawolf discovered this vulnerability on the night he killed Malak, and it didn't remain a secret afterward.

These men must plan to shoot me from a distance with their crossbows and then remove my hand at the first chance they get.

The only saving grace is that none of them will be trained warriors. They may have spent the last ten years working with metal and wood, building up their physical strength, but they weren't part of the city's defensive team, the Wasteland Warriors—who are loyal to the Vandawolf.

Well, I assume the Warriors are still loyal, because I didn't see any of them among the traitors on top of the wall. Each of the Warriors trained personally with the Vandawolf, and each is a skilled fighter.

I can only imagine how Braddock, Nero, and Vincent got the Warriors to stand aside. At best, they were bribed or threatened. At worst, they're dead.

I've taken longer than I should have to catch my breath.

I judge I have no more than three minutes before the humans will reach me, and I can't waste a second of them.

Working at a frenzy now, I drop the shield onto the ground near the tusks, placing it so that its curved inner side faces upward.

I pray there's enough of my magic left within this metal that I can command it to alter its shape one last time.

Pressing my powered hand and the medallion wrapped around it against the metal, I ask the shield to elongate, picturing within my mind the longer, narrower shape I need it to be, along with the ledge I need it to form at one end, where the Vandawolf's feet can rest.

The metal creaks and groans, warning me that its malleability is coming to an end. It responds much more slowly this time—seconds that will surely cost me—finally stretching outward and curving up at the bottom.

Before it stops, I wrap my fist around the handle in its center and ask it to break off. The metal comes away in my hand, but it leaves a knob behind.

I grimace, snatch my hammer from my waist, and smack it against the metal, flattening it as fast as I can.

The clanging sounds ring out around me and I sense the approaching men pausing. It's sensible of them to stop, since they can't be sure what I'm doing or planning, and their caution works in my favor, giving me extra moments to prepare.

I snatch up one of the tusks, position it on one side of the shield, and hammer the edge of the shield around it. It takes longer than I would like, since the shield's metal fights back, and it's only my increased physical strength that allows me to succeed.

I repeat with the other side, my muscles screaming at me while the *clang* of metal continues to ring out around me.

Sweat pours down my face, but I don't stop until I've attached both tusks. Then I draw back, my chest heaving.

I may have created the stretcher, but the Vandawolf and I aren't going anywhere until I've dealt with the humans.

And I still have to somehow figure out how to make it across the exposed wasteland without the humans on the wall killing or trapping us with their remaining weapons.

Hooking my hammer to my belt again, I retrieve the two daggers from the Vandawolf's waist.

Then I drag him as quickly as I can back against the monolith's chest. Once there, I turn him onto his side and position the stretcher in front of him, using it again like a shield, laying it long-side down and angling it back so that it leans across him. It's wide enough that it touches the monolith, forming a triangular barrier that will protect his head, chest, and upper legs from any crossbow bolts fired at him.

I'm sweating with the effort, the heat of the morning sun reaching me even in the shadows, but I don't stop until I'm certain he's as concealed as he can be.

Turning back with a dagger now clutched in each hand, I take a moment to stare down at the large crossbow bolt that had impaled him and then defied my power. If I could command that metal, I could turn it into a second shield.

Seeking Thaden's help seemed wise at the time, but that decision is now coming back to haunt me.

Still, the bolt could come in handy as an oversized spear. It's unwieldy, but I nudge it to the inside of the monolith's right leg, where I can grab it if I need it.

The men's footfalls are much closer now, but they haven't reached me yet, and in those few remaining moments, I prepare myself for what's coming.

For the last ten years, I defended these humans against the monsters that rose in the wastelands.

If I thought they would simply let me leave, then I could allow them to live.

I exhale a deep sigh.

I've been wearing my final medallion on my left palm for several minutes now and in that time, I've stopped distinguishing its cold malice from my own intentions.

In the fight ahead, I can have no mercy.

Mercy will only result in my death and the Vandawolf's end.

I plant my feet, ready the Vandawolf's daggers, and count my heartbeats as the approaching footfalls draw closer.

CHAPTER 3

A man appears on each side of the monolith.

They move fast, dropping to a knee and aiming their crossbows at me.

It's a reckless move since they could shoot each other.

Except that the man on my right adjusts his aim, pointing his crossbow to his left, at the monolith behind me. I don't miss the way he's searching the ground, no doubt looking for the Vandawolf.

At the same time, two other men join him, each taking a knee, also aiming their crossbows at the monolith.

Maybe their plan is for the men on my right to take out the Vandawolf while the men on my left try to kill me. Their crossbows won't get through the shield I placed across the Vandawolf, and I don't intend to let them get close enough to stab him.

The man on my left is already firing at me.

The bolt flies straight and true, its crimson tip glittering in the sunlight.

The metalworkers may have struggled to create weapons large enough to take down monsters, but they're skilled at creating regular weapons for use in combat.

I drop and roll, narrowly evading the bolt. It hits the earth only inches away from my previous location.

The man who fired it is hurriedly reloading his crossbow. At the same time, the three other men who were approaching on that side appear beside him, quickly fanning out around him and shooting wildly.

A new rain of bolts flies toward me. I duck and roll again, and the bolts hit the earth in my wake.

Thud-thud-thud.

My path has taken me closer to them, although they're all still ten paces away and busy trying to reload.

I'm not about to squander my chance to end them.

From my crouched position, I fling a dagger toward the chest of the man who fired first.

He moves at the last second and it misses his heart, hitting his shoulder instead. The force of my enhanced strength accelerates the dagger's speed and the impact is so immense that it knocks him off his feet. He gives a shout and loses hold of his weapon, scrambling in the mud to pick it up even with the dagger jutting from his shoulder.

I would admire his determination if he weren't my enemy.

My second dagger meets another man's thigh—one of the men who was standing. He drops to the ground with a shout.

Leaping to my feet, I prepare to turn my medallion into a spear.

That's when a volley of bolts fly at me from behind.

The air rushes at my back, and the *whoosh* of metal

makes the hairs on my arms stand on end. My medallion suddenly burns against my skin and it's as if the air is charged.

I don't have time to study the bolts up close, but I'm aware of the *thud* as each hits the ground directly behind me. They're all inches short of hurting me, despite the fact that my back was exposed. Of course, if they'd aimed higher, they might have struck their own comrades, so that could explain why they missed me.

Still, the hairs on my arms and the back of my neck continue to prickle.

There are now seven bolts jutting from the ground near the front of the monolith.

Seven. Each man has fired once and each shot has flown wild.

But... *Where is the eighth man?*

I've kept moving and I'm now five paces away from the nearest man ahead of me. In that time, he has nocked his crossbow and points the bolt directly at my chest.

His finger twitches. He'll fire directly into me, but a command flies through my mind to my medallion.

Spear.

The weapon forms in a flash, its length shooting outward from my palm. As I dive to the left, I ram its tip against the crossbow, disarming the metalworker.

The bolt flies wide, the crimson dust on its tip gleaming like a streak of lightning.

Now, my instincts are screaming at me. A danger I can't identify. Something more than the threat posed by these men. I can't pinpoint exactly what it is, but it's a warning I can't ignore.

Gripping the spear, I give a single command and it returns to the shape of a medallion, wrapping itself once again around my left hand as if it belongs there and nowhere else.

The man I disarmed has thrown himself backward, a defensive move, as he leaps for his weapon.

My leg muscles are bunched, ready to follow him and, at the same time, leap clear of the next volley of bolts from the attackers behind me, when a flash of light draws my attention to the top of the monolith's head.

A carpenter crouches there, balancing precariously on the smooth surface. He's holding a burning brand, the flames licking around the bundle of tinder.

The eighth man.

"Go, go, go!" he shouts.

The other men scatter, including the man with the dagger in his shoulder. The metalworker with the dagger in his thigh is hobbling as fast as he can before one of his comrades grabs him and propels him to go faster. Despite his obvious pain, he manages to cast a grin back at me.

A bolt sits beside my hand where I crouch in the mud.

The dust covering half of the bolt's length glitters at me.

Up close, I can now see that a thin, resin tube has been attached to the side of the bolt and it's filled with the same red dust that covered the tip.

My eyes widen.

It can't be.

Not crimson coal...

Crimson coal is the substance Blacksmiths used for their forge-fires. It was mined in the eastern mountains and hauled down to the city—originally by human workers who were well paid for their labors, then by humans who were forced to work for Malak. Braddock was one of the men forced to work in the mines when Malak ruled this city.

We had recently learned that Nero was hoarding crimson coal in contravention of the Vandawolf's laws.

Somehow, the humans must have found a way to crush it.

Once lit, crimson coal burns extremely hot. So hot, it can blaze for days.

In unskilled hands, it's incredibly dangerous.

But this powdered form of it... And a whole tube of it...

It glimmers at me now from all of the bolts littering the ground around me.

My heart plummets.

Up on the monolith, the eighth man is already hurling the burning brand toward the bolts before he turns and disappears, presumably to slide down the wolf's back.

The brand sails through the air toward me.

My survival instincts tell me to run as far and as fast as I can. Out into the wasteland. Let the force of the explosion knock me away from the center of the blast.

Instead, I turn toward the Vandawolf.

All I have to do is reach him and get behind the stretcher. I can use my last medallion to form a greater shield around us.

I can guarantee our survival. Mine and his.

I *can*.

These thoughts race through my mind as my legs pump and I fly across the sodden earth, pushing myself to run as fast as I can.

Behind me, the fire hits the earth.

There's a moment of silence.

A moment where I'm conscious of the breaths rushing through my mouth, of the ashen earth racing past beneath my feet, of the scent of magic in the air, and of the way the rain is finally evaporating, leaving my surroundings as pure as snow again.

The Vandawolf's location is still five steps away, and in that moment, I know I won't make it to him in time.

Then the world explodes.

CHAPTER 4

A tornado of ash and flames rushes at my back, filling my field of view on both sides.

I throw myself across the remaining space between me and the Vandawolf—the final few steps—my back arching with the speed of my leap.

I hurtle into the stone monolith, attempting to turn my right shoulder to take the impact, sensing the crunch of my own bones.

The fire follows me, an unstoppable force that blows me even harder against the rock.

Instead of falling, the intensity of the explosion pins me there, my back to the stone, for an excruciating moment.

A moment of burning pain that fills my entire body.

I'm trying to send a signal to my medallion, trying to turn my left palm outward, trying to scream for a shield to protect me from the billowing flames.

Form a shield! Please!

Even if I could slide down the stone surface I'm pinned

against, it's too late to seek shelter behind the stretcher. I would have to force its edge away from the stone and that would expose the Vandawolf to the fire. Right now, the stretcher is sheltering his body, and I pray that the flames won't lick around the openings at his head and feet.

Somehow, my left arm is extended into the blaze. My hair flies around me like molten strands of silver. The skin on my outstretched arm gleams like forged metal.

The honeyed scent of crimson coal glides down my throat, as if the air has become syrup.

I'm screaming.

Burning and screaming as waves of power beat across me, causing my thoughts to become incoherent. A jumble of impulses are streaming into my mind from the medallion, and all I want is to survive.

Take control, take control, take control...

Be mine, be mine, be mine...

I stop fighting the cruel malice, welcome its icy embrace, and scream into the fire. *"Be mine!"*

The blaze grows hotter, the syrupy taste in my mouth increases, but then—

The pressure eases and I'm falling.

Finally, I'm falling.

My body weight takes me down toward the stretcher and I have two choices: throw my weight to the side and roll down the stretcher to the scorching-hot ash, or grab the edge of the stretcher and slip between it and the stone.

My intention is to roll down the outside, but my body has other ideas. My left hand snaps down to the tusk at the side of the stretcher, pushing it outward so that I'm falling toward the Vandawolf.

The air around him is startlingly cold, a different kind of burn that beats upward.

Because he's lying on his side, I knock into him, pushing him onto his back before I get my right hand down into the narrow space between him and the rock. My left hand releases the upper edge of the stretcher and it falls back toward me, leaning against my left shoulder.

There's a gap between the stretcher and the stone now—a gap caused by my body in between the two—but that isn't my greatest concern.

Instinctively, my left hand descends toward the Vandawolf's chest and it takes everything in me to avoid making contact.

As my fall comes to an abrupt stop, I find myself balancing on my right hand mere inches above him, my body as stiff as a plank, only the barest contact between my right forearm and his side. My left arm is bent and pressed to my chest.

My ears are buzzing, my head is pounding, and my heart is thumping.

I'm aware of the receding explosion above me, the spiraling cyclone of flame and ash that washes up across the monolith and into the sky. I'm conscious of the amber light flickering across the Vandawolf, lighting up all the dark rivulets of metal threaded across his torso.

The light above me is so bright that I don't cast a shadow over him. No darkness, despite the cold metal I've fused to his body.

My only certainty is that the flames never touched him.

But that's where my relief ends.

As I wait for the explosion to abate, I'm afraid to shift my focus to my arm—to my visible skin. I'm afraid of what I'll see.

Surely, I'm badly burned.

Certainly, these must be my last moments.

I'm merely experiencing a last burst of energy keeping me alive before I'll sink to the Vandawolf's chest and die here. It isn't the worst place to perish.

He once said to me that creatures like me and him rarely have the chance to grow old.

Above me, the amber light is finally fading, leaving behind a darkness that seems to hang over me, but still, I'm breathing.

I force myself to look at my arm and acknowledge the damage.

My right forearm is gray, my skin tarnished like old silver that hasn't been cleaned. My muscles are trembling, but I'm not sure if it's from the effort of keeping myself in this position one-handed or because I'm about to crumble like rust flaking off old iron.

There are no obvious burns and it's far less damage than I was expecting.

I'm suddenly aware of an intense patch of cold against my chest, which seems to be from my left arm.

When I extend that forearm a little, fighting the wobble in my right arm as I try to stay elevated, I'm startled to see that the veins in my left arm are threaded with black.

But my palm...

My eyes widen and I swallow my scream.

The titanium medallion is no longer sitting against my hand.

Its edges have sunk into my flesh, seamlessly fitted to my skin as if it were always a part of me.

No. This can't be!

Panic floods me.

Despite the heat I'm sure I'm about to launch myself into, I push myself away from the Vandawolf, the muscles in my right arm screaming as I use it to propel myself backward. In my frantic rush, I knock the stretcher aside. It falls softly into the ash, kicking up a plume of dust as I throw myself clear of the Vandawolf.

I come to a stop at a crouch in the only clear space between the Vandawolf's feet and the monolith's front left leg.

Through my panic, I'm still aware of my surroundings.

The explosion has abated, but the air is filled with thick smoke. It's so opaque that I can't see farther than a few feet in any direction. It's so bad that I can no longer see the Vandawolf's shoulders and head only a few paces away.

In the distance, farther out in the wasteland, there are brighter spots, hazy and amber. I recognize the locations as belonging to skeletal trees. They must still be on fire, their dry trunks continuing to blaze.

The ash beneath me is hot, but not so much that it burns through the soles of my boots.

An eerie silence has fallen around me, but I find no peace in it.

My focus is only on the medallion.

Frantically, I scratch at it, attempting to dig at its edges, trying to gain purchase so I can peel it off.

Get off! Get off me!

It can't be a part of me now.

I'm digging at my own flesh, drawing blood, gasping for breath as I fail to remove it. I've left red welts around the band and now all I can think about is the way I flung my left hand out into the flames, begging for a shield that never came.

My own scream during the explosion echoes back at me.

Be mine.

Amid my anxiety, there is clarity.

The explosion of crimson coal must have created forge-fire. It's the same fire that was used for centuries by Blacksmiths into which they cast metal, heating and preparing it to be hammered into a new form.

I cast my own hand into the forge-fire. In fact, my whole body was forced into it. And now...

The medallion has become part of me.

Fused to me, even more surely than the streams of metal coursing across the Vandawolf's chest.

Now I don't know what has become of me.

A new wave of fear washes through me as I abandon my attempts to remove the medallion and scratch at the tarnish on my forearms instead.

The tarnish doesn't come off.

I drag at my burnished hair, finding it consistently blackened, as if it's coated in dust that also doesn't come off.

My heart is pounding as I swallow the scream rising to my throat.

It's a cry of fury because with every passing second, my own thoughts are disappearing.

Even my panic is fading as my feelings grow as cold as my skin and so much less like my own emotions.

So much less like *me*.

With every heartbeat, the hatred in the band is smothering the humanity within me and filling me instead with calculated anger.

Too much cruelty floods me, until my shoulders are hunching, my fists are clenching, and my lips are twisting.

I am filled, not with defeat, but with acceptance.

If the malevolence within this medallion is now a part of me, then I will use it to stay alive.

I consider my surroundings with cold eyes and await the dangers coming my way with an even colder heart.

In the distance, I can now hear whispers. The men who attacked me with crossbows seem to be calling to each other, checking that their comrades are still alive.

I identify at least five different voices. Their whispers are quickly joined by calls from farther back—presumably from the wall because I recognize one of the voices as Braddock's.

"Find Asha Silverspun's body!" he roars. "Bring it to me. We will hang it beside the Vandawolf's corpse for all to see."

Calls from the ground acknowledge the order.

Judging by their voices, the men on the ground aren't that far away from me. They must have dived for cover behind the monolith.

But they won't be able to see me. This pall of smoke is so dense and must stretch for at least half a mile in each direction, made worse by the still-burning trees.

I should be choking on the smoke, but for now, it continues to taste like honey on my tongue.

Crimson coal belongs to Blacksmiths.

My brows draw down and my lips twist.

They thought they could destroy me with forge-fire?

Fuck them.

Rising slowly, I listen intently to their footfalls, identifying that the nearest man is now about twenty paces to my left.

I glance back at the Vandawolf. His body is vulnerable now that the stretcher lies in the ash beside him.

I take a moment to consider my chances of maneuvering him onto the stretcher and pulling him away under the concealment of the smoke.

I'm certain I could make it a good distance, but the sound of the stretcher being dragged would attract attention. The men would know I'm alive and they would set upon the Vandawolf where he lies vulnerable on the makeshift bed.

No. Better to attack my enemies while they think I'm dead and escape before more humans are sent down from the wall.

Carefully, I angle the stretcher back up over the Vandawolf, taking my time to ensure I don't make a sound.

Once I'm done, I plant my hand on the monolith's leg and leap over it, landing silently on the other side.

It's only when I touch the ground and rise back up that I'm aware of a stabbing pain in my left shoulder. It has to be the wound I sustained in the fight with the wolf. My armor was split there and the flesh was impaled by the wolf's sharp fur.

I have a higher pain threshold than humans and, until this moment, it was the least of my worries.

Craning my neck to examine it, I find the skin mottled and rough. It looks like the fire licked across the exposed flesh. It must have happened before I got my hand up into the flames.

The wound appears to be cauterized—at least the edge of

it that I can see—but it hurts like the aftermath of a real burn and sends a dangerous signal to my brain.

Pain.

It was only days ago, but it feels like a lifetime, that the Vandawolf warned me Malak's cruelty was strongest when he was hurt.

Well, now *I'm* hurt.

The hatred within the band now fused to my hand intensifies, obliterating every other emotion.

Nearby on the ground is the abandoned crossbow bolt, metal that glows red hot and ready to be molded into a new form, except to achieve that, I will need to hammer it, and hammering will draw attention. What's more, I would need an anvil—or some other hard surface—to hammer against.

The monolith isn't hard enough. I put cracks in that stone with my hammer when I removed the tusks.

I take a step forward, examining my surroundings in case the fire has hardened some part of it. My steps bring me to the edge of the explosion, where I pull up short, my lips parting in surprise.

The blast cut into the ground. Right down to the bones of the earth.

Within the cut, old tree roots writhe like snakes and between them, a glowing mass of dust appears to slowly swirl.

I struggle to breathe as I see for the first time the full extent of the magic that has sunk into this earth, a seething mass that glistens with a kaleidoscope of colors.

It looks almost like oil sitting on top of an iron surface.

Beneath the oily rainbow of energy, I can make out bones.

I glance back at the stone wolf. Monsters like that wolf must have once been real creatures, their bones mutated and given life by the transformation magic I'm now looking at.

Directly below me, I make out the leg bones of what might have once been a four-legged creature. Judging by the shape of its skeleton, it might have been a deer.

I've never seen a real one.

Neither has the Vandawolf. I promised him that if I saw one on my journey beyond the city, I would tell him all about it.

He said: *"Don't waste a second of your freedom."*

I didn't know then that he was trying to send me away forever. To live my life. Make my own choices. Be *free*.

Because of the smoke, I can't see how far the crater stretches, but it doesn't descend too deeply at this edge. Crouching, I dare to hover my left hand above the swirling surface.

It's the same move I use to detect the location of a monster—or, as I discovered earlier this morning, to identify the location of another Blacksmith, since I unwittingly tracked my own sister this way.

Energy leaps up to meet my palm, biting my skin and tingling through the medallion.

It's so much stronger than when there's a buffer of soil covering it.

This energy…

It seems to be constantly building. Gathering. Working on the bones in the ground. A tumult of transformation power.

Currently, it's strengthening around a spot in the near

distance where, undoubtedly, the bones of another animal must lie.

My lips rise upward because I'm certain that another monster will rise from that spot soon enough.

If it forms before the smoke clears, the humans won't see it coming.

I feel no sympathy for them.

This situation is of their own making.

My cold smile broadens.

Whether or not a new monster rises, the men now approaching my location won't be alive to fight it.

CHAPTER 5

As quietly as a wraith, I glide back to my feet.

I've paused for long enough that I've given the men the chance to approach around the side of the monolith to my left. Their footfalls tell me they're moving as a group, but I can't see them yet, which means they can't see me, either.

It sounds like one of the men is limping—no doubt the one I stabbed in the thigh.

"We need to find her body," one whispers.

"We should cut off her hand before we take her body back," another says. "Make sure her power's destroyed."

"Why the fuck are we whispering?" a third asks, speaking more loudly than the first two. "Nobody could have survived that fire. Not even that fucking Blacksmith whore."

I let the insult wash over me. The Vandawolf would visit my bedroom at night and Braddock seemed happy to spread stories about it. Ironically, the Vandawolf only came to me under the cover of darkness when he wanted me to interrogate and kill his enemies. Sadly, that didn't include Braddock. I can't fathom why the Vandawolf kept the ruddy-faced man alive all this time.

Silently, I prowl directly left, staying close to the monolith's front leg, where I'll come up behind the men.

If anything, the pall is growing thicker the longer the trees in the distance continue to burn, so there's no chance they'll see me until I'm upon them.

The only danger is that the new smoke is from wooden branches, not from crimson coal, and I'm certain it will hurt my lungs.

Soon, I won't be able to breathe.

But that time is not now.

I move quickly, listening carefully as I follow in the footsteps of the last man. The group is veering wide of the stone wolf, headed toward the heart of the explosion, which makes sense if they're looking for me since it was the last place they saw me.

The straggler's silhouette becomes visible to me. He's tall with a wiry frame.

It's hard to tell from behind, but he appears to now be wearing a mask tied around his lower face—probably to guard against the smoke. He isn't carrying the holster with extra crossbow bolts and when I check his hands, it appears he's only carrying his axe. The men won't want to accidentally shoot each other while they can't see far and, if they believe I'm dead, they'll think they don't need the extra weapons.

I surge quietly toward the straggler's back, matching the back-and-forth movement of his left arm, mimicking its swing and judging the exact moment I can strike.

His arm sways back.

My left palm brushes his elbow as gently as a breeze. As softly as...

Smoke.

The command flits through my mind, the briefest thought before the man's entire body disintegrates into a puff of white.

It's soundless.

He doesn't shout. His mind wouldn't have had time to register the danger before it became nothing. His body has simply become part of the fog hanging around us.

Not so for his weapon and clothing.

I catch his falling axe but allow his clothing to settle to the ground since it drops so softly.

I crouch and find the material he was wearing around his face: a wet flannel. It will protect me from the wood smoke building in the air, so I quickly wrap it around my nose and mouth, trying to ignore the man's scent lingering on it.

Tipping my head to the side, I take a moment to check for any shouts of alarm before I step over the remainder of his clothing.

The unimpeded sound of movement ahead of me indicates that his friends are none the wiser.

I follow their footfalls in the direction of the crater.

As I glide onward, my heart grows even colder, and my actions feel more distant. The throbbing pain in my left shoulder beats down my arm to the medallion, a constant drip of anger that courses back up to my heart.

I catch the men's whispers.

"Where is the bitch?"

"We should have killed her years ago."

"And the Vandawolf. We deserved better than to be ruled by a fucking animal."

These humans with their false bravado. They're no better than the smoke I will make of them.

A second and third man are walking side by side directly ahead, their silhouettes becoming clearer as I draw nearer to them. They're slightly behind the others, which makes them perfect targets.

Still, I'll need to take them out one by one, which means the others could raise the alarm.

Shadowing their footsteps while I assess their gaits, I calm my breathing and time my attack for the moment one of them looks away from the other, peering into the fog.

"Her body must be up ahead," he says.

I identify his voice as the one who called me a whore.

As he speaks, my left palm brushes the other man's lower back. That man's clothing billows as his body turns to fog, but the weapon at his waist drags the material down faster.

I choose to let the axe fall and it thuds softly onto the ash. Puffs of white dust waft upward around the empty material, but it isn't my focus.

The man who insulted me swings back. His startled eyes meet mine, but my left palm is pressed to his heart.

"Mist," I whisper.

His throat visibly constricts as if he wants to make sound, but already, he is nothing more than fine droplets in the air.

His form is gone. His clothing and axe fall to the earth in soft, swooshing thumps.

I'm intrigued to see that the swirling smoke I made of the other two men wafts in the direction of the crater in the earth, as if it's drawn there.

It probably shouldn't surprise me since, after all, Blacksmith magic gravitates toward itself.

I return my focus to the remaining men and increase my pace.

They must be proceeding in a tighter group, but their footfalls have stopped. By their voices, I judge their position to be right at the edge of the crater.

"Look at that."

"What the fuck?"

I can't be entirely sure if they've halted because of the crater's eerie appearance, although it seems most likely. If they'd heard the falling material of the dead men's clothing, I'm sure they'd be hurrying in my direction.

I'm still gripping the axe of the first man I turned to smoke.

It's a strong weapon. A good weapon. The blade is no doubt crafted by the metalworkers while the handle would be fashioned by the carpenters.

I may not appreciate their allegiances, but I can admire their work—and the effectiveness with which I can use it against them.

Just as they used my weapons against me.

With a silent snarl on my lips, I slip through the smoke, abandoning my quiet approach. The men are too close together for me to take them down individually without detection.

I swing the axe at the back of the first one's neck, my muscles tense, all of my enhanced strength giving me momentum.

The blade cuts clean through.

His body drops to the ground, his knees hitting first and sending the white smoke in the air pluming around him.

I'm not done with him. Still gripping the weapon, I veer sharply to the right. My left hand lands on his shoulder as I race past.

"Stone."

Let him remain there for the humans to see what happens when they try to kill me.

The man to my right shouts, half-turning, trying to leap away from me, but his reflexes can't match mine.

The sound in his throat strangles as my left hand rams against his turning shoulder.

"Ash." The command leaves my lips and his body instantly fragments and collapses, dust raining onto the earth at my feet.

Thankfully, the mask I'm wearing stops me from inhaling it.

Two more men rush toward me on my left. One of them is bare-chested, his shirt wrapped around his shoulder. He's the one I attempted to stab in the heart.

I duck the axe he aims for my throat and slide past him through the muck. His arm is raised, exposing his ribs, and my left hand brushes his side.

A second later, he, too, is nothing more than smoke.

I spin to the final three men, one of whom has a shirt wrapped around his thigh. He hurries backward, and I let him go for now because he won't get far.

I hurl the axe into the chest of one, this time hitting the mark. As he falls to his knees, I duck the second one's weapon, plowing into the dirt as my left hand slaps against his thigh.

Another pile of ash falls to the earth.

I scoop up his dropped axe and prowl quietly after the final man, following his unbalanced footfalls.

He's managed to get quite a few paces away from me, but his silhouette soon becomes clear in the smoke.

He spins back to me, throwing his hands up, while trying to stumble away from me.

"Don't kill me," he pleads. "We can make a deal. I'll let you go. I'll buy you time so you can escape while the smoke clears."

It isn't a terrible proposal.

However...

His voice may be muffled behind his mask, but I recognize it from before.

He's the one who called the Vandawolf an animal.

Pity.

"Better to be ruled by a fucking animal," I say, watching as the man's eyes widen, "than be torn to shreds by a Blacksmith."

I swing my arm back, preparing to fling the axe at his neck, coldly calculating the angle needed to account for how far he'll get before the weapon strikes him.

He shouts, but the blade flies toward his throat.

It does its work, stopping his speech.

I wait the second it takes for his body to hit the ground and then I drop beside him in the mud, press my left palm to his chest and command him to become stone. I've left the axe where it fell. Once the smoke clears, he will be another gruesome reminder to the humans that they have made an enemy of me.

Slowly, I rise back to my feet.

My chest should be heaving, but I'm completely calm.

Blood drips from my fingertips. The wetness across my cheeks tells me blood is splattered across the exposed parts of my face and undoubtedly in my hair.

All of the rain may have evaporated from the ash beneath my feet, but the snowy surface is no longer white.

Human blood taints it now. For the first time in ten years.

My heart should be cracking, but it isn't.

I should regret what I've done, but I don't.

Even if I wanted to... I *can't*.

I can't feel anything except the sensations that my physical senses detect: the honeyed air mingling with wood smoke; the way my boots sink a little into the ashen ground; the pain in my left shoulder continuing to beat down to the medallion in my hand.

I turn my palm over.

I never would have chosen this.

The humans did this. This is of their making.

With a snarl, I hurry back to the Vandawolf. He's still breathing and that's all that matters.

I push the stretcher onto the ground and reach for him, my fingers leaving smears of blood on everything I touch.

With every breath I take, I'm transported back to the moment I first saw him.

He had towered over me, his bare chest splattered with blood, his pants torn, and his breathing harsh. The strands of his hair had fallen across his eyes, the gore so thick that I couldn't see what color the strands were or discern the parts of his face that had become wolf from those that were still human.

To me, he was the beast my people created.

I didn't see then that we were connected.

Now we are. Irrevocably.

Just as Malak created the Vandawolf, the humans have forged me, their own worst enemy.

I am the beast now.

CHAPTER 6

S moke fills my chest, burning my insides as I hurry as quickly as I can across the wasteland toward the Sunken Bog, dragging the stretcher behind me. The mask I'm wearing is a poor barrier against the intensity of the fumes now.

I lifted the Vandawolf onto the stretcher and used the men's clothing as straps to tie him in—multiple pairs of long pants and shirts knotted together and wrapped around his chest, hips, and legs. I also wrapped some of their shirt material around my hands to give me enough traction against the smooth, onyx poles to pull the stretcher along.

I took several of the men's flannel masks so I could switch them out as I need to, wrapping one around the Vandawolf's face. It wasn't an easy task while using only my right hand and my teeth, since I need to keep my left hand away from him as much as possible.

I can't transform my medallion into any sort of weapon now, so I retrieved two of the fallen axes and hooked them to either side of my belt, one of them now sitting alongside my hammer. I considered looking for the Vandawolf's daggers but didn't want to waste time on that task. I also considered hammering the discarded crossbow bolt into weapons, but it would have taken too long and drawn more humans to my location.

Even as I was tying the Vandawolf to the stretcher, Braddock, Nero, and Vincent were calling down from the wall, demanding to know what was going on.

I worked quietly and left while the smoke cover still concealed me.

Tremors continue to run through the Vandawolf's body, but I harden my heart against the pain he must be feeling.

He's alive and I will keep him that way.

When I reach the edge of the wasteland, about to step into the Sunken Bog, I risk one last look behind me at the city.

In the distance, the smoke continues to swirl around the stone wolf, its silhouette vaguely visible against the backdrop of the wall that extends around the vast city.

I wanted the wolf to remain like a guard outside the wall, facing the mountains as a warning to anyone who was foolish enough to try to attack the city.

Now, I wish that the wolf had turned to face inward before it died so that the humans could look upon its fierce face until the time when I can return.

As for the monsters that might rise in the wasteland while I'm gone, if Braddock, Nero, and Vincent are smart, they'll ask their metalworkers to copy the harpoon and create more crossbow bolts. It was the launching mechanisms that had eluded them in the past, and I gifted the mechanisms to them.

As much as I hope those men die at the hands of a monster, there are people in the city who aren't my enemies: Kedric and Maybelle, who raised my brother and sister as if they were their own children; and Mother Solas, as well as her granddaughter, Rachel, who are descended from the last human king. They treated me with rare kindness. Possibly also Genova, who is the head of the farmers' guild—although I can't be completely certain about her loyalties.

I turn away from them now, hurrying onward.

The Sunken Bog stretches out into the east, a marsh filled with misshapen trees that have an eerie, amber hue, their trunks perpetually rotting. Their branches stretch high and cover the ground in shadows, seeming to seal in the moisture so that its muddy surface never dries out. Anything heavier than a small stone sinks into the gunk. Even the trees are constantly sinking.

Some clumps of greenery are so thick that I won't be able to pass through them. I'll need to find trails and gaps, but it's going to be far more difficult with the stretcher.

Far, far worse now that I can only see ten paces ahead of myself. The wood smoke is eye-watering. Despite the visibility issues, I do my best to stay on course, constantly checking the position of the sun as best as I can through the branches overhead.

Thaden described a safe path through the mountain range that sits directly east where the sun rises. He said that there are caverns on the right-hand side of that pass, and that he would lead my siblings there, where they would all wait for me.

I push onward, fighting with every step to stop the stretcher from sinking. The mud sucks at the ends of the tusks as they gouge a path through it, the sodden earth seeming to grab hold and pull down with every step I take.

My muscles are cramping and sweat is heavy on my face, mingling with my tears, but it only fuels my pain, which in turn feeds the medallion.

The Vandawolf's breathing is louder than it was before, but it's a fearsome, rasping sound, as if the smoke is scraping at his throat with every inhale and exhale despite the mask he's wearing.

I travel for hours, navigating between patches of rotting trees, somehow managing to keep moving in the right direction.

Insects buzz around me, but I ignore them. They're harmless. It's the creatures that slither in the mud that are dangerous. They might once have been snakes, but their forms have become grotesque over time.

Each time I was forced to fight a monster in this bog, the reptiles within the soil seemed to have grown bigger and could move faster than they could the time before.

Genova herself said that the magic in the Sunken Bog was getting stronger. She reported that the edges of the crop fields in the south were decaying and becoming covered in slime.

I can smell the sludge on the ground and trees even over the top of the acrid scent of smoke that remains thick around me. The decay. It's only growing worse the deeper into the bog I go.

Until finally, I've traveled far enough that the smell of rotting wood overcomes the scent of wood smoke.

That's when I become aware of rustling in the leaves beneath the trees on my right.

I pause for the first time, fighting the way my muscles instantly cramp up.

I bring the stretcher to rest across the roots of an amber-colored tree that glows so brightly in the shadows, it plays havoc with my vision. Its leaves are tightly curled and remind me of crickets and grasshoppers. Of course, I'll only find out if they *are* insects if I brush the damn things.

Satisfied that the tree's roots are stable enough to support the stretcher for now and keep it from sinking into the mud, I close my eyes and listen carefully.

My breathing, as well as the Vandawolf's rasping, are loud in my ears, but I force myself to focus beyond it.

The strange sound to my right mimics the breeze through the trees, the rustle of twisted leaves, but it's louder than gusting wind. Noticeable enough that I can't dismiss it.

It's a kind of swirling, scratching, swishing noise.

Now that I've stopped moving, I can discern that it's not only coming from my right, but also up ahead.

Also... on my left.

My eyes slowly open, widening.

Damn.

I must be in the middle of a viper's nest, the slithering creatures that pose one of the greatest dangers in this bog.

Considering the projection of hissing sounds from all directions ahead of me, the only safe path is back the way I came. To avoid the nest, I'll need to retrace my steps and then veer wide of this location.

It will cost me hours. Hours of daylight and time the Vandawolf might not have.

The alternative is to try to fight my way through the snakes.

Already, I'm pulling the material off my left hand, exposing the medallion and bending to the ground.

I could cast a command through the roots of the nearest tree, attempt to spread my magic as far as it will go, a cascade that could turn all living things into stone.

I stop within an inch of touching the nearest tree root, though, my gaze following it to the stretcher and the Vandawolf.

To cast my power so indiscriminately may not work—or worse, it could work too well.

I could kill the Vandawolf.

Even if I thought I could proceed through the nest and try to fight off the snakes one by one—which would be impossible with a swarm—the awful reality is that it would only take one to bite him and he would die.

Everything I've overcome this morning would be for nothing.

I slowly rewrap my hand and then I rock forward, knowing I need to move but fighting this moment of defeat.

The environment around the city is extremely dangerous. It's why I didn't attempt to escape with my brother and sister ten years ago. I didn't have my tools then and I couldn't have protected them.

There was a time, before Blacksmith magic polluted these forests and fields, that Blacksmith delegates were sent out beyond the mountains to forge alliances with the kingdoms in the north. That was decades before my birth, and Malak called all of the Blacksmiths home when he rose to power. There would have once been safe pathways across this land and through the mountains ahead of me.

Not so anymore.

When I thought I'd travel through here with my brother, Gallium, and Thaden Kane at my side, I was far more confident we could make it through. We could watch each other's backs and rely on each other's strength.

But alone... and with this stretcher...

I fight my fear as I rock forward, my forehead pressing to the back of my left hand.

I want the cold hatred in the medallion to overcome my anxiety, but it seems that fear and malice go hand in hand.

The more I attempt to fill my heart with ice, the greater my worries grow.

I cut through them with a decision.

I have no choice but to retrace my steps and go around the viper's nest.

Swallowing my anxiety and gritting my teeth, I turn the stretcher in the narrow space between trees, trying to move as carefully and as quietly as I can while fighting not to upend the Vandawolf into the mud.

Finally succeeding, I pull cautiously, listening carefully for the proximity of the snakes.

Hours later, I've backtracked and then veered north, skirting the nest and finally heading directly east again.

By this time, the sun has passed its peak and will soon descend into the horizon behind me.

The smoke has cleared and I discard the mask I was wearing. Many times over the last few hours, I've considered the possibility that the humans will have sent men out after me. It wouldn't be hard to track the stretcher through the mud, although when I glance behind me, the trail that the two tusks are leaving behind is quickly consumed by the sludge.

But I don't hear or see any signs of anyone, so I guess they're smart enough to let me go. At least, for now.

By the time I reach the edge of the bog, the sun is well and truly setting.

I've never been this far away from the city.

Ahead of me, the ground is rocky and barren, an open plain that stretches about a hundred paces wide with a gentle incline that leads up to the mountain range.

The mountains themselves extend left and right as far as I can see, forming a circle around the wasteland. They reach up so high that I have to crane my head in an attempt to see the top of them.

The pass that Thaden described must be up ahead, somewhere amidst the rocky crags, but the ascent to reach it is daunting.

As far as I can see, the landscape consists only of stone. There is nothing living in it. No trees, no greenery in crevices, not even any moss. The stones look loose, as if they'll roll away under my feet. Given that I'll have to pull the stretcher along that uneven and unreliable ground, I judge it could take me another two hours to reach the caverns Thaden described.

By then, night will have fallen.

I take a step out onto the stony plain, but that's when my knees buckle. I find myself leaning against the nearest tree, which, by some miracle, has a solid enough trunk that it bends under my weight instead of breaking. Somehow, I've kept hold of the stretcher behind me.

I lower it to the ground before I drop it, my right shoulder grazing down the solid bark of the tree when my legs wobble violently.

Once the stretcher is safely on the ground, I collapse against the trunk, turning so that my back grazes it as I slide all the way down.

I'm faced with the fact that the additional strength the medallion gives me can't overcome my body's basic needs.

I'm dehydrated. I haven't drunk a drop of water since I left the city before dawn. Since then, I've fought multiple battles and survived an inferno and dragged the Vandawolf through the mud for hours.

I've pushed my muscles beyond their breaking point.

I need water and I need rest, both of which I won't get until I reach my family. They took all of the supplies with them, including mine. Certainly not their fault, since I left everything with them when I went to fight the monstrous wolf.

For a wild moment, I wonder what might happen if I press my left palm to the tree I'm resting against and command it to turn to water.

Could I drink it? Or would it be somehow poisoned with magic?

Malak was the first Blacksmith to change the nature of any living thing with his power. He transformed an ordinary apple tree to make its bark sparkle brightly at night. Until then, no Blacksmith had attempted to change the nature of organic material. Let alone succeeded.

Malak created something beautiful, but it triggered a quest for power that became ugly.

I'm so thirsty that I cast caution to the wind, not caring if the water I create will be poisoned. Twisting and planting my left palm against the tree, I send a command through the medallion.

Water.

It's a testament to how groggy my thoughts are that I don't consider for a moment that turning the solid object I'm propped up against into water will only land me on my face.

Liquid explodes up into the air around me. I fall clumsily onto my side, my outstretched arm buckles beneath my weight, and I bang my head on the rocks.

Fuck!

Water splashes down onto my face and chest. When my tongue darts out, I find the liquid slimy and as stagnant-tasting as the bog smelled.

I suppose it's just as well I didn't get a mouthful of it.

Self-loathing fills me as I stay where I am, a cruel laugh forming on my lips.

How fucking stupid. As if I could do anything good with this power.

I roll onto my back, ignoring the stones that bite into me. Now that I'm facing upward, I can see the clear sky and the first few stars twinkling to life in it.

It's brighter than the night sky above the city, clear of the thin haze of magic that hangs over the entire wasteland.

But I may as well be lying at the bottom of a dark pit.

I tell myself I can crawl out of it.

I have to.

Giving up is not an option.

Rocking onto my side, I force myself up onto all fours, then onto my knees, but once there, I pause because the effort of rising to my feet again, the thought of taking hold of the stretcher and pulling it once more, is crushing.

I tell myself I'll only stop for one more moment to take a breath.

Breathe in. Breathe out.

But my exhalation leaves my lips with a moan of despair and my head is in my hands, the medallion pressed to my forehead.

"Asha."

The Vandawolf's whisper reaches me over the sound of my own moan.

My eyes snap open, my hands jolt away from my face, and my focus flies to him.

He's awake!

CHAPTER 7

I lurch toward the Vandawolf, a new burst of energy giving me the strength to scramble the short distance across the muddy rocks.

I'm reaching out to him before I remember myself and snap my left fist closed, pressing it to my side.

He's staring upward where he lies on the stretcher, his wolf's eye open while his human eye is half-closed. He blinks at the darkening sky. Squeezes both eyes closed. Opens his wolf's eye again. Seems to be trying to open his human eye too, but it remains mostly closed.

His brow is fiercely creased, his voice more agitated. "Asha?"

"I'm here." Heat burns behind my eyes as I dare to press my right palm to his clammy cheek, waiting for him to look at me. "I'm here with you."

He turns his head in my direction, but his eyes are glazed and unfocused.

I draw back a little.

Oh, dear saints.

He can't see.

The way his gaze slides across me, as if he's searching for me, confirms it.

His wolf's energy is in turmoil. It was so often a writhing, furious burn in my senses, but now that he's awake, it's as if it's biting and thrashing, gnawing at the dark energy curled around it. A cage of metal threads have been wound around and through it.

"Where are we?" the Vandawolf asks, the tension in his voice making me shiver.

"We've reached the mountains. We'll be safe soon."

I don't know that for certain. In fact, we may never be safe.

Instead of calming at the sound of my voice, he becomes more agitated.

"You were meant to leave me." His voice grows in strength, becoming a harsh snarl. "I *wanted* you to leave me."

My eyes widen. I know what he wanted. He wanted me to escape with my family. When I asked him to come with me, he refused.

But that was before his people tried to kill him.

I was sure I was too dehydrated to produce tears, but they're leaking down my cheeks. "I'm taking you to my sister. She can heal—"

"No!" His roar makes me jump.

He rips at the material strapping him to the stretcher, somehow tearing through it. Within a heartbeat, he lurches toward me, catching the hand I pressed to his jaw, pulling me toward him.

My reflexes are slow. Evidence of how tired I am.

Before I can move, his arms close around me, crushing me up against his chest. We're both now kneeling on the hard stones. Somehow, I've managed to extend my left arm, holding my power away from his body, my forearm aching from the effort to avoid touching him with it.

That discomfort is nothing compared to the anguish of his body pressed to mine.

I'm hard up against all the cold metal I fused to his chest and it's slowly tearing me apart.

A scream of pain rises to my lips.

How could I have done this to him?

He would have chosen death over this.

His roar obliterates the agony raging through me. "*You were meant to leave me!*"

And yet, he's holding me as if he never wants to let me go.

His right hand is softly cradling my head; his left hand is pressed to my lower back. His cheek rests against mine—his human cheek, the gentler side of his face—and his lips brush the edge of my jaw.

"You were meant to leave me, Asha," he murmurs, his speech slurring now. "I wanted to do... one good thing..."

My right hand is pressed up against his heart, that arm folded between us. Beneath my palm, I sense the slow beats of his heart, and suddenly, I'm whisked back to the very first moment that I ever touched him.

I tried to use my power on him, despite the fact that I didn't have a hammer or medallions at the time, and when I pressed my palm to his chest, all I felt was the heavy beat of his heart, along with the damp of sweat and blood.

But now I wonder... in that moment... how much was concealed from me beneath his cloak of blood?

Did I miss the way his hand softened around my wrist or the way his heart jumped when I touched him, or the way he looked at me so unguarded in that moment?

I try to speak around the sob choking my throat. I need to tell him what I've done to him, because he can't see the metal and he doesn't yet seem aware of it. He must be in terrible pain, even worse than mine, but he must believe it's from his wounds.

Even as I try to force sound through my lips, his body is rapidly growing heavier against me, his head slowly dropping to my shoulder, resting in the crook of my neck.

Whatever burst of energy allowed him to lurch up off the stretcher seems to be fading as quickly as it arose. His body is fast becoming a crushing weight that I could never support without the strength the medallion gives me.

He mumbles against my neck, his fading speech painfully coherent, even though I wish I couldn't hear or understand him, and I squeeze my eyes shut as if doing so could block my ears.

"I wanted you to be free of me. Precious Asha..."

The final heaviness of his body tells me he's unconscious again.

Hot liquid fills my eyes.

I can't choke back my sob any longer.

Somehow, despite the cold energy cloaking my heart, I can still feel this pain.

Empathy, kindness, compassion... All of those are stripped from me, but *this* pain?

Oh, pain is a constant now.

And so is anger.

I want to rage at him for trying to push me away. I want to hate him for all the years he treated me like an enemy.

More than anything, I want to force him to peel back all the shields and cloaks he's layered around his heart.

I want to know everything he's been hiding from me since the moment we met.

All his secrets. All his lies. All his truths.

But I will have none of them until he's healed.

Gritting my teeth, I lower him to the ground, and then drag him back onto the stretcher. I do my best to retie the material he tore. Luckily, I fastened the original knots with plenty of material to spare.

Once he's secured, I continue our journey across the rocky plane, fighting exhaustion with every step I take.

The moon is rising by the time I reach the edge of the mountains. The incline is steep, and multiple times, I nearly lose my footing, sending stones clattering down the hilly landscape behind me.

The pass through the mountains finally looms in front of me. It's about twenty paces wide, and cliff faces soar up on either side of it. The path is not straight, curving along the ground and leading to what appears to be a sharp turn, beyond which I can't see what lies ahead. The cliff faces on both sides are jagged, not smooth, but at least the path is wide enough that I won't brush up against of them.

Thaden said there would be caverns on the right-hand side and that he and my siblings would shelter at the entrance to one of them so I could find them easily.

The promise of reaching my family drives me onward.

Once I get to them, I will be able to remove the life-sustaining titanium from the Vandawolf's body, my sister will heal him, and then we will all be free to choose our future.

Of course, I'm forgetting the band now welded to my hand, but I promise myself I will figure out a way to be rid of it, even if it means losing my power altogether.

I shudder at the possibility that it may require removing my hand, but I'll face that decision if it comes to it.

For now, this power is keeping me alive.

An hour later, I finally approach the first cavern on the right-hand side of the pass. My heart leaps when I see its shadowed entrance and hope quickens my footsteps.

My heart sinks when I peer inside it. The cavern is shallow, extending no more than thirty paces into the cliff face, so it's easy to see...

It's empty.

I fight my sinking heart and carefully place the stretcher on the ground, freeing up my left hand to press it to the ground. It's how I've always detected the location of a rising monster and, early this morning, I also detected my sister's presence this way.

It only works if my brother or sister has awakened their tools and is wearing them, but now that I've reached the first cavern, it's worth trying.

I pray for a streak of energy to travel toward me through the ground, but nothing happens.

Perhaps it's a relief that neither of my siblings has awakened their medallions. If they had done so, it could mean they were in danger.

I force myself to move on.

The next cavern is deeper, and I have to veer inside it to ascertain that it, too, is empty.

I try to bring moisture to my dry lips as I drag myself and the Vandawolf away from the opening and continue along the pass, my hope draining with every step I take.

My footfalls are stumbling and, above me, the moon has risen high by the time I reach what must be the fifth cavern, this one appearing much deeper than the others.

Again, the cavern is empty at its mouth—but this time, I make out the sound of trickling water within it.

I need water.

I immediately swerve inside the entrance, trying to see what dangers could lie in the shadows that fill the space beyond the edge of the moonlight.

When I call out softly, "Hello?" my voice echoes into the distance.

Nothing stirs.

As the sound of my voice fades, there is only silence.

The promise of water lures me farther inside, fifty paces into the darkness while my eyes adjust, right up to a spot where the opening narrows so much that the stretcher won't fit through it. But when I crane my neck around the opening, I can see that the cavern widens again beyond the narrow section. Beyond it is the back of the cave and, on the far-right side of that, is the water source.

Liquid falls steadily down a jutting crevice at the back of the cave not more than ten paces away, cascading into a small rockpool on the cavern floor.

Stagnant water is dangerous, but running water is more likely to be safe.

I'm torn between choices as I lower the stretcher to the ground, rubbing my shaking arms.

If I want to drink, I'll need to leave the Vandawolf here, and I won't have a clear line of sight to him from the rockpool.

Of course, if I collapse from thirst, I won't be able to protect him, either.

Making my decision to drink while I can, I push the stretcher as close to the opening as possible so I'll have a chance of keeping the top edge of it within my sights when I enter the second cave.

I slip through the narrow pass, hunching my shoulders so I don't scrape them on the jagged surfaces on both sides. The intact plates of my armor protect me to some degree, but I don't want to risk needless damage.

There's barely any light within this second cavern, but the walls glimmer with a soft, amber light, the origin of which I can't pinpoint.

I make it to the cascade of water that's as wide as my hand, drop to my knees at the edge of the little rockpool, and quickly unwrap the human material from around my hands before I hold my cupped palms beneath the water flow.

At the last moment, I retract my left hand, using only my right to direct the flow of water to my lips.

I drink, and drink, and drink until my stomach feels like it's bursting and my thirst is finally quenched.

My thoughts clear a little, although I know it will take time for the liquid to replenish me fully.

When I lean back, preparing to rise to my feet and hurry to the Vandawolf, there's a soft, scuffling sound from within the outer cave.

I freeze, half-risen, listening carefully.

Unfamiliar voices reach me across the distance. I identify three of them, all carrying a higher pitch, indicating the speakers are likely female. Each voice is a soft, melodic whisper that reminds me of a gentle breeze passing through branches, but there's nothing soothing about them.

The hairs on the back of my neck have shot right up.

My left palm is tingling. Not the same sensation as when I detect Blacksmith magic, not even the same scent as when blood-rain threatens to fall, but there is certainly magical energy in the air.

The first voice carries a mix of fear and disgust. "What is it?"

"We should kill it." The second voice is followed by the soft ring of steel, as if a weapon has been drawn.

A third woman speaks quickly but firmly. "Whether this creature lives or dies is for the Commander to decide."

They can only be talking about the Vandawolf.

Fury rises within me.

The location of their voices is close enough that they could be standing over him, but they aren't near enough to the opening between the two caves that I can see them from this angle.

The edges of their shadows become visible as I prowl forward, my footfalls silent. There may be more of the newcomers farther back in the outer cave, but the shadows cast up over the wall confirm that three are hovering over the Vandawolf.

The first woman is speaking again, her voice sly this time. "Commander Dawn is busy checking the other cave. I say we kill this thing and tell her it was dead when we found it."

"With fresh blood dripping from the wound?" The third woman's contempt for the suggestion drips from her words.

"We don't know if it's going to bleed," the first woman snaps. "Look at it. It's covered in metal."

"And with some sort of... tooth. Do you see it?" That voice belongs to the second woman, and her shadow indicates she's leaning right over the Vandawolf.

I'm at the lip of the pass now, concealed behind it, able to see the full extent of their silhouettes cast up on the wall directly to my left—as well as the Vandawolf's silhouette where he lies, unmoving, on the stretcher.

It will only take another step to make my presence known.

My right hand sweeps across one of the human axes, quietly pulling it free, while my left hand clenches around my medallion.

The third woman—the one who objected before—starts to speak. "Even so, we should wait for the Commander—"

"It's nothing more than a beast!" the first woman snaps. "Enough talk. I'm killing it!"

Her shadow looms closer to the Vandawolf, the outline of a blade visible above his neck.

I slip through the opening with a snarl on my lips. "He may be a beast. But he's *my* beast."

I raise my left hand, palm out, my fingers curling like claws. "If you want to kill him, you'll have to kill me first."

CHAPTER 8

The three women all react at once.

The woman holding the dagger jumps to her feet with a cry of alarm. She's slightly shorter than I am with a petite frame, golden hair, pale skin, and brown eyes.

The woman to her left also jumps to her feet, revealing a taller frame, but her features are startling to me. Her skin is also fair, but her hair is pale pink and her eyes are a soft, peach color.

The third woman is the only one who backs away, both of her hands raised. Her hair appears to be the darkest black, but as she moves, the strange amber hue in the darkness around us catches the strands, revealing dark-purple highlights. Her eyes are a surprising violet.

She is visibly the youngest of the three, possibly no older than sixteen. No older than me when I protected my siblings and offered my life to the Vandawolf.

All of the women are wearing raven-black armor that

covers their bodies from their necks to their feet. Their armor seems to blend into the dim light so that, despite casting clear silhouettes against the wall, their bodies are harder to see in the shadows. Especially as the bright moonlight gleaming at the far opening of the cave doesn't come close to reaching this location.

Their armor is so seamless that, if their boots are separate from their armor, I can't see where the tops of them lie. Each of the women wears their hair in a single, tight braid that falls over their shoulders.

As the other two brace, the woman with the violet eyes continues to back away, crying out, "Dusana! Bethoc! Step away!"

I recognize her voice; she's the one who objected to killing the Vandawolf on the spot. I follow her focus as it flies from the golden-haired woman—presumably named Dusana—to the pink-haired one—apparently called 'Bethoc.'

"Get away from the Blacksmith," the violet-haired woman continues to shout.

My eyes narrow. She knows I'm a Blacksmith. *But how?*

"What do you know of me?" I demand of her, my focus momentarily on her.

Dusana and Bethoc don't miss their chance while I'm distracted.

Bethoc sweeps her right hand across her left shoulder.

To my shock, a blade appears, seeming to peel off the surface of her armor where it must have been conforming with the shape of the material. For mere seconds, it looks like it's made of liquid, completely malleable and flexible, but then the handle and blade solidify in her hand.

She's now holding a sword with a wickedly gleaming blade.

With a scream, she leaps over the Vandawolf, her sword cutting the air toward my throat, her pink braid flying off her shoulder with the force of her jump.

If I weren't her target, I'd be impressed with her strength, speed, and agility. What's more, my position is not great. The space between us is small. I'm blocked in by the narrow pass at my back and the Vandawolf's stretcher lying so close to my feet.

But I'm not helpless.

Of all the monsters I've ever fought, this pink-haired woman is certainly the smallest.

My muscles are already reacting, my reflexes instant.

I don't make a sound as I leap sideways, aiming for the space between her flying body and the far side of the stretcher. At the same time, I twist, my left hand flying outward, my trajectory perfect.

My palm connects with the sword midair.

Clang!

My intention was merely to deflect the blow, but the collision of the sword and the medallion creates a sound as beautiful as any melody. It's a clear, ringing bell as pure as the sound of my hammer on iron.

Light explodes between us, a shock of energy that bursts across the Vandawolf below us, lighting up the mess across his chest, brightening Bethoc's features and making her pale skin appear like delicate porcelain. Even her black armor seems dazzling in that heartbeat.

Oh, but the power that blasts through my body is like nothing I've felt before.

Her blade can't be made of ordinary metal.

I realize this in an instant.

If I'd had any doubt about its form, I'm now certain that it's infused with magic.

Not Blacksmith magic. This power is foreign to me. It feels like the heat of sunlight, the rush of winter wind, the strength of a solid tree, and the beat of a heart—the essence of life encased in this single blade.

I may not recognize this power, but it's as susceptible to my strength as if it's made of living flesh.

In that instant, as Bethoc flies past me and our bodies are on the cusp of being blasted apart, I close my fist around her blade.

It's a terrible risk. The sword's wickedly sharp edge could cut right through my fingers.

It doesn't.

Bethoc's eyes are already wide, but now I sense her fear, like a streak of energy through her hand where she grips the blade. Her emotions seem to pass all the way through her sword into my body.

It's a terrible, stomach-sinking horror that's reflected on her face, as if she's witnessing her own death in the bright air, seeing it before it happens, and there's nothing she can do to stop it.

Her blade turns to putty in my hand a mere fraction of a moment before the explosion takes hold and we're blasted apart.

Time seems to speed up again, and I crash against the cave wall a few paces from the narrow opening. My back hits the rock with a *crunch* that rattles my bones and for the second time today, I'm pressed against rock. This time, it's only for a second before I land on my feet, swallowing my cry of pain at the impact.

Bethoc's sword is in my hands and it's like holding on to a living thing, the blade molded where my fingers press into it, leaving peaks of metal between my digits.

Bethoc has a shorter path since she was already leaping at the side wall that the Vandawolf's stretcher is pressed up against. Her shoulder was turned toward it as if it had been her intention to cut off my head on her way past me before she would protect herself from the impact and rebound off the stone surface.

Instead, her arms have flown wide. The blast carries her back at a sharp angle.

She smacks the stone hard, the back of her head bouncing against it with an awful, cracking sound.

She crumples to the ground, landing at the Vandawolf's feet, where she doesn't move.

Dusana has tumbled across the cave floor, somehow managing to land on her feet and keep hold of her weapon despite the blast.

She's now ten paces away from me, rising back to her full, albeit short, height, her wide eyes passing wildly from me to Bethoc's still body.

The corners of my mouth turn down as I decide to give her one chance. "Let me pass, and I'll let you live."

She doesn't even appear to think about it. Switching her dagger to her left hand, her right hand is immediately sweeping across her shoulder, mimicking the same motion Bethoc performed.

A sword peels from her shoulder, gleaming like the one I'm holding.

"Don't do it, Dusana," the violet-haired woman cries from the side of the cave. She wasn't as close to the center of the blast and has remained on her feet, although, judging by her current location, the impact must have forced her much closer to the wall on that side. "You can't win against a Blacksmith."

"Shut up, Gliss," Dusana snaps. "If I beat this bitch, nobody will deny me the chance to challenge the Commander at the next Winter Ascending." Her lips twist. "*I* will stand at the head of the Queen's army, not your fucking sister."

I have no idea what power games Dusana is playing, or who the Commander is—or the Queen she mentioned, for that matter—but I don't have time to ask questions.

All I know for certain right now is that I want nothing to do with these women.

"Bitch?" I repeat softly to myself as I move to stand in front of the Vandawolf. "I suppose I've been called worse."

I latch the human axe back onto my waist and reposition Bethoc's sword. Its blade quickly become solid again, but the indents remain and I rapidly run my fingers over their points, creating a deep serration with sharp tips that resemble teeth.

"You've made your choice," I say to Dusana.

I'm about to launch myself at her when the silence behind me arrests my attention.

The Vandawolf's breathing has become soft and shallow again.

It's barely audible.

I risk taking my eyes off Dusana and Gliss to cast him a quick, panicked glance.

His face is paler than before, a horrible, gray color, and

the tremors in his hands have stopped. He lies more still than he has since the crossbow bolt hit him this morning.

"*No.*" A denial rises to my lips and I don't care if the other women hear it.

I kept the Vandawolf stable. The medallion stopped the bleeding.

He woke up before. He spoke to me. He can't be fading now.

Not now.

I can't lose him after all this.

I have to get past these women and find my sister.

I need to do it *now.*

With a scream of rage, I abandon all caution, throwing myself at Dusana.

My sword clashes with hers, the ringing sound echoing around us. Both of my hands are wrapped around my weapon's handle, and I sense my power streaming through the blade with every collision as I beat her back across the cave floor.

She's physically strong—certainly stronger than a human. But I'm stronger.

Within moments, I've pushed her toward the far wall and around again.

She's on the backfoot, her eyes wide, and I sense the tension in her arm muscles as she attempts to block the blows I aim at her head, chest, and neck.

The only way I'm getting past these women while dragging the stretcher is if I put them both out of action. Otherwise, one of them could stab me while my hands are busy.

If that means killing them, then so be it.

Dusana stumbles and that's all I was waiting for.

Her defenses are down for a split second and her free hand—the one with the dagger she hasn't yet used—is lowered, opening up the space between my sword and her neck.

I picture my serrated blade ripping through her flesh and ending her swiftly.

I swing, but she drops to the ground before the blade can meet her body, throwing herself into a slide beneath my arms.

Before I can evade the blow, her dagger meets my side.

CHAPTER 9

Dusana's blade breaks through my armor and slices across my ribs.

I sense my skin splitting, sense the physical damage as I catalog the increased pain. Logically, I'm aware that it's only because of my armor and the angle of her blade that it didn't travel farther and pierce my lungs.

I'm breathing, moving, functioning, so it can't be a fatal blow.

Dusana continues her slide across the rocky ground, jumping to her feet behind me, her blade dripping with my blood.

She gives me a triumphant smile as I spin to face her.

I don't bother checking the wound, even though her focus flashes to it as if she expects me to be worried about it.

I shake my head at her, a slow, deliberate movement. "You shouldn't have done that."

Malak was at his cruelest when he was in pain.

Dusana's eyes widen with apparent surprise when I drop

the sword I was holding, letting it clatter to the ground and leaving both of my hands free. My fingers flex around my medallion.

At the side of the cave, Gliss cries to Dusana, pure panic filling her voice. "Yield, Dusana! You know she can kill you. Yield and let her pass!"

But beneath the sound of her voice is an absence of noise that's crushing my heart.

The Vandawolf's chest has fallen still.

In the space of moments, my hope has died.

To Dusana, I say, "Do *not* yield. He is on the cusp of death and you have stolen the time I needed to save him. For that, you will pay with your life."

Dusana's expression falls a little, some of her confidence draining from her brown eyes, but my focus is not on her face any longer. It's on the exposed spaces between her weapons. All the vulnerable places and all the chances I have to simply lay my hand on her.

No matter the damage she causes to me in the meantime.

Without another word, I charge at her, aiming for her shoulders.

She swings her sword and thrusts with her dagger, but my fists collide with her inner forearms, one after the other, knocking her arms wide and forcing her off-balance before I punch her to the ground.

My left hand closes around her sword's blade as we fall, turning it to putty before we hit the dirt. I rip the weapon from her hands, flinging it off to the side before my right hand collides with her clavicle.

Her armor is filled with the same earthy energy as the sword. My only explanation is that it's somehow organic, akin to flesh and blood, which in turn, makes it vulnerable to my power.

Even as she lands heavily on her back, my fists are crunching into her chest, caving the armored plates across her ribs.

I'm aware that she's trying to stab me with her dagger. I can't risk grabbing it with my non-powered hand, and I'd have to twist to take hold of it with my powered hand, so I let the blows land.

I can't care how many times her blade pierces my skin.

If I'm experiencing pain, it's only feeding my rage and making me stronger.

I have nothing but furious impulses, not even a care for my own life, and for the first time, I understand...

When I was five years old, Malak went on a rampage.

His sister, Milena, had supposedly been killed in a human uprising. It was said that she was the only Blacksmith he truly trusted. In his rage and grief, he stormed through the human population, killing indiscriminately.

I understand it now.

There's nothing left of myself to pull me back from it. No other emotion. No honor. No empathy.

I'm suddenly aware that Dusana is quiet beneath me and I'm not sure when she blacked out. All I know for certain is that she's still breathing because her chest is rising and falling, her breaths rattling loudly.

My fists become still where I straddle her chest.

Judging by the state of her armor and face, I've broken her ribs and her jaw. Probably one of her arms.

I've completely immobilized her, yet my rage only worsens.

Why should she breathe when the Vandawolf's chest no longer rises and falls?

Once again, I'm at the bottom of a pit and there's no way out of it.

Nothing to hold on to, nothing except the knowledge that I will leave this woman to die on the cold stone beneath her.

I rise to my feet and prowl toward Gliss.

The younger woman shrinks against the cave wall, her violet eyes wide and her face draining of color.

"Please—" she begins.

"What will I make of you?" I ask quietly. "Will you be ash or smoke? Or maybe stone? Something other than alive, because that's what I can do." I nod to myself. "I can make you dead."

Hot, unwanted tears fill my eyes as I force myself not to look at the Vandawolf or listen to the silence where he lies.

"I can kill monsters. But I can't save them."

I ram my left hand against the stone beside Gliss's trembling shoulder.

Her lips part, but the sound she makes is strangled. "Asha Silverspun. Please. *Don't do this.*"

My voice is low. "How do you know my name?"

She stumbles over her speech, her gaze flitting from me to the Vandawolf. Then across the other two women. "I... We..."

As she speaks, my hand clenches and unclenches against the stone, my fingernails rasping against it. I'm not blocking her other side and that's the way she shuffles, sliding across the rock in the direction of the opening.

Maybe she thinks she'll escape that way and—who

knows?—maybe she'll make it to the mouth of the cave before I end her.

Or maybe she won't.

Her armor scrapes along the stone, a screeching sound in the quiet.

"I'm sorry." She gasps.

"For what?"

"I'm sorry they called him a beast."

My eyebrows arch. *That's* what she's sorry for?

A dark laugh rests on my lips. "He *is* a beast."

He's a *dying* beast. With no hope of being healed now. The hard reality of my situation has already taken root within my mind.

I won't find my sister.

She's long gone, and I don't know where to find her.

As for the Vandawolf, I've kept him alive for longer than should have been possible.

He spoke to me earlier and those will be his last words to me, telling me I should have rid myself of him.

Gliss focuses on my face, her gaze following the tears dripping down my cheeks.

She suddenly stops sliding away from me, planting her feet and looking me in the eyes, the terror in her face seeming to fade, and I'm not sure why.

"I'm sorry he's dying," she says.

My helpless rage has nowhere to go but into my fists.

I smack my left hand against the stone again, and it occurs to me to wonder why Gliss has abandoned her efforts to escape. Why she's suddenly facing me with a look of sadness in her eyes.

Is it compassion or is it pity?

I'm not sure why she would have either for me now that I've certainly killed one of her friends and left the other to die.

Memories are playing havoc with my mind, because once again, I'm transported back to the moment when I first met the Vandawolf and he demanded to know if I pitied him.

I told him: *"I have no pity for you."*

Now I have to ask myself: Will I kill Gliss even if she doesn't try to fight me? Even though I don't know who she is or what she's doing here or how she knows my name?

Will I kill her simply because I can?

Isn't that what a real beast would do?

Isn't that what the Vandawolf should have done to me all those years ago if he really was the animal my people thought? If he didn't have a heart and a mind and the capacity to love?

All I wanted was the chance to know: Would he still be my enemy if we were both free to make our own choices?

All I wanted was the answer to that question.

Another scream rises to my lips and my fingernails scrape down the stone. I don't care that I'm drawing my own blood, only that the pain feeds the malice in the medallion and it halts my memories in their tracks.

"Go," I whisper, stepping back from Gliss and letting my bloodied hand drop to my side. I hate that I stumble a little now that the stab wounds in my side are taking a toll. "Go before I change my mind."

She hesitates and I don't understand why she hasn't darted away from me.

"Go!" I roar at her, making her flinch. "Leave!"

I squeeze my eyes closed as the memory of the

Vandawolf's earlier cry echoes within my mind. *"You were meant to leave me."*

Still, Gliss stays where she is. "But he's dying and I can—"

Her voice is cut off by the sound of running footfalls.

Many footfalls.

At least eleven women converge on the mouth of the cave, maybe more.

They're all dressed in that same black armor that, despite the moonlight pouring across the path outside the cave, makes their silhouettes more difficult to distinguish from each other.

The magical energy rising off each of them sends a shiver down my spine.

One woman surges ahead of the others, shouting, "Halt, Blacksmith!"

As she moves, the other women quickly spread out to fill the space between the sides of the cave at its entrance, blocking all escape.

Well, maybe if I were someone else.

I picture the smoke they will become and the ease with which I will walk through it.

Provided I make it that far.

I finally check the state of my side, a snarl rising to my lips at the mess Dusana made of me. Blood seeps through multiple gashes in my armor and I can feel it trickling down my side.

The woman hurrying toward me wears a red crest, resembling a flower, on the left shoulder of her armor. Her hair is as black as Gliss's with the same deep-purple highlights, and her eyes are the same shade of violet.

She rapidly takes in the fallen women—Dusana and Bethoc—before her focus reaches the Vandawolf in the distance. If she can see the detail of his appearance from her position, she doesn't show any surprise about it. It certainly doesn't slow her down.

Her final glance is for Gliss and in that brief meeting of their eyes, I read fear in the approaching woman's expression. It's a deep fear. The kind I saw in my siblings' eyes when they were frightened for my life.

The newcomer pulls to a halt only five paces away, her focus returning to me and her gaze now leveled with mine.

"I am Elowynn of the Dawn, the rightful Queen's Champion and Commander of the fae army," the newcomer says. "You will stop where you are, Asha Silverspun. Or I will *make* you stop."

CHAPTER 10

I step back from Gliss and focus my attention on Elowynn.

There was a lot that Elowynn crammed into her speech and I don't have time to contemplate it all right now.

Fae. The rightful Queen. Champion. Commander. An army.

Explanations will have to wait, assuming I ever get them.

For now, I focus on the threat in front of me—this imposing woman who seems more afraid for Gliss's safety than concerned about the other occupants of this cave.

If her physical appearance is any indication, then she's Gliss's sister.

I shake my head, trying to clear it. The blood loss from my injuries is threatening to make my thoughts fuzzy.

I exhale and focus.

"If you wish to end me," I say quietly to Elowynn, "then I invite you to try."

"I do!" Elowynn snaps, her focus entirely on me now. "I wish to end you. I want all Blacksmiths dead."

My left fist closes around my medallion as I speak again, this time through gritted teeth. "Then *try*."

"I would..." The snarl in Elowynn's voice fades, her lips twist, and it seems that she's caging her anger when she says, "But I can't."

Can't? It's an interesting distinction from *won't*.

"Against my counsel, my Queen has decided to grant you amnesty," she says. "To strike you would be to defy her wishes, and I will never commit treason. You will come with us—"

"Like fuck I will!" I snap. "You expect me to become your prisoner? Well, I refuse."

Her lips thin. "That's not what amnesty means."

I snort. "Isn't it?" I advance on her before she can respond. "Why are you really here, Elowynn of the Dawn? How do you know who I am? What do you want with me?"

Elowynn's expression is now blank. "I will answer all of your questions when you release my sister."

I pull to a stop, casting a sideways glance at Gliss.

They're sisters. My first guess was correct, after all.

"Your sister wasn't trapped," I say. "I told her to go. She refused."

Elowynn's eyes widen before her expression becomes blank once again. "Gliss?"

"It's true," Gliss says, reaching for me, even though I'm a solid three paces away from her now. "Asha's in pain and her friend is dying—"

"Gliss!" Elowynn's sharp voice cracks across the cave,

but it carries a hint of the panic I first heard in her voice. Her tone softens, but not by much. "Come away from the Blacksmith."

An unexpected hint of stubbornness passes across Gliss's face, and her expression reminds me so much of my own sister, Tamra, that my forehead creases.

Still, if she won't move away from me, I will move away from her.

I take deliberate steps toward the center of the cave, increasing the distance between us. Then I incline my head sharply from her to Elowynn and snarl, "Fuck off."

Gliss doesn't hesitate another moment, her footfalls pattering as she races toward the women blocking the way out, pausing beside Elowynn. Despite a clear difference in age, they're the same height, and very similar in appearance now that they're standing side by side.

Gliss reaches out to Elowynn, her fingertips brushing her sister's arm. "Asha wasn't going to hurt me. I'm sure of it."

Elowynn's lips thin again. "Seal off your heart, little sister, and remember the damage that Blacksmiths can do."

They fall silent then, and my questions only increase as I study the unspoken communication that seems to pass between them.

"Go," Elowynn whispers. "Quickly now."

Gliss gives a brief nod before she darts toward women at the front of the cave, zigzagging between them and disappearing from sight.

"Your sister's safe," I say to Elowynn, my voice hard. "Now, either leave me the fuck alone or explain yourself. But if you persist in your desire to grant me 'amnesty,' then speak quickly. I have little time left and no wish to spend it listening to your voice."

Elowynn considers me for a moment. "Your tone indicates that you're accustomed to having your orders followed. What were you to the humans in the *Vadlig Odemark*? A leader? A queen?"

"The what?"

"The Cursed Wasteland."

"Is that what you call the Southlands? No, forget I asked." I wave my hand dismissively. "It's clear you're determined to stall until I pass out—"

"We found your family," she says, throwing back her shoulders, her purple-black braid slipping from her shoulder.

My heart leaps painfully in my chest and I jolt forward before she can say more. "My family! Where are they?"

"They're safe and well," she says. "We were scouting this part of the mountains and found them sheltering in a cave back that way." She inclines her head in the direction I passed to get here. "They were with a creature who calls himself 'Thaden Kane.'"

I bristle at the way she calls Thaden a 'creature.' To my mind, it's one step removed from 'beast.'

"I'll admit our meeting with your siblings wasn't exactly amicable," Elowynn continues. "Blacksmiths have long been the enemy of the fae and we recognized your brother's and sister's power immediately."

Fae.

She mentioned them earlier.

I'm not totally unfamiliar with the fae as a species, but I don't know much about them.

When I was younger, there were books in the Blacksmith

library that mentioned delegates traveling to other kingdoms and forging alliances with them. There were only scraps of information about the kingdoms themselves and the people who live in them. In fact, some books had pages torn out and I wondered if that had been done on Malak's orders.

The three most important things I know about the fae are that they supposedly live far away, certainly far enough that they shouldn't be here; their power is related to nature; and they are a cunning and deceptive race, which means they are best avoided.

I can understand why Blacksmiths might be their enemies, particularly given that my power destroyed their weapons and armor.

It can't make them feel terribly safe around me.

Elowynn is continuing. "Luckily for your siblings, the creature named Thaden Kane stepped between us and them."

"Man," I snap. "Thaden Kane is a *man*, not a creature."

Her eyebrows rise slightly, but she doesn't otherwise respond to my anger. "He convinced us that Tamra and Gallium aren't our enemies. He claimed to have grown up in *Myrkur Fjall*, which is one of the few human villages not aligned with the human kingdom in the north. He told us that he and your siblings were fleeing *Vadlig Odemark*, and he asked for amnesty."

Her lips twist. "His knowledge of our culture saved him —and your siblings. Since he requested amnesty, we were obliged to take them all to Queen Karasi. In our culture, she alone can grant amnesty."

Although the presence of fae in these lands is a surprise to me, the existence of a queen isn't completely startling.

When I was interrogating Thaden Kane before he became my ally, he talked of growing up in the village called *Myrkur Fjall*, which means *in the mountain's shadow.* He described it as a harsh place with barren ground in which it was difficult to grow crops, but he and his father had found shelter there from the war that had raged farther north.

The war between feuding queens.

The Queen that Elowynn now speaks of must surely be one of them. Particularly as Elowynn referred to her as the 'rightful' Queen, implying she has a greater claim to the throne.

Elowynn continues. "Queen Karasi granted your family her protection."

"Against your counsel," I murmur.

Her jaw clenches. "Your siblings requested that Queen Karasi extend her protection to you, which she also granted." Elowynn's focus flickers to Dusana and Bethoc before her voice becomes hard. "It's a decree she can reverse at any time."

Naturally.

Elowynn's gaze moves to the Vandawolf. "Your family didn't mention you would have someone else with you."

"They didn't know," I say.

"Well, whatever *that* creature is, it's up to our Queen if he lives or dies."

I stare back at her, fighting a resurgence of rage, but beneath it is a feeling that I hate more than my wrath.

It's a growing emptiness.

My hope of helping the Vandawolf was stripped away and now... There's a chance I can reach my sister after all, but I doubt it will be in time.

I don't want this new hope, only to have it torn from me again.

"Since that creature is clearly with you," Elowynn says, "it is not permissible for us to harm him until Queen Karasi makes her decision."

"*Man!*" I snap. "He also is a man, and too late! They already tried to kill him."

My eyebrows draw down as I cast a glare in the direction of Dusana and Bethoc. It's curious to me that the other fae haven't tried to retrieve their fallen brethren yet, but perhaps, it's because I'm in the way and, unlike Dusana and Bethoc, Elowynn seems to have a healthy respect for my power.

In response to my statement, her eyes widen and her cheeks flush. If I didn't know better, I'd say she looks angry about it. "That should not have happened."

My lips twist. "You assumed I attacked them and not the other way around."

Elowynn clears her throat, but she doesn't respond to my accusation. "I've explained myself as you asked. Now, you need to make a decision: Accept amnesty and come with us, or refuse our Queen's protection and suffer the consequences."

I have a decision to make but no real choices.

Elowynn could be lying. She might have killed Thaden and my siblings. I can't possibly trust the outwardly smooth appearance of her features because...

I recognize the mask she's wearing.

I have worn it.

A mask so complete that it allowed me to shut myself off from everything bad in my life. It allowed me to show only the emotions I was *supposed* to show, not what I was truly feeling.

I started wearing it the day I picked up a hammer and failed to access my power. I wore it for my parents and for the other Blacksmiths during my childhood years. I wore it for the humans for whom I killed monsters.

I wore it for the Vandawolf for a very long time... Until I didn't.

But I also consider what I know about Gallium, Tamra, and Thaden.

Gallium trained as a warrior with the Vandawolf. Thaden has the strength of a dragon. And Tamra, well, she might not have combat skills, but she's smart and she would have found a way out of danger.

"You're deciding whether or not you can trust me," Elowynn says, nodding her head. "That is wise. But I would urge you to make your decision quickly. As much as I would love the chance to kill you, I also want to leave this place as soon as possible. These mountains aren't safe. It isn't wise to linger in them."

Elowynn takes a step toward me before I can respond. "It would be my preference if we could end this situation amicably, Asha Silverspun. You will put down your tools, we will take you to our Queen, and she can decide whether or not to grant you and that... *man*... her continued protection."

At some point, my hand has come to rest on my hammer.

I drop my arm to my side, giving Elowynn a final hard stare. "My tools are down."

She narrows her eyes at my left hand.

"This one?" I ask, holding my palm up for her to see. "It doesn't come off." My lips twist. "The humans did this to me.

And no, I wasn't their leader or their queen. I was as much their captive as Gallium and Tamra were."

Elowynn's expression changes and for a second, her mask slips completely.

"Humans," she spits. "Perhaps we have some common ground, after all." She gives me a firm nod. "I will accept that your tools are down. Please remain where you are. I'm sure you can understand that our truce is tenuous."

She turns to the women on her left. "Retrieve Dusana and Bethoc. If they're wounded, tell me immediately."

At her command, two of the women on her left break off from the group, steering as wide of me as they can as they race toward their fallen comrades. They both have coral-colored hair and soft-blue eyes.

The woman who rushes toward Bethoc slows her pace before crouching and placing her fingers against Bethoc's neck. She looks to Elowynn and shakes her head.

The other woman reaches for Dusana, kneeling beside her before checking her pulse. "Dusana's alive but hurt," she calls.

Elowynn chews the inside of her lip as if she's chewing her thoughts. "Take her to the encampment. If she wakes up, do not give her anything for the pain."

The other woman's blue eyes widen. "But—"

"Do not question me!" Elowynn's harsh voice doesn't allow for objection. "Dusana disobeyed a direct order from Queen Karasi. That is treason! Punishable by death." Elowynn glares around at her warriors. "I should kill her on the spot. Letting her live is more mercy than she deserves."

The blue-eyed woman is pale. "Yes, Commander."

Elowynn seems to fold her wrath away, blank once again

as she continues. "Bring Bethoc's body. I will deliver the news of her treason to her family, and they will live with the shame of it."

In the next beat, she issues orders to the women on her other side. "Retrieve that man. We will bring him with us for Queen Karasi's judgement. Anyone who harms him will be judged by the Queen herself."

Four women rush from the group, hurrying toward the Vandawolf while also steering wide of my position.

Despite Elowynn's command to stay where I am, I step into their path, forcing them to pull up sharply. "If you wish to live, touch only the stretcher. Do not touch the man."

It isn't an idle threat. I don't know what will happen if they come into contact with the metal on the Vandawolf's chest. Possibly nothing. Maybe something awful.

Although it seems that's not all they have to worry about.

Judging by Elowynn's declarations, their Queen's word is law and breaking it means death. It's a much harsher regime than I would have expected.

Now that I've delivered my message, I turn to Elowynn. "I will walk beside his body. He doesn't leave my sight."

Her eyes narrow a little when I refer to his 'body.' Her lips part as if she's about to question me and I believe I know what she's going to ask: *Is he dead?*

I don't know the answer to that, but time is not on my side and even my rage is deserting me. Soon, I will have to face what losing him means.

Elowynn surprises me when she declares, "We will not be walking."

At that moment, a streak of light bursts through the air at

the mouth of the cave. It's a dazzling explosion of amethyst energy that sizzles around us like lightning.

With it comes an almighty *crack* like a blast of thunder.

A beast like none I've ever seen alights on the ground outside the cave.

CHAPTER 11

My hammer is in my hand, the creature's appearance triggering my fight reflexes, but Elowynn is quick to lift her hand. "Easy, Blacksmith."

The creature's wings fill the space between the rock walls of the pass outside the cave, and its talons scrape the ground as it turns toward us.

It looks like some sort of enormous bird with inky-black feathers and a dark-purple beak. Amethyst light continues to sizzle around its form, snapping and crackling like lightning.

Despite my limited view, I register how serene it seems, how settled, and how beautifully formed it is. Not like any monster I've ever encountered.

It settles onto the ground and I'm stunned to see my brother sitting atop it on what looks like a saddle—a two-seated saddle with Gliss sitting in the front. She must have gone to summon this creature.

"Asha!" my brother cries.

He slips from the saddle, slides down the bird's extended wing, and races toward me, carving a path between the fae warriors.

I can only watch as he runs toward me. I'm afraid that this must be a dream, that the blood loss has finally taken a toll and I'm hallucinating. "... Gallium?"

"I'm here."

"Gallium!" I choke back a sob, my heart responding to his presence, a little of myself surging to the surface despite the darkness that has taken hold of me.

Seeing him again is like being cast a lifeline, a length of rope into the dark pit I'm trapped in, a way to climb out.

He hurries toward me, his brilliant, green eyes filled with concern, his arms reaching for me. There was a time when he was little for his age—a time when I threw myself in front of him like a shield, determined to protect him with my life— but now his presence is like *my* shield.

He's taller than I am. As tall as the Vandawolf and just as broad in the shoulders. His muscles were honed over years of construction work within the human city, along with relentless combat training with the Vandawolf. His eyes are the same shape as our mother's eyes, and his jaw is as strongly cut as our father's. His silver-blond hair catches the moonlight, radiating light around him.

He's wearing what I last saw him in: sturdy-looking pants and a long-sleeved shirt, but his clothing is smudged with dirt and ash, no doubt from the trip through the wasteland.

I need the hug into which he's about to sweep me, but just as he's about to reach me, I remember myself.

I'm a danger to him. Just as I'm a danger to any living creature.

I backpedal as fast as I can, veering to the left and hitting the wall at the side of the cave.

"Stay back, Gallium!" My cry is filled with overwhelming panic. "I could kill you!"

My left hand is up, my palm out so he will see the medallion and understand the threat, but I prepare to retract it quickly.

At the last moment, before he would wrap me up in a hug, his focus falls to it.

He jolts to a sharp stop.

"Asha?" His expression is falling. "What happened?"

"Forge-fire," I say, even though that's hardly an explanation. "I can't get it off."

I pull my left arm back to my chest, closing my hand around the medallion. My breathing is heavy and my shoulders are hunched. Tears are leaking down my cheeks, and I want them to stop.

I wish that my brother's presence and the concern in his eyes didn't have the power to make me feel my heart again.

"Oh, Asha, no..." His gaze passes from my tarnished hair to my arms to my left hand.

"Maintain your distance, brother. I'm no longer myself."

My brother's focus is dropping to my wounds.

The concern in his eyes turns to fear. "You're hurt." His forehead quickly creases. "But those are fresh wounds. They can't be from the monster this morning." His eyes briefly widen with apparent realization before his jaw clenches and his gaze flickers to the nearby women. "The fae did this?"

My response is a low murmur. "Before their commander arrived."

His lips press into an unhappy line. He immediately reaches for his shirt, tugging the base of it clear of his long pants and pulling it up and over his head, leaving him bare-chested.

He pushes the material toward me. "Use this to bind the wounds as tightly as you can. I need to get you to Tamra right away."

When I take the material, careful not to touch him in the process, he steps away from me, but I try to call him back. "Gallium, I'm not alone."

At that moment, the four fae women pass by, carrying the Vandawolf's stretcher. Seeing them, one at each corner of the stretcher, their muscles straining, brings home to me just how large and heavy the Vandawolf is.

I'm not sure how I dragged him through the wasteland for all of those hours and up into this mountain.

Gallium is turned away from me, so I can't see his face, but he stiffens and his voice is strained. "The Vandawolf is with you."

I can't be sure how Gallium feels about the Vandawolf right now. The Vandawolf kept him and Tamra alive for the last ten years, but they harbor justified rage about their separation from me and the way the humans treated me. More specifically, the fact that the Vandawolf was complicit in that treatment.

When he set us all free this morning, Tamra was vocal about her feelings: She didn't want me to go back to help him fight the monstrous wolf. Gallium was quieter about his opinions at the time. He didn't try to stop me, but he must have hoped I would leave my past behind.

"Barely," I say. "The Vandawolf is *barely* with me. I'm not sure if he's still alive, and I can't..." I try to breathe, forcing myself to continue speaking. "He needs Tamra's help more than I do."

Gallium half-turns back to me, his expression closed off, but his response is quiet. "She can't help the dead."

I won't let the Vandawolf out of my sight and I take a quick step after him, staying wide of my brother.

"He isn't dead. He can't be." My voice hardens and I close my fist around the medallion and take hold of its cruelty. "He wouldn't fucking dare."

Gallium seems to reconsider me as he keeps pace with me. His lips part and the tension around his eyes increases. He appears wary of me now—and so he should be. Whatever resurgence of my own mind I experienced when I first saw him, it's disappearing.

He hurries ahead of me. "I'll find out."

As I follow my brother toward the mouth of the cave, keeping the stretcher within my view, I quickly peel up the plates of my armor and slide his shirt around my body beneath them. I try to cover as many of the stab wounds as I can, and then I pull the material tight. I tie it off, knowing it won't stop much of the blood, but it's a start.

Outside the cave, Gliss has slid to the ground. She approaches the bird's head, stroking its neck and quietly murmuring to it, as if she's intent on keeping it calm.

Nearby, Elowynn has stepped up beside the women holding the stretcher and is now standing between Gallium and the Vandawolf.

Gallium approaches her at a quick pace but slows when he reaches her.

I'm surprised at the way her mask slips as she watches him approach, her gaze flitting across his now-naked chest, her lips slightly pursed and her forehead creased, as if he perplexes her somehow.

"We need to get back to Tamra as soon as possible," he says. "But first, I need to check the Vandawolf."

"The what?"

Gallium inclines his head to the stretcher. "That man. He's called 'the Vandawolf.'"

Elowynn stiffens and her eyes widen. "*This* is the wolf you spoke of?" Her incredulous gaze flashes to me before returning to Gallium. "But your sister's protecting him. Why would she defend the wolf you said imprisoned her?"

Her speech surprises me. Only a short time ago, she accused me of being a leader or a queen, and yet now it seems she already knew I was a prisoner because my brother told her so.

I remind myself of what I know of the fae: They're cunning. They will play games. I can't trust anything they say or do.

"Don't ask me to explain my sister's motivations," Gallium replies, and I wish I could see his face because it sounds like he's speaking through gritted teeth.

Elowynn's expression softens. "Very well."

She stands aside and Gallium pauses there for a moment, his head turning, as if he's contemplating the Vandawolf's wounds.

With his back to me, there's only so much I can tell from the set of his shoulders and brief glimpses of the side of his face, and for the life of me, I can't seem to make my legs move beyond the mouth of the cave.

These damn wounds. The makeshift bandage Gallium gave me isn't making much of an impact, the blood already seeping through.

Gallium leans across the stretcher, turning his ear to the Vandawolf's face without touching him.

He straightens. "He's still breathing, but he doesn't have long. With these wounds, it's astonishing that he's alive at all."

"He's fighting to live," I whisper, a cold smile crossing my lips. "He probably wants the chance to tell me to leave him again."

I pull myself away from the rock, forcing myself to use the pain and the energy in the anger that comes with it.

"He has your Queen's protection," I say to Elowynn. "If you don't want him to die on your watch—which I understand could be an act of treason—then you will take him to my sister immediately. She can heal him."

Behind Elowynn, Gliss is visible to me where she has remained at the bird's head. The bird arches its neck to peer in my direction with two very intelligent-looking eyes. Its feathers ruffle softly in the breeze.

As for Gliss, she's staring hard at Elowynn, who turns to her sister, as if there's some sort of silent communication happening between them again.

Elowynn gives Gliss a small shake of her head before she turns back to me.

"It's too dangerous to carry the Vandawolf on a thunderbird," she says to me. "We will walk, as you originally said. If he dies along the way, that's unavoidable."

My brow furrows. My declaration that I would walk beside him was only relevant when I assumed there was no other form of transportation. "How long is the walk?"

"On foot, it will take us all night to reach the outskirts of our encampment."

I grit my teeth. "He won't live that long."

"Well, I'm sorry, but that's the best we can do."

I glare at the creature she called a thunderbird and the saddle with two seats. "No, it isn't. I'm commandeering this beast. I will carry the Vandawolf on it."

Elowynn's eyes widen with apparent alarm. "On *my* thunderbird?"

"Yes," I say.

"No." Her eyebrows draw down, but I'm certain I detect real fear in her eyes. "Your power is too dangerous. You could kill Concord just by touching her."

Concord.

The bird has a name.

The fear in Elowynn's eyes is real. I'm sure of it now. She loves this bird. The same way I love my brother and sister.

Love creates leverage.

I allow my smile to grow as my heart becomes colder and colder and colder...

"That's true," I say, advancing on Elowynn. "My power is a danger to every living thing. But you no longer have a choice."

As I approach, I ignore the way Gallium's lips have parted and how his brow is quickly drawing down. He doesn't like what I'm saying and there's a part of me that understands that.

Still, I plow on, keeping my focus on Elowynn and not

the growing horror in my brother's eyes or the rising anger in the women around me.

"You will either allow me to take this bird while you lead the way on one of the other birds you undoubtedly have circling the air right now," I say. "Or I will kill it."

Elowynn takes a sharp breath. Her hand flies to her shoulder, where I'm sure her weapon lies against her armor.

"Do it," I say, my fist clenching and unclenching around my medallion, my other hand on my hammer's handle. "Draw your weapon, *fae*, and see what happens."

Gallium is shaking his head. "Asha, no."

I cast my focus onto him. "Brother, I love you, but I've fought and bled and screamed. I've kept the Vandawolf alive, and I won't give up now."

"Why?" he asks.

"You've never touched darkness, brother. Not like the Vandawolf has. Not like I have. His fate is intertwined with mine and I will see this through. No matter what it takes."

He steps up to me and I don't flinch.

"Even if you have to go through me?" he asks.

Even without his tools, my brother is bright in my vision. His goodness, his heart, and his honor are untainted.

Take control of the light and the dark.

The impulse is strong.

My response is quiet but absolute. "Even if I have to go through you."

CHAPTER 12

"Stop!"

The cry comes from Gliss. She leaves the thunderbird's head and hurries around the stretcher.

"Sister—" She stops in front of Elowynn and starts again more formally. "Commander Dawn, Concord is your thunderbird. You have the final say in this, but Concord is willing to carry Asha Silverspun and the Vandawolf. In fact, she *requests* to do so." Gliss's voice lowers. "Which you already know, since you understand Concord's thoughts as well as your own."

At Gliss's speech, the thunderbird shuffles a little, her neck curved, her eyes on Elowynn.

There's a silence between them.

Then Elowynn's jaw clenches.

I reevaluate the two dark-haired women. Fae powers are connected to nature, but it seems that they can read this thunderbird's mind. It's unsettling that they might be able to read mine, too.

Gliss's voice lowers to a whisper. "Don't risk Concord's life in the name of pride."

Elowynn's expression is unreadable. Almost. I'm getting better at interpreting the smallest changes in the mask she wears.

She's frustrated.

I don't need to read her mind to know she won't want her authority undermined, let alone by me.

She spins to me. "You have my permission, Blacksmith, but according to your own request, we will not touch this man. Which means we will not help you move him up to the saddle. You must do that yourself."

"That's fine." I've faced more daunting tasks than that today. I'm more concerned about the bird tipping us off once we're on it, but hopefully, that won't happen, given the creature's apparent willingness to carry us.

"Put the stretcher on the ground," Elowynn orders the four women holding it. They look relieved as they place it on the ground, rubbing their arms as they step away.

My brother is once again at my side. "You'll only open your wounds lifting him up there."

"I'm aware of that," I say, trying to keep my voice low. "But you can't help me." I sigh. "Even if I thought you wanted to."

There's a war in his expression, but I don't have time to worry about him.

Hurrying to the Vandawolf, I hook my arms under his shoulders, hauling him upward with a grunt. There's no point trying to keep my left hand away from him now. All I can do is guard my thoughts and impulses and focus completely on lifting him.

With the force of my effort, I sense my wounds open and feel the fresh flow of blood, but the medallion gives me the strength to ignore it. Stomping my foot down on the stretcher to keep it steady, I heave the Vandawolf off it.

I'm aware of the wide eyes of the fae women watching me, particularly the ones who were holding the stretcher and the way they're whispering to each other as I pull the Vandawolf a full five paces toward the bird all on my own.

While the others stay clear of me, including Elowynn, whose lips are pressed into a hard line, Gliss approaches me.

"Carry him up Concord's wing," she says, keeping a small distance between us. "The bone along the top of her wing is strong enough and wide enough to create a platform. I will keep Concord calm and make sure she takes you directly to the widest landing pad at the castle."

"*You* will?" I glance from her to Elowynn. "What about your sister? I thought this was *her* bird?"

Gliss's expression hardens. "Concord was our mother's thunderbird. My sister may have officially claimed her, but Concord is bonded to both of us."

With that, she heads back to the bird, strokes her hand along its large neck and, when it arches its face to her, she presses her cheek to its cheek.

I assume she's communicating with it, but it's impossible to tell for sure.

Across the way, Elowynn has folded her arms across her chest.

I take a deep breath as the bird extends its wing toward me. I identify the edge of it, where the bone must rest.

Breathing out, I tell myself this is no worse than pulling

the stretcher up the mountainous incline and I already accomplished that.

I can do this, too.

With another grunt of effort, I step onto the wing, moving backward and crouching as low as I can to find my balance and stop the Vandawolf from sliding around.

All the while, the stillness of his chest drives me onward.

Finally, I reach the saddle. Because the bird's wing bone is closer to the front seat, I pull the Vandawolf up onto it, fighting desperately to keep him from sliding across and falling off the other side.

The only way to get the Vandawolf to straddle the seat is to sit myself down in the back seat first. While engaging my stomach and thigh muscles, I pull him high enough that I can maneuver his legs to either side of his own seat.

It's awkward and difficult and nearly impossible.

When one of the fae women on the ground giggles cruelly at my efforts, rage rushes through me, giving me the strength to complete my task.

Finally, I lower myself completely onto the saddle.

It has waist straps and I manage to clip one around the Vandawolf, although I have to let the strap all the way out so it will fit around him. Clipping my own waist strap closed is nearly impossible, but I manage it, only to find that it bites into my injuries painfully.

Blood continues to drip down my right leg, all the way down the outside of my boot and onto the stone below us.

The Vandawolf is now facing the bird's tail and, as such, is facing me, his upper body leaning against mine while I pray I'm strong enough to support his weight for the time it will take us to reach our destination.

The pull within me toward the metal plastered to his chest is fainter now, as if it's decreased with his low energy. But the softness of his breath against my neck, the slow and barely perceptible movement of air, reassures me that he's alive.

I exhale some of my turmoil, finding comfort in holding him. This, at least, I can attempt to control.

The moment I'm settled, Elowynn bursts into action. "Bring me Bethoc's bird. I'll ride it back. You two!" She points at two of the women who helped carry the stretcher out of the cave. "Bring that stretcher with you. We'll need it once we reach the camp. The rest of you, fan out in the sky. We don't know what might come at us once we're airborne again."

She said earlier she didn't want to linger here. I shiver a little at the possibility of more threats ahead of us.

All of her warriors jump into action, leaving my brother standing still amid a flurry of activity.

Elowynn approaches him. "You will ride with me, Blacksmith."

He gives her a brief nod and steps away, but he casts glances back at me as he goes.

As soon as the space around us is clear, Gliss cries to the bird, "Fly, Concord. Keep them safe!"

The thunderbird extends its wings and flaps them with a *crack!*

Energy sizzles around us and it's like touching lightning. My heart jumps and misses a beat. I want to run my fingers through the light storm suddenly building around us, but I can't take my hands off the Vandawolf.

Actually, if I weren't so desperate to get the Vandawolf to my sister, I'd be fucking terrified right now.

The energy surrounding the bird creates a visual disturbance that stops me from seeing the retreating ground, but once we're in the air, the light around the thunderbird's body dims significantly until it's a barely perceptible black shadow beneath me.

That's when I can clearly see the mountains, which now sit far below us.

It's dizzying, and I quickly shift my focus to the bird's neck.

Don't look down.

I fight to hold on to the contents of my stomach and pray only to stay on the bird as it soars through the darkness.

I'm vaguely aware of multiple other sparks of light from within the mountain pass I've left behind, tiny pinpricks of bursting energy before they quickly fade and a group of dark shadows rises up into the air behind us.

One of them must be carrying Elowynn and Gallium, but I can't tell which and I can't twist to peer more closely at them.

The space below me is an ongoing blur and I know I'm missing most of it. The mountain range is vast, merging into barren ground and finally giving way to gatherings of shapes that could be a village dotted with sparse trees.

Then there's a forest, and another plain, and far ahead, more mountains, except that those don't appear to be as vast or high as the mountain range we just left behind.

My focus is finally drawn downward as we soar a little lower, across a wide field that rests at the base of the upcoming mountains. It's dotted with triangular shapes that could be tents, but I can't study them for long enough to be sure.

Up ahead, the outline of a castle comes into view.

It appears to have been hewn into the side of the mountain and stretches both upward and sideways.

Light flashes brightly on my far left, and my attention is drawn to the sky at the edge of the field.

Thunder rumbles across the distance and lightning flickers, even though the sky is clear and there's no storm in sight.

Many flying creatures in the shape of thunderbirds seem to be forming a line in the sky there, and unlike the bird I'm riding on, they aren't concealing their presence.

Concord is flying so fast that the stone castle rushes toward us, and before I know it, she's touching down onto a platform.

Firebrands burn at the sides of an arched opening leading into the castle on my left.

My arms and legs are trembling with the effort to support the Vandawolf. At least, I hope that's why they're trembling, and not because I'm going into shock.

Several thunderbirds land around me, at which point a group of armor-clad women rush from the opening on my left. They surge toward Concord, as well as toward the other birds, but pull up sharply when they see me and the Vandawolf.

Luckily, Elowynn has landed right behind us. She slides down her bird's wing, landing lightly on the platform and hurrying toward the new group of women.

"We have Asha Silverspun!" she shouts. "Four of you,

take care of the birds. The rest of you, form an escort to the Queen."

The women ahead immediately form two lines leading to the entrance.

Concord has extended her wing.

I force my fingers to work and unclip the waist strap around both the Vandawolf's body as well as my own. My arms and legs seem to have gone numb, and as soon as the straps are open, I slip to the left, desperately trying to hold on to the Vandawolf at the same time I angle myself along the bird's wing bone.

I only half-manage it. We slip down the top of the wing bone and then off it, tumbling the remaining distance through the bird's feathers to the hard, stone platform below.

"Asha!" Gallium's cry reaches me moments before he appears beside me.

I hold up my hand to ward him off. "I'm okay."

I'm not. But the medallion's influence makes it far easier to lie.

The Vandawolf has landed with his head on my chest, his torso half on mine, his legs on the ground. My left shoulder took the brunt of the fall, but by some miracle, I don't sense any broken bones.

Once more, I find myself staring up at the night sky, except that this time, it's filled with streaks of unnatural lightning and the thunder of wings as a cascade of birds stream toward the castle and veer toward different platforms.

Moments later, the two fae warriors Elowynn chose earlier place the stretcher down beside me. They're joined by two more women, each staring down at me, apparently waiting for me to drag the Vandawolf onto the bed.

I tell myself it will be the last time I need to do this.

I convince myself I'm not already pushed beyond my endurance.

Maneuvering him onto his back, I fight the pain, which has become my constant enemy—or maybe my friend, since it spurs me on.

Somehow, I get him back onto the stretcher and then I drop to my knees beside him, aware of how quiet it is now that all the birds have landed.

The women lift him into the air and then they're carrying him away.

I stumble upright, but I pause for a moment to incline my head in a small gesture of thanks to the bird for bringing us here. "Thank you for not tipping us off. I apologize for threatening to harm you. And for falling through your wing."

Concord responds by inclining her head, her feathers rustling a little.

Ahead of me, Elowynn has been joined by Gliss, although my brother hangs back near me.

Somehow, I move.

I'm too tired to care about the mistrustful expressions of the fae women around me and the way they narrow their eyes, as if I'm their worst enemy.

Perhaps I am.

I stay close to the stretcher as our path takes us inside the castle.

I pray I'm not about to step into a nest of vipers worse than the one in the wasteland.

CHAPTER 13

Elowynn and Gliss drop back so that they're directly in front of the women carrying the stretcher. Gallium stays close on my right as we enter the castle and descend down a wide, sloping walkway to an equally large hallway with arched doorways on either side. The doorways reveal rooms lined with saddles and armor all neatly laid out on shelves or hanging on the walls.

I have no hope of memorizing the path as we navigate a maze of corridors and chambers that extends much farther back into the mountain than I was expecting.

There are no explanations from the women surrounding me, only their constant, soft footfalls.

Just when I think we can't go much farther into the mountain, the path seems to veer outward again and the air becomes fresher. Gallium is a constant at my side, his arm lifting when I stumble, but I steer clear of his touch.

My brother is loyal and kind. My decision to bring the Vandawolf with me may deeply concern him, but there's no accusation in his body language now. Nothing but worry as he risks reaching out to support me.

"Commander Dawn," he calls to Elowynn, who has remained ahead of us. "How much farther?"

Elowynn casts a glance back at us. Her focus lingers on him, but it's sharp on me. "The Queen is in the ballroom, entertaining her chosen companions for the evening. We're nearly there."

Sure enough, the women ahead of Elowynn quicken their pace and within moments, they split to either side, lining the walls and stopping there.

Elowynn and Gliss continue ahead of the stretcher bearers while Gallium and I follow.

We approach a brightly lit opening that's arched like the doorways along the corridors, but much higher and wider. Lilting music wafts from the room ahead, the slight echo in the melody indicating we're about to enter a much larger room than any we passed.

As we approach, my chest fills with a scent I don't recognize. It's reminiscent of the smell of vanilla cakes that would float from bakeries when I was a small child and my parents didn't yet know I would be different than other Blacksmith children. It was a sweet smell that clashed with the harsh reality of the lives of the humans who baked those cakes.

Behind me, five of the fae I thought would remain on guard against the wall peel off as I pass by and follow at my back.

When I finally step into the ballroom, they form a line across the opening as if to block any escape. I pay them no mind. I could decimate them if I wish.

The room before me reminds me of Malak's throne room when he would hold garish parties to show off his latest creations and where Blacksmiths would eat and drink to excess.

My stomach turns at the memory.

Those were not happy times for me.

The ceiling soars high above us, glowing yellow orbs situated all around it that cast light across walls decorated with what appear to be living vines and flowers.

Wooden tables and chairs fill the left half of the room, although there's plenty of space around each of them, giving force to Elowynn's statement that these are the Queen's 'chosen' companions.

About thirty fae with hair, complexions, and eyes of all colors sit at the tables, drinking and chatting with each other. There's an equal mix of men and women. They're dressed in fine clothing, from silvery gowns to dark-as-night pants and tunics, and they wear overly-bright smiles.

Darkly, I wonder what they have to do to be 'chosen.'

A wooden throne sits at the far right of the hall, in front of which is an open stretch of floor about twenty paces wide.

The throne has the appearance of a tree trunk that grew out of the stone at its base and into the shape of the seat, its back extending all the way up to the high ceiling.

Lush vines curl around it and roses drip from them, while a rug of petals has formed at the feet of the woman resting on the throne.

She is extraordinarily beautiful with pale skin dusted with gold and long, blonde hair that falls in waves across her chest. Even from this distance, her eyes remind me of the sun, a glistening yellow color, like that of the sunflowers I saw in illustrations.

But my focus quickly shifts to the two people sitting in chairs to her left.

My sister, Tamra, has hair that is long and silvery, an unmissable color in the soft, yellow light. She's seated closest to the Queen and turned toward the monarch, her hands folded in her lap and her countenance calm.

Thaden sits in the chair to Tamra's left. When standing, he's as tall as the Vandawolf and just as broad in the chest. His hair is bronze—as bronze as the dragon scales that coat his right arm all the way from his neck to his fingertips and down his right side to his waist. Only the scales on his forearm and hand are currently visible since he's otherwise wearing a long-sleeved tunic rolled up to his elbows.

The pull toward Thaden is as electric as the draw I feel toward the Vandawolf. Blacksmith magic was used to change both men's forms and is constantly ignited within them, acting like a magnet when I'm in contact with my tools.

Which I now permanently am.

It's only because of the Vandawolf's waning life that the strength of the pull toward him has lessened.

Three toolboxes rest on the floor between the chairs Tamra and Thaden are sitting on. I recognize the boxes as the ones containing Tamra's tools, Gallium's tools, and the third one—the black one—houses my last, remaining medallion. It's the one I left behind when I went to fight the monstrous wolf.

Elowynn and Gliss precede me and Gallium, hurrying across the open floor toward the throne, where they take a knee five paces from it.

The women carrying the stretcher follow closely behind them, quickly setting it down slightly behind Elowynn and Gliss, but in an open patch to their left so that it will be fully visible to the Queen.

They, too, take a knee.

I try to keep up, but my footsteps are stumbling and, once again, Gallium veers toward me, stopping himself from touching me at the last moment, his jaw clenching as his focus flies to my left hand.

I can feel his frustration like a palpable force as he stays clear of me.

"I'm fine," I murmur, although I'm conscious of the smirks from the onlookers.

Let them think that I'm weak. All it will take is some new pain or anger and my weariness will disappear again.

Ahead of us, Tamra has half-risen out of her chair, craning to see around the women as they settle to their knees. As soon as she has a clear line of sight to me, she gives a cry, her focus flashing across my face and my tarnished hair to the blood now drying on the outside of my boot.

I've left bloody footprints in my wake.

Her bright, green eyes are wide. "Asha! You're hurt!"

She starts to lurch toward me, but the Queen's hand wraps around her arm, moving at a flash and jolting Tamra to a stop.

Tamra's weight is on her front foot, her startled gaze turned to the Queen.

"Still yourself, dear," Queen Karasi says, her face turned up to Tamra's from where she remains seated on her throne.

A hushed silence falls around us the instant the Queen speaks, and now I sense all eyes on her.

It's so quiet that I can hear my sister's sharply indrawn breath. "But—"

"Darkness surrounds your sister," the Queen says, her face turned up to Tamra. "I can sense it. A terrible, destructive evil. It's best if you stay here, where it's safe. I'm sure that's what Asha would want."

With that, the Queen turns her gaze on me, her smile soft while her sunlit eyes are sharp.

Despite the barely hidden calculation in the Queen's expression, I don't object. My sister is safer as far from me as she can be.

"It is what I want," I rasp, emphasizing my speech for the listening fae. "To touch me is to die."

Tamra's chest rises and falls rapidly, but she stops tugging against the Queen, who slowly unfurls her hand.

Tamra's forehead is pinched, tension growing around her mouth as she lowers herself to her seat. She's smart. I can practically read her thoughts: *How can I heal Asha if I can't touch her?*

I give my head a little shake, unsure if she'll read it the way I intend: *You can't heal me. Not yet.*

Maybe not at all. But I'll face that problem later.

"Fuck that." Thaden's voice is a soft rumble as he rises from his seat. He grasps Tamra's hand briefly, as if to reassure her, before he hurries toward me.

I'm on the back foot, surprised by his exclamation. "Thaden, what are you...?"

"I can help you."

All of the fae, including the Queen, are watching him as he skirts around the stretcher and strides toward me. His features tense at the sight of the Vandawolf, but his focus returns swiftly to me.

"No, Thaden." I backpedal as fast as I can—which, in all fairness, is not fast in my current state—but he keeps on coming.

"Asha, you can't hurt me." Thaden reaches out with his scaled hand, his pace only increasing. "The worst was already done to me. Let me make something good of it. Let me help you."

His dragon scales glisten in the bright lights. I'm reminded that they act as a barrier that can withstand the power in my dark medallions. When Thaden was a captive in the Vandawolf's prison and I attacked the Vandawolf out of pain and fear, it was Thaden who disarmed me.

Still, my left hand is up, a visual warning not to come near me.

He doesn't stop, and instead catches my dangerous hand within his scaled palm, enclosing it and covering it.

I shudder to a halt.

The cruel malice within me comes to a blissful cessation that makes me gasp with relief, my eyes filling with tears. I can still feel it, writhing in my arm and hand, but it has nowhere to go. Of course, if I pressed it to his other arm, it would be a different story, but for these precious moments, the burden has lifted.

I don't miss the way Thaden winces at the contact between us before his expression wipes clean.

"It's okay," he says softly, brushing my tear tracks with his other hand. "I've got you."

As his gaze takes me in, he seems to relax even further, as if he has no reason to fear me whatsoever. As if this new

126

version of me doesn't frighten him. I suppose holding my powered hand without suffering any consequences must give him some level of confidence.

"I'm glad you made it. We were worried when you didn't find us." He lowers his voice. "We've gained amnesty for now, but we aren't among friends."

Aside from my brother and sister, most people aren't happy to see me. This isn't new to me. I am hated. My power is hated. My presence is reassuring to *nobody*.

I press my lips together, trying to stop the pain in my chest as he continues. "But it's clear you're in a bad way. Tell me where you're hurt."

I shake my head. Every moment we spend talking, the Vandawolf draws closer to death. "I'm not the one who needs help."

He grimaces. "The damage to your armor says otherwise."

"Please, Thaden," I whisper. "I have time. The Vandawolf doesn't."

He gives a quiet exhale, his hand tightening on my cheek as if he knows I won't like what he's going to say. "I'm not sure that anything can save him, Asha."

"Tamra can."

Thaden's jaw clenches, but I can't read his expression because he twists to glance at the throne.

The Queen has risen from her seat and is stepping toward the Vandawolf—or, more correctly, toward Elowynn, who has continued to kneel near the Vandawolf's stretcher.

The Queen said there's darkness around me, so she'll surely sense it around the Vandawolf, too. I don't know what she plans to do, and I'm already tugging toward her, pulling on Thaden's hand.

To my relief, he supports me without objection as I hobble toward the stretcher.

I stop when I reach it, keeping my distance from the Queen. She doesn't appear to be paying me any attention, but as I draw closer, I can see that she's eyeing me from beneath her lashes.

To Elowynn, she says, "Commander Dawn. Rise and report."

Elowynn lifts to her feet. "Queen Karasi, I've brought Asha Silverspun, as commanded. However, when we found her, this man was with her." Elowynn points to the Vandawolf. "Just as you see him on this stretcher, that's how we found him. We brought him back with us for your judgement."

Queen Karasi barely glances at the Vandawolf, her narrow-eyed focus remaining on me. "Who is he?"

"He is called the Vandawolf," I reply, speaking before Elowynn can. "And he needs my sister's help. If you will just—"

"This is the wolf-man we heard about?" The Queen's speech cuts across me as she aims her question at my brother. "This is the man who held you captive for years?"

Gallium now stands on my right while Thaden is on my left.

My brother nods. "He is."

The Queen turns back to me. "So you captured your captor, Asha Silverspun?"

"No." My voice is hard. "I rescued him from the humans who betrayed him. And now I ask—"

"Well." Queen Karasi's hand flutters to her chest. "How intriguing that you would seek to save the beast that caused you so much pain."

She glides closer to me, her long gown slithering across the floor behind her, until she blocks my view of Tamra in the background.

Given her warning not to get too close to me, she's coming far nearer to me than I thought she would.

All the while, her golden eyes gleam at me. "Despite the darkness that has taken control of your mind, what spark of light must have driven you to forgiveness?" Before I can draw breath to answer, she continues. "Indeed, you must have a story to tell, and I do love a good story."

She claps her hands, two loud claps. "Gallium, will you bring your sister a chair so she can sit at a distance and tell me her story?"

And immediately to me, she says, "Come, Asha, you may sit near the throne. Not too close now. Close enough that I can hear you." She beams at me, as if she's bestowing me an honor. "Entertain me with your story."

Gallium hasn't moved. His focus on me. So, it seems, is everyone else's, including Elowynn, who is reaching for her hidden weapon.

A haze of anger has descended across my vision and a snarl rises to my lips. "*Entertain* you?"

Thaden's hand clenches around mine, but all I needed was this rush of fury to give me another boost of strength.

Standing tall, I wrench my hand out of his grasp. "You would be entertained while someone dies at your feet?"

Elowynn takes a step forward. Beside her, still kneeling, Gliss looks up, her face pale. I sense Thaden close in at my back while my brother also edges toward me—to stop me or support me, I'm not sure.

As for the Queen, my anger seems only to amuse her. Her lips curve upward and her eyebrows rise, her eyelashes batting at me.

"Well, of course," she says, her voice just as serenely melodic as it was moments before. "You live at my whim, Blacksmith. You must give me a reason to keep you alive."

My heart is like ice, but the sensation keeps me focused.

"No," I whisper. "You live at *my* mercy."

CHAPTER 14

The Queen's smile falls away. Her fingers twitch and the air around her suddenly heats. It's a soft heat, far too gentle to combat the freezing cold filling my veins.

When she lifts her hands, the fae at the tables behind me all draw back so quickly that their chairs scrape, but I'm not sure if it's in reaction to her or me.

Farther to my left, Elowynn draws her weapon, a finely crafted sword that she peels off her armor. If she's the Queen's protector, I'm sure she'll know how to use it.

I plot my path between her and the Queen while I remain conscious of the fae at my back and hope that Gallium and Thaden will stay out of my way.

Not so, it seems.

Before I can make a move, Thaden sidesteps me and places himself firmly between me and the Queen. His right hand is extended toward me, the scales that keep him safe gleaming in the light, while his left hand is held, palm up, toward the Queen.

"Stop," he says, and I'm not sure if he's speaking to me or to her until he continues. "Queen Karasi, you've granted us amnesty—"

"Which Asha Silverspun is on the verge of violating," she snaps.

He shakes his head. "If you will allow Asha to speak with her sister, I'm sure this can be resolved without igniting a war between fae and Blacksmiths."

"There is *already* a war between fae and Blacksmiths!" the Queen snarls. "It began thirty years ago and continues to this day."

I'm thrown by her declaration. Thirty years ago, Malak rose to power. I'm not sure what could have happened with the fae at that time.

If Thaden is confused or uncertain, he doesn't show it. "Whatever grievances you may have, they aren't against *these* Blacksmiths," he says. "They are innocent of any past history with the fae, whatever it may be. So again, with respect, I would ask that you honor the amnesty you've granted."

The Queen's shoulders are tense and the friction in the air rises, but then she exhales. "Hmph."

The glimmers of heat disappear from around her fingers and she lifts her chin. "Asha Silverspun may speak with her sister." She raises her hand, one finger held upward as if to make a point. "Then I will have my story."

"Agreed," Thaden says before he turns to me. "In fact, I think we will all need to hear it."

The Queen is already stepping aside, her expression

once again serene, such a complete mask that I would never guess she'd been on the verge of fighting me.

She waves her hand at Tamra. "Come, dear. Your sister wishes to speak with you."

Tamra stands and moves from her seat. She's still wearing the pants and long-sleeved tunic I last saw her in, although there are mud stains on her knees.

Her footsteps are slow and her features are pale and drawn, unlike moments before.

She approaches so cautiously that it draws confusion within me. I'm not sure exactly why she seems so reluctant to move toward me now. She can surely see that those standing near me aren't harmed by my power.

In fact, I'm not sure why she didn't hurry across the room earlier, no matter what the Queen said about my 'darkness.' What I recently learned about my sister is that she will bend, or even break, the rules when she feels in her heart that it's the right thing to do.

For a horrible moment, I consider that maybe the Queen has some other leverage over my family that I'm not yet aware of and of which they might not be able to tell me. Thaden looked relieved to see me and he told me to prepare for a game...

Or maybe it's simply because the Vandawolf is covered in malicious black metal and Tamra doesn't yet realize that I can remove it before she touches him. Malak's anvil was made from this same metal and it was upon that anvil that he siphoned Tamra's power when she was little. It's a trauma I don't think she's ever forgotten.

My heart hurts as I wonder if seeing the Vandawolf like this is triggering memories for her.

While the Queen retreats to stand beside Elowynn, who watches us carefully, Tamra finally comes to a stop a few paces away from me.

"I know what you're going to ask," she says quietly to me. "You want me to help him."

I hurry to reassure her. "I used a medallion to stop the bleeding, but I can pull it away from him so you won't be hurt. I just need you to be ready to heal him before he loses any more blood. Will you trust me? Can you try?"

Her green eyes glisten with tears, and she presses her palms together, chewing on her bottom lip as she stares back at me.

The silence between us stretches for so long that my heart progresses up into my throat.

I try to bring moisture to my lips as a new fear fills me.

A possibility I never considered.

"Tamra?"

Her hands stop wringing. Her expression wipes clean and she shakes her head resolutely. "I won't do it."

My heart plunges into an abyss.

That dark pit is pulling me down again, and I'm not sure if I'll be able to claw my way out of it this time.

I want to believe there's another force at play here, that somehow, my sister isn't making her own choices.

But her expression is clear. She doesn't take glances at anyone else, as if they have sway over her. In fact, both Thaden and Gallium appear surprised by her declaration, their foreheads creased, as if they assumed she would at least try.

"Why?" I ask, my voice barely more than an exhale.

She meets my gaze with an increasing calm that slowly breaks my heart.

"If I heal the Vandawolf, he'll cage you again."

"No." My denial is quiet but instant. "He gave us our freedom. He told us to leave—"

"He had *ten years* to free you!" Tamra snaps back at me, her calm composure breaking. "He didn't."

Her cry rings out around us and I'm aware of the way the Queen is suddenly smiling.

"Well, well," she says, an eager exclamation. "What an unexpected conflict."

Elowynn steps toward us, as if she thinks our disagreement should be stopped in its tracks, but the Queen halts her.

"No, no, dear Elowynn. Let them fight." Queen Karasi licks her lips. "If I'd known this would happen, I would have allowed them to speak much sooner. This is far more entertaining than any story."

Her speech fuels my rage, but I clamp down on it and try to focus on my sister.

I have to change her mind.

If I don't...

"He wasn't free to make his own choices," I say. "Yes, it took him ten years. But he spent those years playing games of survival with humans who hated him. Humans who ultimately tried to kill him when he was already injured and my back was turned. They wanted him dead. They thought of him only as a beast, never as a person."

"He *is* a beast!" Tamra cries, her voice once more cracking through the silent room.

Deep down, I recognize her anger. It's a rage she was never at liberty to feel before now. She could never express her outrage and pain. She was never free to fight back against our situation. I was the leverage used against her, just as she was the leverage used against me. Her love for me imprisoned her.

Now, her cry echoes what the Vandawolf himself told me:

I am a monster. Never forget it.

"Yes," I say, not denying it. "He is a beast. But that doesn't mean he can't make different choices."

Tamra shakes her head at me, her lips pressing into a hard line. "He is who he is. He can't change."

"'Can't change?'" I stare at her, incredulous, before I cross the distance to him, drop to my knees, and brush the damp hair away from his forehead, fully revealing his face. The sharp tooth peeking between his lips on his left side. The wolfish shape of his left eye. Even the texture of his hair.

"Look at him, Tamra. He *did* change. He *was* changed."

I swivel back to her, only to be faced with her unyielding features. I'm painfully aware of the distance between us and the fact that she's refusing to close it.

Still, I plough on. "He was transformed from a man who loved his family into a wolf whose nature pushed and pulled him every second of every day."

"You don't know that he loved his family," she replies, the corners of her mouth turning down. "You just want to believe that because it would make him more like you."

"I know he loved them!" I thump my fist against my heart. "I know he did..."

I'm certain of it. As certain as I am that the titanium hammer resting at my waist belonged to Malak.

At the same time, I'm not sure *how* I'm so certain.

I know nothing of the Vandawolf's past except that he spoke of a father and a younger brother, and that there was pain in his voice when he talked of losing them.

A pain I will feel if I lose *him*.

"If you heal him, he will have the chance to decide who he is," I say. "His first real choice that isn't influenced by obligation or expectations or fear. He doesn't have to go back to the humans. He can forget that cursed city and the humans who betrayed him. He can make a new life."

With me.

It's a hope I can't express because it's too fraught with uncertainty. What I need is to know who he is without all the walls between us. The chance to discover if the glimpses I saw of him in our cage in the sky were real.

Tamra's expression softens. "You don't want to give up on him."

"I *can't* give up on him."

If I give up on him—this beast, who was Malak's creation—then it means I will have given up on myself.

Because I, too, have been poisoned by Malak's power.

As long as there's hope for the Vandawolf, then there's hope for me.

I need to explain this to my sister. I need her to understand.

But her expression is already hardening. "I'm sorry, Asha. I won't risk your freedom," she says. "Or mine."

She takes a step back toward the throne. "I will heal *you* as soon as it's safe to do so, but I won't heal *him*."

My thoughts are suddenly bleak.

It won't ever be safe to heal me. Not as long as the

medallion is fused to my hand. A fact I'm refusing to acknowledge and will have to face soon. For all I know, my life is already slipping away, but with all this power clouding my mind, I'm oblivious to the danger.

It's the Vandawolf who still has a chance and yet she's refusing to help him.

I drag air in and out of my chest, trying to control the storm of resentment and powerlessness and disbelief raging within me.

Nearer to Tamra, Gallium has stepped up, reaching for our sister. "Tamra, won't you consider—"

"No, Gallium." Her rebuke stops him in his tracks. "Like Asha, you want to see the good. You don't want to see the bad. The Vandawolf closed his fist around her heart the day he let us live. She won't be free unless he's dead."

Gallium has no response to that, his quiet gaze meeting mine a moment before Thaden speaks.

"I don't pretend to know what you've experienced," he says. "But I know what it is to live each day pushing back the darkness within." He swallows visibly. "If I were in the Vandawolf's position, I don't know if I would—"

"No, Thaden," she rebukes him, too, but more softly. "You may battle the dragon whose soul you carry, but you are not a beast. You didn't kill my people or cage my sister or use her love against her." She gives him a rueful smile. "You didn't hurt us or keep us apart. Since you came into our lives, there's been hope."

She gives a heavy exhale before she turns back to me. Her eyes fill with tears and I recognize the deep pain behind her resolve. Ten years of pain.

"My hope lies with you, Asha. Don't break my hope."

She presses her lips together, her eyes beseeching me. "You have to let the Vandawolf go."

I can't.

So help me... I *can't*.

My only rationalization is an instinct. Because surely, it's true that I could never love a man who held me in a cage in the sky.

All I have is an undeniable and overpowering sense that I need to keep him alive. I don't even know if it's for me anymore or for some other reason.

My only certainty is that I will fight any battle to ensure he lives.

I try to speak past the constriction in my throat. Trying one last time. "Tamra, please. I kept him alive when he should have died. I fought the humans and escaped them. I carried him through the wasteland, even though I should have failed... All through it, he stayed alive. He needs to live."

My voice breaks, but I force myself to continue. "I have fought and I have killed and I have bled..."

I look up at my sister, to where she stands in a position of power over me, and I beg her. "*Please.*"

She takes another step back. Now, her voice is harder than I've ever heard it. My sister, who doesn't have a heart of darkness like mine, is speaking words I never expected to fall from her lips.

"I won't do it, Asha. Don't ask me again."

As I listen, everything around me seems to drop away.

A horrible thought rises within my mind.

I could *make* her do it.

All it would take is to lay my hand on her.

I could make her do it.

I could fucking... make her...

But I would never hurt my sister like that because I love her. And the Vandawolf was right.

Love is more powerful than hate.

I rock forward, my arms clutched around my stomach, too much fury billowing up within me to contain it.

My pain has nowhere to go but into a scream.

I roar it out, a frightful sound that echoes around and around the ballroom.

Tamra jumps, the watching fae lose their garishly eager smiles, and the Queen herself jolts backward.

I pour all of my pain into my voice, knowing that when I stop, I'll have to face what I have to do.

So I scream and scream until my chest is empty of air and I have no choice but to draw breath and prepare for the terrible act that will follow.

CHAPTER 15

As if my scream dragged him back to consciousness, the Vandawolf stirs and his low growl sounds. "Asha."

His eyes open, revealing the amber iris of his left eye. It's pale and both eyes are blank, just as they were this morning.

His blindness hasn't changed.

The sight of his wolfish features causes a stir among the nearest fae, their whispers becoming a hum around me.

"Asha!" The Vandawolf grips the sides of the stretcher, attempting to rise, but he barely makes it an inch upward.

Ignoring everyone else, I press a hand to his shoulder, just above the location of his heart.

"I'm here," I say, leaning over him, my tears dripping down onto his chest, onto the metal, where he won't feel them. "You're not alone."

His left hand wraps around my wrist, but his hold is weak.

"What kind of hell is this?" he asks, his sightless eyes somehow finding me. "How is there so much snow?"

Snow?

I reconsider him, but I shouldn't be surprised by the sickly color of his skin or the way his voice has become a mumble.

I exhale my acceptance of his deteriorating condition.

He must be delirious.

He won't know what he's saying anymore.

"I have to get you out," he says, still struggling to rise, his hand tightening around my wrist. "Your fingers are blue. You won't survive the night. I'm supposed to hate you, but I can't leave you here. I can't let you freeze to death..."

The breath rattles from his chest, his voice trails off, and his head drops back to the stretcher.

I think he's fallen unconscious again, but then his lips move. A barely audible murmur.

"I'm tired, Asha."

His speech slows, and I have to lean closer to catch his voice.

"I'm tired of digging in the snow. Let me sit beside you, where it's peaceful. Let it end here with you and me. In the pure... snow..."

He closes his eyes and now, he falls silent.

I swipe at the tears dripping down my cheeks.

I don't know what he was talking about. I don't know why he thought snow was falling, but somehow, I feel his words in my bones.

Let it end here with you and me.

"Thaden," I say, choking back my sob. "You can help me now."

"Anything," he says, in a low rumble.

"I need you to bring my toolbox."

There's a pause and I sense Thaden's wariness. When I look up, I find him poised on his front foot and his forehead creased.

"Why?" he asks.

"Because I need the medallion in it."

He still doesn't move, although the tension in his shoulders increases. "But that medallion is dangerous."

It's the medallion that Thaden used when he helped me forge the weapons for the city wall. He wrapped it around his right palm, which could withstand its power. In that way, he enabled its power to pass into the iron that he hammered into shape.

In doing so, unknown to us at the time, he also filled the medallion with the dragon's rage.

When I accidentally came into contact with the medallion afterward, the fury in the metal nearly tore me apart.

Yes, the medallion is dangerous, but right now, I am even more so.

"Will you make me fight you, Thaden Kane?"

He exhales heavily, his shoulders sinking a little. "I'll do as you ask."

The room is so quiet now that I clearly hear his retreating footfalls, then the soft, metallic clatter as he picks up the toolbox, then his approaching footfalls once more.

He crouches to place the toolbox beside me.

"Please open it," I say.

His lips press together for a moment and his voice is low. "Asha, what are you doing?"

"Open it."

"Promise me you're not giving up."

So that's his fear. I meet his eyes. "Don't worry. This is not about me."

"Okay, then." He pushes the lid open to reveal the single medallion lying within it. The titanium band is imprinted with the pattern of scales that exist across Thaden's palm.

"Whatever you need this for, let me use it for you," he says, still gripping the box's lid. "I can at least do that much for you."

He was the one who convinced me not to destroy this medallion. As he said, he *is* the dragon. Its rage and pain are part of him. He told me that if I ask him to, he will use the medallion to defend me.

I meet his eyes. "You kept my family safe, as you promised. For that, I will be forever grateful. But I could never ask you do this for me." I shake my head. "I'm the one who has to finish it."

He studies me for a long moment, searching my eyes, before he gives me a solemn nod. "I'm sorry, Asha. I truly am. This isn't how I thought things would turn out."

He rises to his feet and steps back toward Tamra, who has retreated even farther away from me. The throne is directly behind her, and her figure is so brightly backlit in that position that I can't see her expression.

I turn away from her and retrieve my hammer from my waist.

Gone is the silvery sheen that would come over my body when I used to pick up this hammer. Now, my skin remains like an unloved pot.

To use the medallion in the box, I must first awaken it by tapping it with the hammer, which I do. Just once.

A spark of dark light shoots up from the medallion, a fierce glow, and the sound it makes is terrifying. It awakens with a roar, a dragon's voice that rises all the way to the high ceiling and rushes around the room.

The watching fae flinch and draw even farther away from me than they already were, some of them knocking over glasses and chairs as they seek to take cover.

The Queen darts behind Elowynn, who takes up position in front of her like a shield.

My family braces as the roar rages around them.

Only Gliss rises up, her head tilted to the side, as if she's listening intently, appearing unafraid, her forehead creasing slightly.

I'm not sure why and it's not my main concern.

As the sound finally fades and the onlookers settle warily back into their seats, my heart only beats faster.

Touching this medallion could kill me. I suppose that's why Thaden was so concerned.

However, a medallion wasn't already fused to my left hand the last time I touched this dragon-imprinted band.

Now, I'm counting on it to protect me.

Carefully, angling my hand so that one medallion will press neatly against the other, I close my fist around the imprinted metal.

Power strikes through me.

Dark light bursts outward beneath my palm. Heat blasts through my arm and torso, as scorching as dragon's breath billowing over me.

I clamp down on my cry of pain.

Sweat breaks out across my body while I fight the storm of power as hard as I can.

Again, I sense the beast's rage in its last moments, the distortion of its brilliant light into icy darkness. An act so cruel that I feel it in my own heart. I'm assailed by sensations and images: burning stone; bronze scales; a black hammer like the one I hold. I can feel how young the dragon was, and yet its fire is beyond anything I've ever experienced, far hotter than any forge-fire.

My instinct is to let go of the imprinted medallion and for a terrible moment, I think I might need to, but then...

As I hoped, the pain lessens.

The medallion already fused with my skin is finally protecting me from the worst of the dragon's energy.

It's enough that I can give the imprinted metal a single, snarled command. *"Form a nail."*

The metal obeys me, its edges pulling in and thickening, transforming into a tip at one end and a flat surface at the other until a large, black nail rests in my palm, the dragon scales still visible on its surface.

I press the nail's tip to the Vandawolf's chest, right over his heart, as I grip my hammer firmly in my other hand.

Gallium flinched at the dragon's scream when the medallion awakened, but now he edges forward. "Asha, what are you doing?"

I inhale a shaky breath.

Anger is my defense now.

Not love.

"The Vandawolf is suffering," I say. "I've kept him alive in the cruelest possible way. Now I have to end it."

I could try to turn the Vandawolf's body to ash or smoke,

but unlike the humans, and even the monsters in the wasteland, he has Blacksmith metal fused to the outside and inside of his body. He has another soul—the wolf—within him. Blacksmith magic was used on him in the rarest of ways.

All of that combines to make him entirely unique. Set apart even from Thaden.

I have no idea how his body would react to my raw power and I won't risk causing him more suffering than necessary.

So instead, I will rely on a blade of my making.

"I will hammer this nail through his chest and stop his beating heart as quickly as I can."

Gallium's shoulders are tense. "You don't have to do this, Asha. He won't last long. You can simply... let him go."

"Your empathy can't help me, brother!"

My shout echoes in the silence.

I love my brother for his compassion, but it can't ease my burden right now. "Every breath the Vandawolf takes is hurting him. Every beat of his heart is pumping cold malice through his body."

I twist to meet my brother's eyes and then I focus on my sister, whose features remain shrouded in light.

"Do you not remember Malak's anvil?" I ask. "Do you remember how it made you feel?" My voice rises. "Have you forgotten how the Vandawolf made sure you never had to touch it again?"

I glance back at the maze of metal twisting across the Vandawolf's chest. "*That* is what I've done to him."

Desperately trying to breathe now, I pull in air, only to let it rush out of me in a low snarl. "Oh, if you wanted revenge on this man for all the years he kept me in a tower, then believe me, I've delivered it tenfold."

I lower my voice to a cold whisper. "I'm worse than Malak. I've shrouded my cruelty in kindness."

The distance between me and my sister—even my brother—feels wider right now than it ever did, wider even than when I lived in a tower high above them.

I may as well be alone.

Keeping the nail poised, I speak quietly to the Vandawolf. "You can stop fighting now."

I lift the hammer, preparing to hit the nail, but there I pause, my hand shaking.

My breathing is harsh. My heart is pounding.

I'm hesitating, not because I'm about to cause the Vandawolf more pain before his death, but because I know that once I end him, a part of me will break.

And I will never mend.

CHAPTER 16

The Fae Queen's voice cuts across the chill air. "I can heal him."

I look up at her, barely able to focus, my voice an incredulous whisper. "What did you say?"

"I can heal him." She glides around Elowynn, her gown once again slithering behind her as she approaches me. "Well, not me personally. I can command one of my people to do it."

She can have him healed?

Outrage floods me. I fight the new snarl rising to my lips. "You let him lie here, clearly suffering, when you had the power to help him?"

Her only response is a shrug. Her demeanor is so nonchalant that I tell myself I can't believe her.

This must be a sick game and I am, once more, her entertainment. Any moment now, she'll burst into beautiful laughter and tell me to get on with killing him.

Surprising me, she holds up a finger. "I want something in return."

Oh. So that is the game.

I force myself to breathe. "You want to make a deal."

That would explain why she waited so long to speak up. No doubt, she wanted me to be so desperate that I'd be willing to bargain for his life.

But deals haven't gone well for me in the past.

It was my deal with the Vandawolf that landed me in a tower. I offered him my life in exchange for my siblings' safety, and instead of ending me as I'd expected, he'd kept me alive.

Behind the Queen, Tamra suddenly makes a move, attempting to maneuver around the monarch's long dress.

She cries, "No more deals—"

"Hush, darling," Queen Karasi croons, her dress swishing as she spins to my sister and blocks her way. "I'm afraid you made your feelings clear. It's too late to help your sister now."

As soon as she speaks, though, she purses her lips, as if she's reconsidering what she just said. "Unless you really have changed your mind? Now that you know Asha will have to reach an agreement with me, will you choose to heal this wolf-man after all?"

Tamra chews her bottom lip, while Queen Karasi's sunlight eyes gleam.

"Will you doom Asha to the Vandawolf's oppression once more?" the Queen asks softly.

Tamra finally shakes her head. "I... can't do it. I can't heal him. If Asha makes this choice, then the consequences are hers alone."

Her words strike at the heart of me, but I try very hard to close off my feelings. I tell myself I can't feed the medallion with more pain right now, but I know that's an excuse. A way of putting away what I'm feeling, of making it cold, because if I don't clamp down on it... my rage will turn on my sister.

Carefully, I focus my thoughts on simple movements, placing the nail back into my toolbox and my hammer back onto the belt at my waist.

The Vandawolf is still breathing, but I have no capacity for hope, and it's just as well. "Name your price, but do it quickly," I say to the Queen. "Or he'll die and you'll lose your leverage."

"Very well," she replies. "I will ensure the Vandawolf is healed and in return, you will hunt and kill the Blacksmith known as Milena Ironmeld."

I'm not sure what I expected, but it wasn't this.

Milena Ironmeld was Malak's sister. She was thought to be dead. She made her presence known, however, when she captured Thaden Kane and used her power on him to merge him with a dragon, in the same way that Malak created the Vandawolf by merging him with a wolf.

She sent Thaden to the Vandawolf with a clear warning: She wants her city back. It was the threat of invasion that caused the Vandawolf to send me out to hunt Milena. My orders were to kill her before she could attack the humans.

From that point of view, this deal with Queen Karasi is remarkably easy to agree to.

But it was never going to be an easy task.

There are no guarantees I'll survive a fight with Milena. What I know of her tells me she's as dangerous as her brother was and just as cruel.

I want to ask why Queen Karasi wishes Milena dead, but her reasons won't change my decision.

The Vandawolf's life hangs on my response.

Queen Karasi lifts her chin, her head held high, as she waits for me to speak. "You have my offer, Asha Silverspun."

I have no choice but to make this deal, but this time, I won't be agreeing to it unconditionally.

"It's an unequal deal," I say. "Your healers, whomever they are, have only to give some of their energy right here, right now. You're asking me to give up potentially months of my life searching for, then fighting, one of the most powerful Blacksmiths who has ever lived."

The Queen shrugs. "You're quite right. The Vandawolf's need is dire and it gives me the upper hand. But finding and killing Milena is the only thing I want from you. Therefore, my offer is what it is."

"No," I say softly. "You will give me more."

Her eyebrows rise, but I continue quickly. "You will allow my brother, my sister, and Thaden to stay here, if they wish. You will give them a safe and comfortable home for as long as it takes for me to return."

Gallium has edged forward, and I sense he's about to interject. Possibly, he will want to come with me, and that would be fine with me, but there will be time for that discussion later. Right now, I need to know that my family will be safe if they need to stay here while I'm gone.

Of course, I already foresee the flaws in the wording of my request. A safe and comfortable home could amount to being imprisoned in an opulent room. And I learned firsthand how a promise can be misconstrued.

I continue. "They will be free to move around the city

and free to leave whenever they want. They will not be harassed, imprisoned, or mistreated."

Queen Karasi barely glances at my siblings, but her gaze narrows slightly at Thaden. There's a barely perceptible tension around her eyes when she looks at him. I imagine it's because to her, he must be one step removed from the Vandawolf, whom her people, like the humans, called an "animal."

"None of that will be a hardship," she declares. "Although I request that they don't spend their days idly. If there is some activity they wish to take part in—say, the harvest—then I trust you won't take the view that I'm treating them as laborers."

"That's fair," I say.

Queen Karasi inclines her head at the Vandawolf. "What of him?"

"The Vandawolf will come with me. We will not be separated at any time."

Until we leave this place.

The Vandawolf can make his own choices about where he goes after that.

She gives me a nod. "Then we're agreed. I will heal the Vandawolf and provide safe haven for your family, and you will bring me Milena Ironmeld's body."

"We are agreed," I say. "Now send for your healers."

"No summoning is required." She arches an eyebrow at her champion. "Elowynn, I believe my wishes are clear. You and Gliss will heal the Vandawolf now."

My eyes widen, and the rage I've been choking back rises like poison to my throat.

Elowynn and Gliss have the power to heal him?

Suddenly, I'm remembering the way Gliss had refused to leave the cave back in the mountains; the way she'd pointed out that the Vandawolf was dying. I wonder if she would have offered to heal him then and there if her sister hadn't arrived.

I guess I'll never know.

Now, Elowynn's expression betrays nothing of her true feelings, although Gliss is quick to move as they kneel on the other side of the Vandawolf's stretcher.

Elowynn shouts orders at the warrior fae gathered at the side of the room as she settles into position just behind the Vandawolf's right shoulder. "I want purified water and clean cloths. Bring them quickly."

Remaining on his left side, I turn my back on the Queen, directing my rage at Elowynn. "All this time, he was in pain and you could have helped him."

"You don't tell me what to do, Blacksmith," she snaps back, loudly enough to be heard by the entire congregation. "I follow my Queen's orders." In the next breath, she continues. "I assume you can remove this dark metal. If you do it slowly, we will heal him as you go and prevent any further blood loss."

I narrow my eyes at her. "Can you do that without touching him?"

She nods. "We can direct our power into him from a small distance. It lessens the effect of the power slightly, but not enough to make any real difference."

Several warrior fae reappear then, placing buckets of water and baskets of cloths beside Elowynn and Gliss before they retreat again.

The two women each dunk a cloth in water, wring it out, and then pause.

"We're ready," Elowynn says to me. "Begin."

I don't hesitate a moment longer.

The metal on the Vandawolf's chest is still awake, so there's no need for me to tap it with my hammer. It will respond to my commands.

Extending my left hand toward the Vandawolf's wounded right shoulder, which requires leaning against the side of the stretcher to reach that far, I experience a moment of fear, not knowing what's going to happen next.

When I plugged his wounds with the metal, I didn't already have a medallion fused to my palm.

With the wrong thought, I could just as easily kill him as help him.

CHAPTER 17

Taking a quick, anxious breath, I empty my mind of all impulses, everything except the need to call the titanium back to me.

I close my eyes and sink into the icy darkness of the medallion until I can no longer distinguish the metal on his chest from the titanium on my hand.

Come away, I whisper within my mind. *Come away quietly from his flesh and bones and skin.*

Come away like drips of blood.

Drop by drop.

Little by little.

I feel the metal move beneath my palm, and it is as slow as I wanted. Gradual and careful. Behind my closed eyelids, I'm conscious of the drips of water from the wet cloths and a dark glow building.

When I open my eyes just a little, careful not to break my concentration, I take note of the tension in both Elowynn and Gliss. They're poised over the Vandawolf, both hands extended, one emitting dark light, while with their other hand, they're carefully cleaning the wound, an efficient but apparently well-practiced process as they work in unison. The cloths sit between their fingers and the Vandawolf's body, ensuring they don't directly touch him.

Their lips are tightly pressed together and their shoulders are stiff, their fingers flexing and their hands trembling.

When the dark light emitting from their palms touches the Vandawolf's chest, he shivers, an alarmingly significant movement.

"What are you doing?" I ask them.

Elowynn answers me. "The violence that was done to him was committed with malice. To heal him, we must meet darkness with darkness. We must draw it out like a poultice. Otherwise, he won't heal."

"Don't be alarmed by what you see," Gliss quickly assures me from the other side of the Vandawolf. "Queen Karasi has given you her word, and we will not disobey it. We won't hurt him."

Despite her assertion, an inky darkness is filling her eyes. It looks like black smoke.

I probably shouldn't believe her, but I have no choice.

Taking another deep breath, I continue my work, moving from his shoulder across his chest and down to his hips, making sure I stay ahead of Elowynn and Gliss, but not by so much that the Vandawolf loses any more blood.

Slowly, very slowly, the metal comes away from his body and the dark light finally changes, shifting to a golden color.

We work for so long that the Queen dismisses the congregation, ordering only the warrior fae to remain. She orders them to rearrange the chairs, inviting both my brother and sister, as well as Thaden to sit with her as she watches me from close by.

Despite that, in the moments when I open my eyes, I find either Thaden or Gallium pacing the floor behind the chairs while my sister sits hunched in her seat, her hands folded in front of her, her head bowed, and the curtain of her hair concealing her face.

They don't speak among themselves, but the friction grows in the air around them, particularly between my siblings.

Finally, the Vandawolf is healed enough that I'm able to assess what has been done. New skin has formed across his wounds and his breathing has become more even. The edges of the new skin aren't completely seamless, though, and I suspect many scars will form.

His face has remained deathly pale, but it isn't quite so horribly gray as it had been.

Finally, my hands hover near his heart, where there's a shallow cut that didn't need to be filled with metal.

My brow furrows because my eyes are telling me I've removed every drop of the metal that constituted the medallion. In fact, it's formed a perfect band once more, resting on his chest and ready to be stored in my toolbox.

Yet an icy chill flows up from his chest to meet my palm.

When I glance at Elowynn and Gliss, I find them also hovering, neither of them declaring that their work is done.

"There's more," Gliss whispers. Her cheeks are drained of color and sweat beads on her brow.

We've been working for hours, and both she and Elowynn appear exhausted.

As am I.

But I can't take the risk that I've left some part of the medallion within the Vandawolf. Even the tiniest sliver could be too much.

"I'll retrieve it," I rasp, my mouth so dry now that I struggle to form sound.

I want to ask for water. The swishing of the cloths in the bucket is driving me mad, but I don't want to break my focus.

I move my palm in small rotations in the air above his chest, seeking the location of the last piece of metal, sensing the growing intensity of the icy cold that reaches up toward me as I draw nearer to the source.

My brow furrows again when I identify it near the base of his heart.

I'm sure I didn't direct any of the medallion's metal to flow there, because his heart was undamaged. It was why he survived the crossbow bolt.

"It's here." Cautiously, I press my left hand against the remaining shallow wound, wary of the possibility that this last piece of metal could do more damage during its removal.

Come away, I whisper again inside my mind. *Slip through the spaces and let him go.*

Leave him whole.

Carefully, I tug the magic toward me, sensing its source shift and then—

Power strikes back at me and in that moment, a terrifying rage assaults me—not from within my own heart, but from within the Vandawolf's.

It's as fierce as the slash of a wolf's claws slicing across my chest.

My eyes fly wide. A scream rises to my lips.

Then, in the next heartbeat, there's a soft *clang* and the rush of power stops.

The Vandawolf jolts. Color flushes across his chest, up his neck, and through his cheeks, as if his heart is finally pumping properly, although he doesn't wake up.

Something hits my palm, but I don't yet have time to check what it is because fresh blood rushes from his wound and now a cry of fear leaves my lips.

"Please!" My eyes meet Gliss's, but she's already moving, leaning across the Vandawolf and beating her sister to the spot.

Golden light floods from her hands once more and within seconds, the awful rush of blood has stopped and his skin has healed.

My fear doesn't abate until she leans back and gives me a nod. "There was some damage, but I've fixed it. He'll be okay."

Even Elowynn exhales heavily, as if she'd been holding her breath.

I suppose if he'd died, she would have failed her Queen.

I rock back on my heels, my heart thumping hard in my chest.

He's okay. He's finally okay.

I fight the wave of exhaustion that assails me now that I'm not battling to save his life, and I push at the fact that I'll have to face my own injuries soon.

My arm trembles as I first turn my attention to the object enclosed in my fist.

When I unfurl my fingers, my confusion grows.

What...?

Far from the misshapen lump of metal I was expecting,

the object is small and rounded at the edges, no bigger than the end of my thumb. It's made up of so many finely interconnected and interlocking parts and layers that I can't possibly identify them all.

Within its circular shape is the design of two wolf heads —or rather, the top halves of two wolf heads. They're on their side with their teeth interlinked between them.

Behind me, I sense my brother and Thaden, along with the Queen, craning forward to see what I'm holding, and opposite me, Elowynn and Gliss wear puzzled expressions as they peer at the object.

I don't know what it is.

A flicker of fear passes through me, a horrible dread, along with a sudden, undeniable need to keep the object to myself.

Quickly, I close my fist around it and then I deposit it, along with the reformed medallion, into my toolbox and firmly close the lid, resting my hand on the box.

I'm not certain of much in this moment.

The rage in the mechanism echoes back at me, buzzing at the edges of my mind.

What I *am* certain of is that the mechanism is made of the same titanium as my hammer and medallions—titanium that belonged to Malak—and that makes it extremely dangerous.

CHAPTER 18

I pull my toolbox onto my lap, trying to ignore how hunched with fatigue I am.

Across from me, Elowynn clears her throat loudly and raises her voice. "The Vandawolf will sleep now," she says, drawing attention away from me. "Possibly for several days. When he wakes up, he will be well."

"What about his sight?" I ask, barely able to raise my head.

Damn it, if someone wanted to take my toolbox from me, I wouldn't be able to put up much of a fight.

"I've restored his sight," she replies, sounding affronted that I would doubt that fact.

"Very well." Queen Karasi rises from her chair, brushing down her dress as she takes charge once more. "Please escort Asha and the Vandawolf to the north wing. Gallium, Tamra, and Thaden are to be escorted to the south wing."

Gallium immediately protests. "We should stay with our sister."

The Queen raises her eyebrows at him. "But I promised you would be safe here. There's no saying what the wolf-man will do when he wakes up in a strange place and hears about Tamra's betrayal."

My sister flinches and Gallium's expression darkens, but I'm the first to respond.

"Nothing," I rasp, sighing at the Queen's inflammatory choice of words. "He won't do anything. He's smarter than that."

My sister lifts her head for the first time in what must be hours, her cheeks tear-stained and her eyes glassy. "Queen Karasi is right," she says without looking at me. "We should stay away from him."

My jaw clenches with frustration. I'm not sure if she's motivated by the belief that she *did* betray me or because she thinks the Vandawolf could hurt her.

My chest quickly deflates. Either way, the fact remains that the Vandawolf obliterated nearly our entire race. The first memory Tamra has of him is terrifying. He was a mess of blood and sweat and gore, a towering beast whose mere shadow paralyzed her with fear. His vengeance against the Blacksmiths was justified, but so is Tamra's wariness.

Gallium, on the other hand, appears torn. Just for the chance to speak with me, he spent years training with the Vandawolf to become a Wasteland Warrior. For me to be separated from them now, when we should have been free to be a family again, is painfully cruel.

To my surprise, it's Thaden who protests loudly. "Asha should be with her family. Surely, there's some way to make that happen."

The Queen scowls at him. "There is not," she snaps.

"Not within the terms of our agreement."

He looks prepared to argue, and I'm grateful for it, but I speak up first.

"It's okay," I say quietly. "I made a choice."

The Vandawolf is healed, so the Queen's largest leverage over me is gone. Separating me from my siblings will help ensure I stay in line until I leave.

"My choice has consequences." With a groan, I scoop up my toolbox and attempt to rise to my feet, wobbling and barely making it up.

"Then I'll come with you," Thaden says, reaching for me with his scaled hand.

One look at the Queen's pinched features and I give Thaden a little shake of my head. "Not a good idea," I murmur.

His jaw clenches, his expression tense as he steps back.

As soon as I stand clear of the stretcher, four warrior fae hurry forward to pick it up.

The Queen continues with her orders, addressing Gliss this time. "Gliss, you will go with Asha to the north wing and heal her there."

Gliss looks taken aback, but apparently, it's not about healing me so much as waiting to do so. "Wouldn't you rather I healed her here, my Queen? She may not make it that far—"

The Queen sucks in a breath that sounds like an indignant hiss.

Gliss immediately bows her head. "Of course, Queen Karasi."

The Queen's command to wait doesn't make a lot of sense. I'm of no use to her if I'm dead. But I also recognize that she must view me as a far lesser threat to her while I'm wounded. After all, if I weren't struggling to stand, I could rage around this room and kill all of the fae now that the Vandawolf is healed. I imagine the Queen doesn't like the thought of being around me when I'm at my full strength. Certainly not right now, while emotions are running high.

"I'll make it," I say to Gliss. Then to Gallium and Thaden, I add, "The Queen has granted you full freedom to move around. If you want to come see me tomorrow, please do. No matter what, I'll leave as soon as the Vandawolf is awake and ready to move."

They exchange glances before they each give me a solemn nod.

"We'll stay safe," Thaden says.

"Thank you." That's all I can manage before I move on, dragging my heels.

Somehow, I make it through the maze of hallways, following Gliss and the stretcher bearers and not letting the Vandawolf out of my sight. I can only *trust* that we're moving in a northerly direction since my senses are now completely dull.

What I do notice is that once again, we seem to be traveling farther into the mountain itself, such that any sort of natural light is now far behind us and our way is lit purely with lamps positioned high on the walls.

Along the way, two more women join us. One carries a bucket of what I assume is purified water and the other brings a pile of cloths, on top of which are folded garments that I hope are clean clothes.

Finally, we reach a doorway carved out of rock with a wooden door and a humbly furnished room beyond it. It contains a bed, three chairs, and a little table beside the bed, along with another small table near the wall. There appears to be an adjoining room on the far side that could be a bathroom, but I won't know for sure until I have the energy to explore it.

My senses may be dull, but I recognize how enclosed we are now, with no way out except the long hallway behind us, which I'm certain will be guarded by warrior fae.

A small group of five men is busy within the room, making the bed with clean-looking sheets, wiping down the surfaces, and placing food and water onto the table—what appears to be a few bread rolls and some fruit.

When the women enter, the men quickly finish up, each of them bowing to Gliss before they disappear down the hallway.

The fae carrying the stretcher place it on the floor at the base of the bed while those bringing the bucket and cloths leave them on the bedside table.

Gliss raises her voice at all of them. "Two of you will guard the hall at the far end. Everyone else will leave."

The women don't dawdle and within seconds, they've closed the door behind them.

I place my toolbox on the bed beside me before I slide onto it, mumbling about getting blood on the sheets.

"The men will bring clean sheets," she replies, filling a glass of water and handing it to me to drink. "This is sugar water. Our warriors drink it before and after battle. It hydrates your body and boosts your energy."

"Your men clean up after you?" I squint up at her as I take the glass. In human society, women tend to do the household tasks.

"Fae men are born with little to no power. In our culture, fae women rule over men."

She takes the glass from me once I've swiftly drunk its contents. *Sugar water* is an apt description. Its sweetness lingers on my tongue.

"In Blacksmith culture, men marry into their wives' families," I say, slumping back onto the bed. "My mother was Silverspun. My father was Copperbound. He took her name and joined her family."

I'm rambling now and I have no idea why I told Gliss any of that. My head is increasingly woozy.

She worries at her lip. "Asha, I need you to focus. You have to remove your armor on your own. I'll be able to heal you from a distance, but I can't risk touching you in the meantime."

My movements are labored as I reach for the plates across my chest and begin unstrapping them.

When I get to my tunic's lapel at my left shoulder, I pause, my hands hovering.

Gliss leans forward. "What is that?"

I peer down at the mangled silver pin that was concealed behind the material until now.

"It was my grandmother's," I whisper.

The human woman called Mother Solas gave this pin to me. She and her granddaughter, Rachel, are the last of the human royal line in the city I left behind.

Rachel called me 'Lady Silverspun' and treated me with rare kindness. Mother Solas, too, viewed me without hatred. She told me that the pin was the last object my grandmother ever forged. She said my grandmother poured all of her goodness and heart into this trinket.

Apparently, she hoped that the next generation of Blacksmiths would rise up against Malak and that her pin would contain enough power to help them.

It wasn't to be. Her own daughter killed her. Such was my mother's loyalty to Malak.

The pin had been shaped into a crescent moon, which was the emblem associated with the Silverspuns. Now it's misshapen and partially melted, the crescent turned in on itself in places and spread outward in others so that it resembles nothing more than a rope of twisted metal the length of my thumb.

Whatever light was contained in this pin, it clearly couldn't compete with the immense darkness in the medallions that surged during the forge-fire.

My voice slurs with fatigue as I continue. "This pin is harmless."

I remove it with trembling hands and place it on the bedside table, slipping it between the bucket and the pile of cloths.

Finally, I finish removing all of my armor, along with the ripped tunic underneath. I tug on the sheet and pull it over my nakedness where the injuries don't extend.

The wound on my left shoulder that was cauterized by the forge-fire is a twisted mess of burned skin. But the series of cuts down my torso are awful to behold. I take one look and then stare at the ceiling. Better not to dwell on them.

"You're lucky Dusana has an overinflated opinion of her own skills," Gliss says as she examines my injuries and sets to work. "She missed all the parts of your body that could have done you real harm."

"Is she still alive?" I ask.

"Her family will have found a way to take her to other healers. So, yes, undoubtedly. But she'll be punished for disobeying the Queen's orders."

While Gliss works, my mind drifts, but not to the point that I'm oblivious to how her power seems to grow weaker as the minutes extend. Or the fact that she seems determined to attend to the cauterized wound too.

"You're exhausted," I murmur, eyeing the increasing tension around her eyes and mouth, even though I'm grateful for the effect her power is having on all my wounds. I may end up with very few scars after all. "I'm surprised you didn't object to the task of healing me."

In fact, I'm surprised that she dismissed the warrior fae to stay here with me alone.

"I'm less exhausted than you," she replies. "You should have passed out hours ago."

I allow my head to sink more deeply into the pillow. "I'm a Blacksmith. I'm stronger than a fae."

It's a statement of fact based on my fight with them and thankfully, Gliss doesn't seem to take it as an insult.

"It's why defeating Milena has been so difficult." As soon as she speaks, she freezes, her gaze flashing to me. A grimace forms on her lips.

"Do you regret speaking so plainly?" I ask. "It's obvious she's your enemy or your Queen wouldn't want her dead."

Gliss resumes her work. "That may be so, but Milena Ironmeld wasn't the first Blacksmith my people learned to fear."

My eyebrows rise. "Oh?"

"No," she says. "It was her brother, Malak Ironmeld, who caused my people to hate yours."

CHAPTER 19

A strange sort of disappointment blossoms within me. I shouldn't be surprised. Malak left hatred in his wake.

But once again, he is the lynchpin that pulls together the threads of my life. Without him, the fae might have considered me a friend and welcomed me without fear or reservation.

"What happened?" I ask, fighting the bitterness rising into my throat.

"I only know what I've heard," she says. "Years ago, Malak was part of a delegation sent to form an alliance with the fae. Instead, he assassinated our former Queen."

Once again, it seems Malak brought death with him.

"Queen Karasi rose to power after that," Gliss continues. "She has never let us forget our hatred of Blacksmiths."

"Why would *she* hate him?" I ask wryly. "He's the reason she became Queen, no?"

Gliss peers at me, her eyebrows raised. "That's a very cynical way of looking at things."

"Are you telling me fae are immune to political intrigue?"

She gives a cold laugh. "Oh, far from it. Our Queen is the finest of manipulators."

She quickly presses her lips together and glances at the closed door, as if she's afraid someone may have heard her.

I picture the length of the corridor outside this room.

"Unless they disobeyed your orders, I doubt they can eavesdrop from the end of that very long hallway," I murmur, fighting to stay awake now that my pain has lessened.

"You don't know anything about my people, do you?" she asks, the sudden sharpness in her voice causing me to become more alert.

"True," I say, speaking more carefully. "But why point that out right now? Unless you mean to insult me because of my ignorance?"

"I speak with regret, not contempt." Her shoulders relax a little, but the tension in her face remains. "If you knew more about the fae, you would know that there are many among my people with the power to snatch the very air from your mouth and hear the words you say from any distance. Including from beneath closed doors and along hallways."

I give a heavy sigh. "Well, that's wonderful."

"You would also have known that my sister was a healer from the moment she introduced herself."

My brow furrows. "How so?"

"Our power is in our name." This time, Gliss's expression carries a hint of pity that rankles me. "Every fae belongs to one of two classes: Sunstream or Eventide. Fae in the Sunstream class have powers that reflect the seasons. For example, Solstice fae draw their power from the sun and therefore control heat and fire. Queen Karasi is of the Solstice. Our *former* Queen was a Frost fae. She controlled wind and ice."

"Wind," I murmur, thinking it through. "I take it the Frost fae are the ones with the power to snatch the speech from my mouth."

She nods. "Our former Queen was a master at making use of what she heard."

"What about you?" I ask, considering what I know of Gliss's power to heal, but I'm not sure how that would relate to one of the seasons.

"I'm in the Eventide class. We're rarer," she says. "We control the elements of night and spirit. There are only two types of Eventide fae: Dusk fae, who can commune with animals, and Dawn fae, who are healers."

Damn. "Your sister introduced herself as Elowynn of the Dawn."

Gliss nods. "Elowynn of the healers."

I groan at how powerless that lack of knowledge had left me.

"You shouldn't be angry with yourself," Gliss says. "Even if you had known, Elowynn would have refused to help until she had Queen Karasi's orders."

I consider Gliss darkly. "I would have *made* her help me."

"Oh?"

"I would have taken you hostage."

"Hmm. Well, that would have been a very bad move. Elowynn may be loyal to our Queen, but if you had laid a hand on me, she would have stopped at nothing before she killed you."

"She loves you."

"To a fault."

Now that I understand more about their class system, I'm puzzled by something. "You said Dusk fae commune with animals while Dawn fae are healers. You implied it's one or the other, but you clearly have healing power while you also seemed to understand your bird's wishes."

Gliss hesitates. "My sister and I are... unusual. Our mother is a Dawn fae, hence we take her name and have healing power. But our father is an uncommonly powerful Dusk fae. Elowynn and I inherited both powers. Elowynn's healing power is stronger than mine, while my ability to commune with animals is stronger than hers."

She grimaces. "Most queens choose their champion— their personal protector—from the Sunstream class because they have greater strength in combat. I'm sure you can imagine the damage that, say, a Solstice fae can do with fire. But Elowynn's dual powers make her particularly useful to the Queen."

"In what way?"

Now, Gliss hesitates. Her focus flashes again to the door. She chews her bottom lip for a moment before she returns to her task without answering me.

The silence stretches and, after a few long minutes, I assume I'm not going to receive an answer. I guess it wouldn't be smart for Gliss to speak about the Queen's weaknesses or vulnerabilities with anyone, let alone with me.

My eyes drift closed.

I must have fallen asleep because the next thing I know,

Gliss is leaning over me with another glass of clear liquid in her hand.

Relief floods her face.

"Oh, good. I was worried I'd have to poke you with something to wake you up." She gestures to the liquid. "You need to drink more sugar water."

"The Vandawolf," I mutter, my voice hoarse. "He needs water, too."

Gliss shakes her head. "There's no way to safely give him any liquid without risking that he'll choke on it. Don't worry. Elowynn's healing power is particularly strong and it will sustain him while he sleeps."

Relieved to hear it, I take the glass and gulp the liquid down. Once again, it tastes like syrup, a little too sweet, but I feel better afterward.

Gliss gestures to the bedside table where the flask sits. At some point, she must have taken away the bucket and cloths because they're now lying on the floor near the door. "Drink all of the sugar water and then sleep. You won't be disturbed."

She retrieves a clean tunic from the small pile of clothes and leaves it beside me on the bed where I can reach it.

Then she pauses, her focus on a spot to my right. It takes me a moment to remember that's where I put my toolbox.

Damn. I should have been guarding it more closely—

"Don't be concerned. I didn't touch your tools," she says. "You can rest assured that no fae will lay a hand on that metal. Its darkness would only hurt us."

She sounds so truthful that my instinct to protect the contents of my toolbox with my life feels a little silly, but even now, I can't shake it.

She continues to hover. "My ability to commune with animals..."

Her gaze slides to the Vandawolf where he lies on the stretcher near the end of the bed, his head and shoulders visible.

I stiffen. "The wolf."

I haven't sought out its energy since I carried the Vandawolf through the wasteland. I couldn't stand to see its pain.

"You were wrong about it," she says quietly.

I consider her carefully. "How so?"

"The wolf wasn't pushing and pulling against him. It was his friend. They trusted each other." Her forehead creases, as if she's trying to find the words. "They're a pack. Or maybe more accurately... they *were* a pack... when their families were alive."

I try to process this information. Of course, she could be making it up, but somehow... I believe her. Mostly because I can't see what she would gain by lying.

She gives me a sad smile that quickly disappears. "You *were* right about the Vandawolf's family. I saw it in the wolf's memories. The Vandawolf loved them and fought for them. When he lost them..." Gliss's face is suddenly pale. "It broke him."

She pulls the sheet to my chin as I consider what she told me.

I want to ask more, but she's already stepping back.

"I've said more than I should have, since I listened to the wolf's thoughts without permission." She swallows and hurries on. "I should explain... Normally, I need to seek permission from an animal before it will share its thoughts with me. But the Vandawolf was dying and his wolf was vulnerable. I took advantage. I shouldn't have done that."

I remember the way she looked at me back in the cave and said she was sorry the Vandawolf was dying. I wasn't completely sure of her expression at the time, but now I'm certain it was sadness.

She takes a deep breath. "I won't listen again unless the Vandawolf gives me permission."

With that, she leaves me, her footsteps heavy, and I imagine she'll drag herself to bed now.

I'm left to drink the sweet water, swallowing the syrup even as I contemplate the bitterness of the future that lies ahead of me.

I wake to a heavy silence.

I'm facing the back wall, curled up with my knees bent and the sheet tucked around me, its smooth surface like silk against my skin, an unfamiliar luxury. The tunic I managed to pull on before I fell asleep is softer than any I've ever worn.

For a moment, I can believe that everything is okay.

Nothing is wrong.

Then I focus on my blackened hair where it falls across my face. Through its strands, my left hand is visible, palm down, fingers peeking from beneath the sheet and resting on the pillow beside me.

For that one blissful moment, I can't see the medallion, I

don't sense the darkness within it, and I can imagine it isn't there at all.

In the next heartbeat, cold malice rushes through me like icy water, a destructive assault that forces me up into a sitting position, my hair falling around my shoulders and a cry on my lips.

"Stop," I whisper, swallowing my scream as I wrap my right hand over my left palm, as if I can somehow make the medallion disappear.

Hot tears trickle down my cheeks. "Please stop."

A low growl sounds behind me. "Asha?"

I jolt and spin, my heart in my throat.

The Vandawolf!

He towers over me as he straightens at the side of the bed, his arm outstretched, as if he were reaching for me. His broad chest rises and falls, as if he's carefully controlling his breathing. He's naked to the waist, still wearing his bloodied pants. Faint scars crisscross the muscles of his chest and stomach. His ashen-black hair falls across his face, matted with dried blood and hiding his expression from me.

His appearance is so much like it was the first time I saw him that my heart misses a beat.

"Vandawolf," I whisper, my eyes wide. "You're awake already."

I don't know if 'already' is accurate, since I have no way of knowing how long I was asleep, but I'm certain it hasn't been days like Elowynn predicted.

He's very quiet and it throws me. I expected instant rage. Distrust. A storm of questions, at the very least.

His voice remains a growl, but it's soft. "That isn't my name."

He tips his head to the side, his hair falling away from his eyes.

My breathing stills as I take in what he said, as well as the changes I can now see in his face.

His amber wolf's eye is gone.

It's... just... gone...

So is his sharp canine tooth.

The color of his irises takes my breath away. No more amber wolf's eye. Both of his irises are deep-gray, like the color of the sky when the sun has gone down and night is falling.

His hair is the same shade as it was before, its strands still resembling a wolf's fur, but it no longer strikes me as a crown of darkness, but more like a pelt falling across his broad shoulders.

His jaw remains as strong, his lips as full, and his gaze just as piercing, but the savage characteristics of the beast are...

Simply gone.

No longer do I sense a wolf writhing within him, beating at the cage of his body.

He seems completely calm. Far calmer than I expected. Possibly calmer than he should be.

I'm sure I've stopped breathing altogether and that my eyes are as wide as saucers.

Every part of his face is somehow *new* to me. The cut of his cheekbones, the curve of his lips, the slight crease in his forehead... as if he's a little uncertain of my reaction.

His entire face has transformed, and he is breathtakingly beautiful, even as he wears the scars of battle.

I try to bring moisture to my lips, helped only by the trickle of tears that reach the corners of my mouth. *"How...?"*

How has this happened?

One corner of his mouth hitches up a little, a hesitant half-smile that takes me by surprise.

He lifts his hands, palms up, as if to reassure me that he doesn't mean me any harm.

"My name is Erik," he says. "I would appreciate very much if you would never call me *Vandawolf* again."

CHAPTER 20

"Erik," I whisper.

He breaks into a smile that makes his eyes crinkle at the corners, but it quickly fades as he follows the tear tracks down my cheeks.

Unwilling to acknowledge them and afraid of all the unknowns, I ask, "How long have you been awake?"

It isn't the most important question. Not even close.

He answers it all the same, speaking with a level of detail he never gave me before. "Long enough to know that two women guard the very long corridor outside this room, that they carry concealed blades, and that they talk about you as if you're dangerous, yet they describe you as their guest, not their prisoner."

He gestures to the door. "Long enough to sense the abnormal shifting of air beneath the doorway, which I plugged with cloths since whatever magic was being used reeked of subterfuge. But don't worry—there are air vents there and there." He points to two spots in the ceiling. "Also long enough to study the striations in the rock around us, which tell me we're in the northern mountains."

His observations about the guards and the air indicate that his wolf's senses must still be fully functional, giving him the ability to hear and smell things from very far away. But his comment about the mountains surprises me.

I can't imagine him ever having been anywhere near these mountains before. "How do you know that?"

"My wolf's pack once roamed this land," he says, before he continues without missing a beat. "I've certainly been awake long enough to wonder how we got here, what you had to do to save my life, and why my face has changed, but none of that, Asha..."

He takes a step toward me, right up to the edge of the bed. In doing so, his body blocks out the lamplight behind him and drops me into shadow.

It seems like the place where I belong.

His voice lowers and his dark gaze cuts through to my heart. "None of that is as important to me right now as knowing why you're in pain."

I'm intensely uncertain. In the last real conversation we had, he raged at me, roared at me to leave him, but he still hasn't shown any signs of anger or distrust.

He hasn't ordered me about or demanded information.

There was simplicity in our relationship before.

He commanded me. I obeyed him.

We had clear boundaries that don't exist anymore, and I wish that I had woken up before he did, because then I would have been composed and ready.

I would have been in complete control of my feelings, and I would have already thought through my next steps.

Instead, he's asking me why I'm hurting and he's waiting for my answer. Quietly waiting for my answer, as if he'll give me all the time I need.

I swipe at my cheeks, trying to stop the hot tears that persist in flowing.

For some reason, that's when he takes a step back, allowing the light to shine onto me once more.

His shoulders hunch, although his growly voice remains low and soft. "I understand... There's no trust between us. When you started to give me your trust, I chose to break it."

He doesn't look away from me, the same way I would always look him in the eyes.

Oh, his eyes.

I never saw them when they were both human, before he became the Vandawolf. I have no way of knowing for sure that this is how they looked, but...

Damn. It's like falling into the night and discovering layers of starlight intermingled with the darkness.

"I chose to break your trust on the day I took you from the throne room with your brother and sister," he says. "I closed my fist around your hope, and I shattered it. Every time I sensed trust growing again, I would destroy it again." He takes a deep, shuddering breath. "I told myself that I needed your hate. I convinced myself that your hate was safer for *you.*"

He takes another step back.

"I think that's still true," he says.

His gaze flickers to the door and becomes slightly distant, as if he's sensing things beyond this room. "They'll let me pass. They don't want me here. They'll be happy to see me gone. I can disappear from your life like a distant shadow." He's nodding to himself. "This is for the best."

He's already near the door and now he's moving fast. Of all the emotions I could feel right now, there's only one that assails me and it's far colder than it should be.

Anger.

"Stop." I slide to the edge of the bed and off it, my feet finding the floor. "You will *not* leave me."

He pauses at the door, only two steps from it, half-turned back to me. His hair brushes his shoulders as he moves and his gaze is steadily on me.

I prowl toward him. My left fist closes tightly around the medallion and I'm conscious of the slight narrowing of his eyes when he glances at it.

I haven't fully revealed the medallion yet, having swiped at my tears with my right hand, but he must see the edge of the band where it sits across the side of my hand beneath my thumb.

If it alarms him, he doesn't show it.

"Erik," I say, rolling his name around on my tongue.

He gives me a single nod.

"Erik what?" I ask. "Humans have family names."

He turns to me fully and folds his arms across his chest. "My father cut ties with his family and left their name behind."

This is curious information. Human families were separated against their will under Malak's rule, which meant they were more often fighting to stay together. They weren't willingly estranged from their kin. "Why?"

A glimmer of a smile flickers around Erik's mouth, but it isn't a calm smile anymore. It's a dangerous one, and I sense the growing tension in his muscles, the way his hands dig into his biceps where his arms have remained folded.

"My father was descended from a long line of warriors who adhered to a particularly harsh way of living. They call themselves the Einherjar and believe there's glory in death. When my brother was born, our father left his family behind."

"But..." My thoughts are suddenly churning because I've never heard of the Einherjar. They certainly weren't a group that existed within the human community back in the wasteland.

"I wasn't born in the Blacksmith city," Erik explains before I can become more confused. "I didn't grow up there."

My eyes widen at this new information. There has always been a void when it came to information about Erik's past and his family. This could explain why.

"My father believed in destiny and omens—that much of his people's culture stayed with him," Erik continues. "He followed the wolves far from the north and made a home for us in the western mountains where he believed we would be safe. And we were. For a time."

In the last few moments, Erik's told me more about his past than I ever knew. Far more than I expected him to tell me.

Oh, but something has shifted within him.

A change so significant that I feel like I'm only seeing the surface of it.

Now, his jaw clenches and his tension increases. "Every choice my father made was intended to protect me and my brother. It was a creed he drilled into me." The light in Erik's eyes darkens. "Protect the people you love at any cost."

His chest rises and falls more rapidly and his words are raw, as if it hurts to speak them. "I broke his creed. Only once. I thought I was doing the right thing. It cost me everything."

He hasn't moved toward me, but the gap between us feels smaller.

I wish it didn't.

Because right now, his pain is like a tangible force curling around my heart—tiny, unseen barbs biting through the broken organ within my chest.

I raise my left hand and unfurl it, fully revealing the medallion and the way it's part of my flesh now. "This is why I'm in pain."

He's immediately riveted by it, unmoving, and other than the steady rise and fall of his chest, his focus is fully and completely on the band melded to my palm.

In those heartbeats as I wait for him to respond, I read a myriad of emotions in his features. Feelings I could never guess before that are somehow exposed to me by the minutiae of little shifts in his human face.

The press of his lips, the smoothing and creasing of his brow, the lines around his eyes, the tension in his jaw and shoulders...

A flicker of fury. A wash of regret. Then a startling *need* and an unsettling determination as he closes the gap between us far more rapidly than I was expecting.

"Give me your hand."

His command echoes within my ears like his shout from long ago when I'd expected him to cut my hand from my body and leave me even more powerless than I already was.

Instead, I pressed my palm to his heart and gave him control of my fate.

"No," I say softly. "I won't."

Now, he steps right up to my outstretched palm, the barest inch from once again enabling me to press it to his heart, and there he stops.

Even though the need and determination in his eyes only grows stronger.

"How did it happen?" he asks, his focus now on my face, as if danger doesn't rest an inch away.

He knows what I can do with this power.

He knows I could kill him on a whim.

"What do you remember?" I ask, watching the play of his features, the small shifts that are like a puzzle for me to decipher.

"I remember the wolf that rose from the ash, and I remember you turning it to stone. You pulled me into the shade of its stone body."

His hand rises, parallel to mine, but he reaches, as if for my face, mimicking the way he'd pressed his hand to my cheek after I'd pulled him to safety. At the time, I could hardly see through my tears because of the damage the wolf had done to him.

"I was more truthful with you than I should have been," he whispers. "But I thought... fuck it... I was dying. What was the harm in telling you what I really felt for once?"

His expression closes off, those little shifts smoothing out all of a sudden. "But you asked me to come with you and that's when I knew I should never have been so honest with you."

My voice is a bare whisper as I remember that moment. "We can have more than a cage in the sky."

That's what I said to him.

The corner of his mouth tugs up, that surprising and unsettling hint of smile. "I wanted to say *yes*. With every shred of my being, I wanted to go with you."

His gaze flows across my face, taking in my features as though nothing about my tarnished skin, my blackened hair, or the medallion I've kept resolutely raised toward him worries him.

Thaden contemplated me like this, but with Thaden, it was as if he'd accepted all the changes without fear.

With Erik... the look in his eyes...

I can't make it out.

"What do you see?" I ask him, my heart so fragile that I'm sure it will soon crack.

"I see you with my wolf's eyes." His hand moves in the air. "You are just as beautiful as you were the first time I saw you."

Tears burn behind my eyes, but they're tears of anger and disbelief. He hated me in those first moments. I was sure of it. And as for now...

I snarl. "There is nothing beautiful about what I am now."

He tilts his head a little, a flicker of surprise in the rise of his eyebrows. "Your heart beats clear and true, Asha. I can hear it. You love just as fully as you did before. Your need to protect the ones you care about is as strong as ever. Nothing could destroy your heart, Asha Silverspun."

"Only break it," I whisper. "Why wouldn't you come with me?"

His hand stills in the air, frozen there as his jaw clenches. "The only way you'd be free was if I wasn't by your side."

My lips purse. "How could you possibly know that?"

"Because I had years to work through every scenario. Years to watch my people plot and plan, to consider every move and countermove. To make sure you and your siblings were strong enough—to train your brother, to wait for your sister's healing power to return. It took years for the way forward to become clear and when it did, I chose the path that would guarantee your freedom."

My heart is slowly sinking, as heavy as a stone in water.

Before he sent me out of the city, he told me that we would never have a world where there were no moves or countermoves, no commands, no subterfuge, and no treachery.

He was always two steps ahead of everyone else.

Always planning. Always plotting. Always influencing outcomes.

When he set me free, I knew that he had arranged it meticulously, right down to the timing of my departure and the ruse he'd created to ensure my sister came with us.

He'd predicted everything before it had happened.

Everything.

"I made one mistake," he says, his voice so low now that I can barely hear him. "I thought I'd pushed you away hard enough, treated you badly enough, that you wouldn't turn back to fight the monster."

A chill has taken hold of me and now it thrums through my body, beating into the medallion and rippling back from it. "I wasn't supposed to come back for you. Was I?"

He doesn't look away. Just as I never looked away from him.

He meets me eye to eye.

The expression on his face now is plain for me to see. It's the same one he wore when I raced toward him across the ashen ground, running back to help him fight the monstrous wolf.

He glared at me and told me: *"You shouldn't be here."*

"My people had the weapons they needed to fight any monster," he says. "You were free. I'd done what had been needed. It was over."

My heart is pounding, the blood whooshing in my ears as I speak my fear aloud. "You knew the humans were going to kill you."

Softly, he says, "You weren't meant to see me die, Asha. For that, I'm sorry."

CHAPTER 21

Hot as a dragon's fire, fury burns through me. "You accepted your death."

"It was time for them to rule themselves. Mother Solas and Rachel were ready. Genova was mobilizing her followers. The Wasteland Warriors were in position. Whatever battle for control was about to play out, I did as much as I could to influence the outcome. My time was done. Now, it's up to them."

I close my left fist, my knuckles turning white where my hand hovers in the air, fighting the icy cold. I care about what happens to Mother Solas and Rachel, and particularly about Kedric and Maybelle—the humans who raised my siblings. But right now, my pain has another cause.

"In all your planning and preparedness, you didn't once consider that your death might matter to me?"

His jaw clenches, but still, he responds quietly. "I hoped it wouldn't."

"You... *hoped?*" My voice rises. "You *hoped* I wouldn't care?"

With a scream of rage, I launch myself at him, my right hand thumping his chest.

He moves in a flash, ignoring the blow and instead catching my left hand by the wrist and keeping it from touching him.

The force of my attack drives him back against the wall, but instead of trying to push me away, he pulls me closer with his free arm, wrapping it around my back, immobilizing my right arm by wedging it against my chest even as he keeps my dangerous hand captured and outstretched.

Our bodies collide in an explosion of heat that's nearly my undoing.

There's barely anything between us but a few bits of material and his will.

His nearness siphons all of my anger and leaves only a terrible burn, an awful need, because there's still too much distance between us.

I tip my head back, only to meet his eyes and all the terrible pain in them.

"Why *would* you care?" he snarls at me, the fury I was expecting from him finally surfacing, except that it seems to have nothing to do with where we are or how we got here, but about my feelings for him. "I controlled your life. I had power over you. What sort of sick delusion would I be living under if I thought I had a right to your love?"

"Not a delusion," I say, sliding my hand up his chest, my fingertips brushing the underside of his jaw. "A determination that one day you *wouldn't* control my life. And then we could find out..."

"Find out what, Asha?"

"If we really are enemies."

His gaze lowers to my lips. "You speak of dreams."

"I speak of hope."

He shakes his head at me. His hold on my powered hand is easing and the hard lines in his expression are smoothing out. His free arm shifts across my back, his fingers flexing against my spine.

"Hope will only betray you," he murmurs.

My left hand is pressed to the wall now. "Hope is all I have."

He searches my eyes, his hand stilling on my back and his voice harsh. "What did you have to do to save my life?"

The medallion burns at the memories of fire and blood.

Ice flows through me again.

Despite myself, I grin at him, a suddenly dark smile. "I did everything I had to do."

His hand tightens on my back. "Tell me."

I narrow my eyes at him. "Is that a command?"

His focus flashes to my left hand, as if he can sense the flood of dark magic rushing from it.

He moves without warning, so fast that my heart has barely skipped a beat before I find our positions reversed. My back is pressed to the wall, his left hand pinning my shoulder, his other hand still wrapped around my left wrist, pressing the back of it against the wall, although now he's leaning toward me.

"Where is your grandmother's pin?" he suddenly asks me.

My forehead creases. I don't know why he's asking, but I have no reason to hide it from him. "It's on the table."

He cranes his neck, seems to see it, and then just as suddenly releases me. Hurrying across to the pin, he studies it briefly without touching it. He makes an unhappy humming sound in the back of his throat, possibly because it's now mangled beyond recognition.

Rapidly turning away from the twisted ornament, he casts his gaze around the room, evidently searching for something else.

His eyes alight on the stretcher and he heads straight for it, crouching and quickly wrapping his hands around one of the onyx poles.

I lean against the wall, puzzled by his actions, the ice in my veins momentarily halted by my curiosity. "What are you doing?"

And why is he doing it?

"I need a surface that will act like a hammer," he says. "Not a Blacksmith's hammer. Just a regular one."

I'm not sure how he thinks he could use any part of the stretcher for hammering, but my eyes widen when he grips the metal at one side of it, which is currently wrapped around the pole. He appears to be trying to pull the onyx tusk free.

I hammered that metal into place, after commanding it to do my bidding. I'm certain that nothing could move it.

Erik's biceps bulge and in the next second, the metal shrieks as it lifts upward, freeing the black tusk, which rolls out onto the floor.

Surprised, I watch as he retrieves the pole and carries it like a spear, its sharp end pointed upright as he heads toward the bedside table.

Using the tip of the pole, he knocks the pin onto the floor

—again without coming into contact with it—and then he kneels beside it where it landed on the floor.

He raises the flat end of the pole above the pin, his muscles flexing. "Remember what you are."

He isn't speaking to me. Right now, that's all I know for certain.

A moment later, he smacks the end of the pole down onto the pin.

The mangled ornament bounces beneath the hit, but that's all.

Erik's hands tighten around the pole and again, he rams it down. "Remember what you are!"

I'm not sure what he's trying to achieve, but again, nothing about the pin looks any different. It isn't even flattened.

I take a step away from the wall, but I don't move any closer because now his jaw has clenched and I sense I should keep my distance.

He shifts his position from a crouch, taking a knee instead. He bows his head as he lifts the onyx pole above the pin, holding the tusk there for a long moment. "Remember who you are."

A split second before he taps the pin with the end of the tusk, a charge fills the air, and the hairs on my arms suddenly stand on end. I imagine, for a moment, that there's a burst of light down his arms, but it's gone too soon to tell.

The onyx pole hits the pin.

A bright, melodic *ting* peels through the room as clear as a bell.

The energy swells and ripples outward.

Erik braces as it billows around him with such strength that he slides backward.

The ripple of power reaches me in the next instant, shoving me up against the wall before it seems to quickly retract and flow back to the pin. The silver metal slowly untwists, its surface smoothing out until it forms a solid band in the shape of a long rectangle.

The hairs on my arms continue to stand on end, the palpable energy spiraling around me. "It's a medallion."

"One of your grandmother's tools. She disguised it as a pin so Malak wouldn't destroy it."

Erik hurries to the bedside table again, takes the empty cup resting there, and uses it to scoop the medallion up off the floor. The band is long enough that it extends beyond the cup's lip.

As he approaches me, more slowly now, he asks, "Will you... please... give me your hand?"

"Why?" I ask, feeling wary, my left arm held close to my chest.

He tips the cup toward me. "You can cover the black medallion with this. It will help."

I'm shaking my head. "I can't use ordinary medallions."

"You don't need to use it or command it. Your grandmother designed it specifically for the purpose of diffusing Malak's dark magic. All you have to do is reach for it, and it will fulfill its purpose all on its own."

My brow furrows. "How do you know this?"

"Because your grandmother told Mother Solas, and Mother Solas told me."

The energy within the room hasn't abated, the glittering

force swirling, gentle beams of dancing light emanating from the medallion.

Erik's voice washes over me, becoming a hum in my ears as he continues to explain. "It was after I killed Malak. I scoured the city for all Blacksmith tools, intending to destroy every last piece of Blacksmith metal. Mother Solas offered up the pin and told me its story. I let her keep it on the condition that she would hide it and give it to you when I asked her to."

My head is swimming as an impulse that I've pushed away from the very first moment I picked up Malak's hammer pulses back at me.

Erik is still speaking, but I no longer hear him.

Take control of the light and the dark.

It occurs to me, perhaps for the first time, that my impulse is not only about darkness.

It's about light, too.

I reach for the medallion in the cup, my outstretched arm trembling as the power within the dark metal embedded in me pushes me backward, away from my grandmother's medallion, while the energy within the silver metal pulls me closer. Two opposing forces, both equal in strength, and only my will can determine the outcome.

"Take control of the light and the dark," I whisper when Erik falls silent. "Fight the old and find the new."

I'm aware that Erik's focus no longer rests on the band, but on my face, as if he's searching for something in that moment.

I'm not sure what it is or if he finds it.

My palm brushes the tip of the silver medallion and it instantly adheres to my hand, curling upward like a vine.

It slides across the titanium band, end to end, and spreads farther outward on each side, becoming like silver liquid that thins out until it covers the darkness completely.

I now have a thick, silver band of metal across my palm and wrapped around the sides of my hand, completely concealing the dark band beneath it.

The energy around me fades.

The anger within me calms.

My heart warms, and it's like stepping out of shadows into gentle sunlight.

The tarnish on my skin remains. My hair is just as charred.

And the darkness within me...

Well, it remains full and strong, but now, so is the light. Neither power is blocked, but neither dominates the other.

It's a balance I've never experienced before. Strength with unity.

I run the fingers of my other hand over the silver metal and feel the way it acts like a barrier.

My eyes fill with tears as I realize... I can hug my family now.

Without fear of hurting them.

"Thank you," I whisper to Erik.

His hand lowers to his side, the cup still gripped in it, and then he becomes very still, except for the small changes in his expression: the lightest press of his lips, the slight crease in his forehead, the tiniest hitch in his breathing.

My head is clear and my thoughts are finally my own again, but suddenly...

So is responsibility for every choice I've made since I stood between Erik and his people.

It all rushes at me at once and the warmth I experienced only a moment before disappears.

Every death at my hands, every drop of blood I spilled, every wound that was inflicted on me, every strike of fear, every angry word I spoke... Everything the medallion protected me from caring about, all of it floods over me.

It's too much.

Erik's features blur as I stumble backward, gasping for breath, clutching at my pounding heart before my legs collapse beneath me.

CHAPTER 22

E rik leaps forward and catches me before I hit the floor. His arms wrap around me, but I can barely feel them.

All I feel is the forge-fire billowing around me again, the memory so strong that I'm trying to throw myself backward, away from the flames, even though in the very next second, the air is filled with smoke and my hand is once again brushing up against human flesh, transforming it into the very smoke I was breathing. My ears fill with hissing vipers and my feet are sinking into mud I can't escape from, and then my hands are smacking into rock as I decide whether or not to kill a fae...

Erik's voice is far away. "You're going into shock." His hands rest on either side of my face. "Oh, Asha, what the fuck did you *do* to keep me alive?"

His hands tighten. "Tell me! You *have* to tell me. You have to extract it like poison. Speak the memories so they'll let you go."

I can't form words, can't focus.

Sharp stones are biting into my back and a dark, night sky is swallowing me whole. Now, all I can hear is my scream, echoing through the ballroom as I fought to constrain my power so I didn't hurt my sister.

I'm vaguely aware of Erik gathering me up into his arms and carrying me toward the bed. Somehow, he manages to scoop up the blanket before he carries me into the next room, where it's darker.

He takes me into the farthest corner, away from the light, where he pulls me into his lap and wraps the blanket around us both, pulling the material up and over our heads so that it drops us into darkness.

My panicked breathing slows.

"This is our den," he murmurs against my ear. "It's a safe place. A place where fear can't reach you."

My memories rush all the way back to the first time I saw his bedroom. The mess of clothing, blankets, pillows, and random belongings all strewn about like burrows. Places to hide.

Finally, that's where my memories stop.

His lips brush my forehead and then my cheek before he urges me to rest my head in the crook of his neck. "You're okay, Asha. You'll be okay."

I shudder wildly as I curl up as tightly as I can, his arms squeezing around me.

"The crossbow was propping you up," I whisper, knowing that I have to start somewhere. "I wanted to kill them all."

Now that I've started speaking, I don't stop.

I tell him everything and leave nothing out—not the way

I used a medallion to stop his bleeding, or how the humans tried to use forge-fire against me, or the number of humans I killed. I describe how I made the stretcher and pulled him through the wasteland under the cover of smoke and then up into the mountains. I tell him about my meeting with the fae, of killing one of them, and of flying him back here.

Then I recount my interaction with my sister and the Fae Queen, and the deal I made.

He listens and doesn't interrupt.

The more I speak, the more I wish I could read his expression in the darkness beneath the blanket. The material gapes open a little at his left shoulder, letting the air in, but there isn't enough light for me to see him properly.

Yet I have no doubt that he can see me.

He may have lost his visible wolf features, but his senses seem as strong as they were.

When I finally fall silent, he asks a question I wasn't expecting.

"Why are the fae this far west?"

I thought he would focus on my sister or on my deal with the Queen or maybe on the mechanism I pulled from this chest—all of the things that impact him directly.

My forehead creases. "I don't know. It wasn't exactly my focus at the time."

Did the corner of his mouth rise a little? I'm not sure.

He seems focused on his question. "For the last ten years, I've been cut off from the rest of the world, just like you were," he says. "At the time when my wolf's pack roamed these lands, the north was occupied by humans. The fae lived far east. When Thaden Kane said there were feuding queens in the north, I expected them both to be human. Some squabble between them, at most. The fae have no right to these lands and should have no reason to be here."

"What are you saying?"

"That the fae are invaders. Any claim they purport to have over this land is certainly false."

I shiver at how emphatically he speaks.

"The question is why?" he continues. "Why would they leave their bountiful lands to press into barren mountains?"

Oh, to think like him.

To always suspect the motives of others and recognize when a game is being played.

I wish I had that instinct.

But perhaps... I am acquiring some of that skill. "What does Milena have to do with it?"

I may not be able to see the detail of Erik's expression, but I feel him nod.

"We're missing something." His arms tighten around me further. "We should find out as much as we can before we leave."

I bite my lower lip. "*We* leave?"

"I'm coming with you." He pauses. "Yes?"

"Yes."

Slowly, he pulls the blanket down, letting the dim light in and leaving his hair a mess.

His arms ease around me in the process.

I reach up to run my fingers along his jaw, my head tipped back to see him.

"Is this what you looked like before you were changed?"

He shrugs. "I was ten years younger then."

I try to ask the question that matters most to me in this moment—not about the fae or the future—but I'm not sure how to phrase it. "How did this happen? Where has the wolf gone?"

His lips pull back into a smile that looks very much like a snarl. "Not gone."

I scowl at him, completely unintimidated. "You're evading. I don't like it." I hurry on. "It's okay if you don't know, but I need to understand what happened. I need to know if..."

My shoulders hunch, which only takes me closer to his chest. "I need to know whether or not, in the midst of all the darkness, I did a good thing."

"You did a good thing." His response is immediate. "Malak used that mechanism to transform me. That device was his greatest creation. The source of his pride. When he cut my chest open and implanted it in my heart, I knew its dark power was never going to let me go. Only an equally dark power could coax it out."

Blacksmith magic is drawn to itself.

"Malak's own power," I whisper. My next question is more hesitant. "Did you hope that I might remove the mechanism one day?"

"Fuck, no," he says, his voice emphatic. "I thought removing it would kill me."

"Oh." My eyes have widened. "I'm glad I didn't know that."

It nearly did kill him. It tore through his body on its way to my hand. It was only because Gliss acted so quickly that he didn't die.

I'm horribly aware that the detail with which Erik described the mechanism means he may have been conscious for at least some of its implantation. I try to shake that off.

Only terrible pain could have created the beast he was when he first came upon me in the throne room.

"What about unintended consequences now that it's gone?" I ask.

"None so far," he replies. "Let me prove it to you."

He scoops me up and rises to his feet, letting the blanket fall away. "See? Arms and legs working fine." He tips his head to the side, his focus becoming distant. "My senses are working normally. I can hear the guards in the far distance talking about dinner. Night birds have started singing in the forest outside this place—their song is drifting in through the air vents. I know it's a forest because I can hear the leaves rustling in the trees. The sun must be going down, for the birds to start calling."

He inhales, as if to test his sense of smell, but his focus falls to me. "You have blood in your hair."

"So do you," I retort.

He arches his eyebrows at me. "The blood in my hair is my own. The blood in yours belongs to multiple people." He gives me a garish grin. "My sense of smell is working fine."

"And so is your mind. Clearly."

I glance around. I didn't pay any attention to this little room before—I couldn't.

Now I see that it is, indeed, some sort of bathroom, as I had first suspected. A sink is carved into the wall and there are cloths piled on a chair in the other back corner.

Without the darkness of the medallion and the panic of its removal, I'm very conscious of how little I'm wearing. Only a thin tunic. Not that Erik hasn't seen me naked many times before.

This feels different. He was the Vandawolf then.

Now, we're in unknown territory.

He follows my gaze to our surroundings. "We both need to wash, but where is the bath?"

He slides me to the floor, scoops up the blanket, and wraps it around me again. After tugging it tightly, he veers toward the left wall. His fingers dance across it.

"I hear water flowing," he says, pausing at a spot halfway along. "Right here. Which means there must be... Aha!"

His fingers wrap around a mottled knob of rock protruding from the wall before he gives me a triumphant grin.

In the next moment, water pours down onto him, but not from low on the wall like it would for a bath. It pours from the ceiling, instantly flattening his hair.

With a yelp, he leaps clear of it.

He lands lightly, outside the downpour, which cascades directly from the ceiling a full foot wide of its central point.

His shoulders hunch as he growls up at the water, as if it triggered his fight reflexes. "Instant rain? What the fuck?"

Water droplets drip down his head and chest before he shakes himself off.

He clears his throat and straightens. "It's perfectly warm."

I bite my lip. It's not often that something startles him. "It must be a fae invention."

He said the water was warm so I step straight into the spray, tunic and all, letting the liquid flow down my hair and face and body. The waterfall is so wide that it nearly extends from one end of my shoulders to the other.

I stay there for a moment, my eyes closed, letting it wash over me, conscious of Erik remaining quietly nearby.

Then something soft presses against my arm and I open my eyes to find him holding a small cloth out to me.

"I'll leave you to it," he says.

My hand closes around his before he can withdraw. The cloth drops to the floor, but I ignore it. The impulse to pull him under the spray with me is strong.

Before I can move, he turns my hand over.

It's my right hand.

He traces the lines on it with his thumb, one side then the other, following them from my wrist out to my fingertips.

He kisses each one, taking his time, and he's so intent on it that it feels...

More than happy.

More than calm.

"Stay," I whisper.

CHAPTER 23

I know he hears my request, even with as quiet as my voice is.

He drops a kiss against my palm, his touch light. Another kiss closer to my wrist and now my breathing is rapid.

I've moved forward out of the middle of the spray, but it cascades down my back and across my shoulders, droplets running between my breasts and legs.

"You don't have power over my life anymore," I say. "I'm free to choose."

His lips linger on my hand, a caress that makes my thighs clench.

He doesn't come any closer and I'm not sure if he's waiting for me to explicitly ask him to.

My lips part, the invitation on my tongue, when he speaks.

"I've walked a line with you from the day I first met you," he says. "A line between keeping you alive and ensuring you stayed at arm's length from me. At first, I didn't want to build that wall between us, but then I realized that neither of us would survive without it. So I did everything I could to inspire enough hatred of me that you would construct a wall for me. And it would never come down."

He's speaking softly, without a hint of fury.

I can't stop my smile. "It came down."

The corner of his mouth tugs up. "You *dragged* it down."

I challenge him. "You let me."

"I wanted to let you."

But his shoulders suddenly hunch, shadows building in his expression, and the abrupt change makes my smile fade and brings an emptiness into my heart.

"This connection between us has only ever brought pain," he says. "Right from the start, Asha. Loss and pain. For you. And for me."

The ache in my heart only deepens, a heavy sadness settling in.

My people killed his family.

He killed my people.

We met in a moment of blood and fury and terror.

My eyes suddenly fill with tears and I'm not ashamed of them. "I want to go back," I say, my pain and hope bleeding into my voice. "If I could go back, I would find you before Malak changed you. I would ask you to run away with me."

His eyes widen and for all the world, I can't imagine a look of greater regret on his face than the one he wears now.

An instant later, he's shaking his head and pulling away from me, but I close my hand over his and hold on tightly with the strength the medallions give me.

"I would fight," I say, meeting his deep-gray eyes. "I

would fight as hard as I did to bring you here. I would pull all of us through the mud and slime and jagged rocks. I would carry Tamra and you would carry Gallium. Together, we would keep them safe, and your family would come with us too—your father and brother—and we would help each other, and we would never..."

My voice breaks. "We would never be lost."

His gaze clashes with mine as he steps forward into the spray, pulling me close, his hands running the length of my spine, up into my wet hair, down to my lower back, and tracing back up to my neck, setting my body on fire.

His lips stop a breath from mine, lips that utter words of hope and regret. "I would give anything to change what happened, Asha."

"Then let's choose our future," I say, closing the gap between us and brushing my lips to his. The contact sends a shock of pleasure straight to my core, so intense that I gasp against his mouth.

He freezes, and in that heartbeat, I comprehend that I kissed his full lips. No sharp tooth to keep me at a distance.

I lean inward, my body already plastered against him, my face turned up to his. I trace the contours of his cheeks and jaw, brushing the hair from his temples before I trail my fingertips to the corner of his mouth where his tooth used to be.

All the while, he stays perfectly still.

Then, with a groan, his lips meet mine.

Skin on skin. The contact drives every doubt and fear from my mind, a heady pleasure filling my body with need.

His hands tangle in my hair. My hands grip the back of his head. The water mingles with our kiss and splashes against my eyelashes, droplets slipping down my arms and legs.

Pressing against him, I drag my hands down his back, holding tightly, needing him closer.

For a moment, I'm aware of the light and dark in my left palm, the metal barrier between his skin and mine, but then my consciousness of it vanishes, overtaken by the force of his kiss and the desperate need building within me.

Before I can second-guess myself, I reach for the hem of my tunic and slip the material up over my head while staying as close to him as I can.

My bare chest crashes back into his and he catches me, pulling me close again. His hands knead my back, sending warmth spearing through me, while his mouth travels to my chin and down my neck, following the droplets to my chest.

When his mouth closes over my breast, his tongue swirling against my nipple, heat fills my head. I lose myself as he kisses and strokes every inch of my wet skin, from my breasts to my hips.

I take everything from the contact, every strike of heat, every slow burn of sensation. All of it heightened as I explore the shape of him, my hands traveling across his shoulders, his chest, up his neck, down his back, my fingertips tracing his scars and the skin in between them.

I'm conscious of the blood running off us both. Conscious of the way the water drives it from his body and mine.

Until he's kneeling in front of me, paused where one hand rests on the new scars across my side. The stab wounds.

He looks up at me then and my breath catches at the

darkness in his expression. The tension in his jaw. The snarl on his lips.

But the way his focus is on my healed wounds tells me his anger is not aimed at me.

"It's okay," I whisper, my fingertips gliding through his hair.

The growl in his throat only grows deeper and the shadows in his eyes only increase. Maybe I should be afraid, but fear is the furthest emotion from my mind.

My hair swishes to the side as I tilt my head, a whispered question on my lips. "What do you want from me?"

"All of you," he snarls. "I want all the beautiful and all the dark. All the fear and all the rage. All the warmth and all the hurt. All the kindness and all the cruelty. All your strength and all your vulnerabilities. I want it *all*."

I teeter on the edge of a precipice and I'm not sure if I'll crash on the other side.

I choose my response carefully, and I mean it with all of my heart. "Then give as much as you want to take."

He doesn't hesitate another moment, his mouth closing over my center. His tongue finds my core and a fire ignites within me.

Moaning, I brace against him, gasping as his tongue moves on me, stroking my body into a frenzy of need.

When my hands close around his shoulders, he pulls away from me, rises to his feet and draws me out of the spray, kissing the water from my lips as he carries me back to the bed.

I wrap my legs around him and my arms around his neck, my lips pressed to his, taking his breath and giving him mine.

I'm not sure when my back meets the bed, only that he hasn't stopped touching me. Not even to remove his pants. His mouth demands access to my body from my neck to my breasts to the sensitive nub between my legs until my breathing is rapid and my exhales have become moans.

The last time we were in this position, this was where he stopped us, but not this time.

He rears back, slides to the edge of the bed, and takes hold of the top of his pants, but he struggles to get them off, the material visibly sticking to his skin. Not surprising since it's waterlogged.

"Fuck," he mutters, pushing at it.

His muscles bunch, rippling across his back and bulging at his biceps, and I can't help but take some delight from it.

Fuck me, he's beautiful.

Rising into a sitting position behind him, I run my hands over his shoulders and around to his chest, planting kisses across his shoulder blades.

He stills at my touch, his breath hitching when I slip to the floor to stand in front of him.

His gaze passes from my face to my hips and back up again, and the desire I see in his eyes makes my toes curl.

I'm not about to stand here under his heated gaze forever.

With a soft snarl, I plant my hands on his chest and push him back onto the bed so that I can take hold of his pants and peel them off him. Not easily or quickly, but when I'm done, I pitch them into the corner of the room with a triumphant smile.

Only to find him coming for me.

He scoops his arm around my waist and pulls me back

onto the bed, twisting so that I'm lying on my back again. With two quick sweeps, he guides my legs around his hips.

But there, he slows. He takes a moment to draw his lips across mine. Brush his chest against me so that my nipples tighten. Nudge my ear and send a trickle of need into my stomach before he whispers the question I want to hear. "May I fuck you?"

My answer is a low moan before I force it into speech. "Yes."

His eyes flare with desire before he leans back to take hold of my hips and positions himself above me.

He takes it slow, stopping when my muscles clench hard around him. My body tightens with the new sensations, my muscles clamping, but need and want are paramount.

I have no fear.

Meeting his movement, I pull back a little, drive forward a little, back a little, forward a little more, every time taking him deeper as my body adjusts to his size and length.

He lets me take control, becoming very still, his fists clenched around the sheets on either side of my head, the desire in his eyes making me burn. With every slow slip back and forth, the movement eases until I take a deep breath and drive upward with a groan.

He takes back control—or maybe I'm still in control. I don't know which and I don't fucking care.

Our bodies clash and every thrust takes me higher. Toward a peak I didn't know existed. More pleasure than I thought my body could take, more than I thought I could possibly feel.

His arms slide beneath me, drawing me up closer,

supporting me as he drives into me and everything around us disappears.

There is only this.

His body and mine. His mouth on mine. His hands stroking my breasts, reaching between us and stroking my core.

There is only a blur of heat and need and movement.

The final thrust takes me over the edge, my senses spiraling before I crash into pure bliss that cascades through me, wave after intense wave, for so long that I'm gasping and gripping his back, barely able to anchor myself. Barely wanting to.

Slowly, slowly, I come back to myself.

I'm trembling, shivering, and covered in sweat.

So is he.

With a soft growl in the back of his throat, he drops his lips to mine, tasting my mouth before he rolls onto his back, taking me with him so that I'm straddling him.

He's so deep in me that our bodies stay joined.

His hands glide down my back, then up and forward, tingling past my neck to capture my tarnished hair where it falls across my face. He brushes it back, his thumbs soothing my heated skin as he strokes my cheeks.

My body clenches around him, sending echoes of pleasure through me.

His deep-gray eyes take me in and a hint of a smile plays around his lips, his serious expression lifting. "Asha."

"Mmm?"

He rears up a little beneath me, his stomach muscles bunching so he can plant a kiss on my lips before he drops back to the bed, his dark hair splaying across the sheets.

The movement takes him out of me.

I'm surprised at the rush of warmth from my body and the puddle now forming on his lower stomach as gravity does its work.

The mechanics of sex aren't a surprise to me, but even so, I'm not sure what to do, my cheeks flushing with uncertainty.

Without fuss, he grabs the edge of the sheet and sweeps it between us, cleaning up before he pushes the sheet away again and rolls us onto our sides.

The kiss he gives me drives every other thought from my mind. A kiss on my lips. Another on my chin. One at the base of my neck. Two more above my heart.

A whisper against my breast. "You are everything."

For long minutes, he strokes my skin, his fingers gliding across my curves while I press closer to him, soaking in the contact.

I close my eyes.

More than the heady pleasure of sex, this peace between us, this feeling that nothing else exists beyond this room, is all I want in this moment.

Too soon, I sense him adjusting his position and I open my eyes to find him contemplating me.

His expression has become serious again and I want to fight against the reality that's trying to push back in on us.

I trace his jaw, trying to ease his tension. Trying to read the suddenly haunted shadows in his eyes. "Erik... What is it?"

His hand slides down my arm to my hip, making my skin tingle, a pleasant sensation that contradicts how subdued he's become.

He speaks slowly. "I want to believe that if I'd made different choices ten years ago, a different path would have been possible for us."

"What choices?"

"Split-second choices. Mere heartbeats of time." He shakes his head. "It wouldn't have mattered. Your family would never have let you go."

My forehead creases. I'm not sure what choices he thinks he had, but I'm certain that he's wrong about my family. "They would have been happy to be rid of me."

"No." He props himself up beside me. "Malak would never have allowed you to leave."

I'm even more confused now. "Malak ridiculed me. He made me go to classes with the other Blacksmiths my age just to stand me in front of an empty anvil without a hammer. They mocked me and hurt me and—"

I close my eyes. I will *not* remember.

Erik's voice is low. Gentle. "He wanted you to learn to hate."

Sudden tears leak from my eyes. "How would that benefit him? If I hated anyone most of all, it was him."

"He wanted to destroy your heart because he *knew*." Erik's jaw clenches. "He knew you were left-handed like him."

CHAPTER 24

I'm a storm of disbelief.

Erik's hands are soothing on my cheeks, brushing away my tears. I could wonder how he's so sure that Malak was aware of my power, but I already have the answer.

"Malak told you all his secrets before he died."

Erik nods. "I forced him to tell me everything."

"If he knew... why would he keep me powerless?"

Even as I speak, I suspect I know the answer. Before I left the cursed city, Genova, the leader of the farmers' guild, had warned me about games of power between men and women.

She had asked me: *What does a powerful man do to a woman strong enough to challenge him?*

It was the same thing Malak tried to do to my siblings, who were also born powerful. "He wanted to destroy me so I wouldn't challenge him."

But Erik shakes his head emphatically. "If he wanted to

destroy you, he would have had you killed or he would have siphoned your power like he did to your brother and sister. On the contrary, Asha. You were the first Blacksmith who was like him. He wanted you by his side."

My face drains of blood. "What?"

"He wanted you to hate the world as much as he did. He was looking for a way to make you a hammer because it was his fault you didn't have one."

Now, I'm baffled. "How so?"

"You needed a special hammer like he did. His sister was the hammer-maker, but by the time he realized you were like him, she was gone. He'd had all the other hammer-makers killed years before. He'd done it to maintain control over Blacksmith power—who received a hammer and when. But it meant that once she was gone, there was nobody to make a hammer for you."

I chew over what I know, but there are more questions than answers. "Milena disappeared—was supposedly killed —soon after I first picked up a hammer."

Erik gives me a wry smile before he pulls me closer, resting back on the bed so that I nestle into the crook of his arm. His voice rumbles in my ear. "I only have Malak's version of those events, but in the days after your power failed to materialize, Milena was evasive about it. It was her job to understand every Blacksmith's individual power. When he pressed her for answers, she refused to give them. Then, a few nights after, he discovered that his prototype device was missing—the one he eventually perfected and used on me. He went looking for her only to find that she'd fled.

"He believed she'd taken it. She had kept your nature

from him and kept a hammer from you so you could never join him. She'd betrayed him. To save face, he destroyed part of the city and concocted a story that she'd died in a human rebellion. That may have been false, but his rage was real."

I shiver. "Many humans died in the days that followed her supposed death." I try to shake off the horror and focus on what Erik is telling me, tipping my head back to see him. "If Milena stole the device, that could explain how she changed Thaden Kane. In all the years since then, she could have created many replicas of that device."

Since Thaden Kane's arrival, it's been my fear that Milena is creating an army.

Erik doesn't immediately agree. "Until Thaden Kane arrived, I didn't think Milena would try to use it for her own purposes. I had this notion that maybe..."

I wait for him to continue. "Maybe what?"

He shrugs. "I thought maybe she was trying to stop Malak. By stealing his device, she set him back years. Along with ensuring your power wasn't available to him, she practically cut him off at the knees."

My forehead creases. "But if he was so unhappy that I didn't have a hammer, why didn't he let me use his?"

"Because nobody other than his sister knew he was left-handed and she had loudly pronounced that you were defective." Erik gives me a piercing look. "For you to use his hammer would have cast aspersions on his power. Even his most loyal followers had ambitions and could have used it against him. He couldn't expose himself to that risk. Well, not until he'd proven he could successfully combine a human with an animal."

"Not until he created you," I whisper.

Erik nods.

My head is swimming, but I try to cut through to what this means for the path ahead of me. "When you were dying, you told me it was my choice whether or not to find Milena." I speak carefully. "But what you really meant was... it's my choice if I want my own hammer."

Again, he nods. "You could have tools of your own."

Assuming I can ever dislodge the dark medallion embedded in my palm...

Even now, a battle is being fought between the two medallions. The balance between light and dark is fragile, and yet Erik is so damn calm as he contemplates me. So much the opposite of me, as if we've switched places and I'm the volatile one.

My shoulders slump. "I should never have tools of my own."

He strokes my hair back, searching my eyes. "Why do you fear your power?"

"This isn't power. It's death." My chest hurts as I curl my left hand against my side, closing my fist around the medallions. "I can take something beautiful and alive, and I can twist it. I can make simple, perfect things ugly and cruel."

He continues to study me quietly. "Do you believe that when *you* use your power, it can only be dark and malicious?"

"I know that's all it is. I've taken life, turned living flesh into stone and ash."

"In the defense of others."

"A horrible defense."

"Death is never anything but terrible." He strokes my

back as he speaks. "Your power doesn't have to mean death, though, Asha. Milena could make you a hammer of light, not darkness."

"Would she, though?" Bitterness rises within me because I'm not so sure. "When Thaden Kane first arrived, he relayed a very clear message from her: She thinks I'm a traitor to all Blacksmiths. Even if I hadn't made this deal with the fae, she didn't give me the correct hammer when she had the chance. If Malak told you the truth—and he could have fabricated all of it—then it means she actively chose to leave me powerless."

"True," Erik replies. "But you're a Blacksmith. There are very few of you left. And you were my prisoner, not a traitor. It has to make her think twice about ending you."

I grimace. "My vow to kill her..."

"Could work in your favor," he says. "She may seek to bargain with you—a hammer for her life."

I chew my lip. "Maybe."

"As for Malak, he didn't make it up. At least, not the parts I told you. I verified his story over time, piece by piece, by asking questions of those who saw and heard parts of events."

"Like Genova." I nod. "She said you asked her about the night Milena disappeared."

"She confirmed Milena came to see her that night and that she was terrified."

I remember what else Genova told me. "Milena brought a baby with her that night. Genova said she was sure it wasn't a human baby."

"It was a Blacksmith child, but I don't know more than that."

He doesn't? I peer at him. "But something Malak said must have caused you to ask."

He nods. "He mentioned it in passing in the context of how normally his sister was behaving that night, as if she hadn't been about to betray him. He said she went out to welcome the latest Blacksmith baby into the world so she could begin the process of fashioning a hammer for them. Apparently, she liked to meet all Blacksmith children soon after birth.

"He was angrier about the fact that she would have known from the time of *your* birth that you were like him, and she never told him."

"So... the baby wasn't important, after all."

"Maybe. Or maybe not." Erik's jaw clenches. "When I crushed the Blacksmiths, I drew a line. I wouldn't kill children. But in the end, I didn't have to. Other than your siblings, the youngest Blacksmiths were around our age. And by fuck, I had no problem taking them down."

He ends on a snarl and his intensity doesn't surprise me. All of those youths walked in their parents' footsteps. Their age didn't make them innocent. In fact, some of them treated humans more viciously than their parents did. They thought they could gain favor with Malak that way.

Pushing away the memories, I rapidly work through the passage of time in my mind from the baby's birth when I was five years old—when Erik would have been six—to the time when I was sixteen and he brought down my people.

"That child would have been eleven years old," I say. "Maybe twelve, at most, depending on exactly when it was born."

"That's right," he replies. "And yet, I didn't encounter a Blacksmith child of that age."

He's peering at me as if I might have information about it, but I shake my head. "My life was dictated to me. 'Go here.' 'Go there.' 'Do this.' 'Do that.' I didn't meet every Blacksmith or know about all of them." I peer right back at him, since he's had far longer to think about it than I have. "You must have a theory?"

His expression is shadowed now. "Malak was enraged that his sister had pretended everything had been normal by going to see that child. My suspicion, as fucking awful as it is, is that the area of the city he destroyed included that child's home. Especially if he had a sense that the child would grow to be powerful."

Genova described how the baby had bent a spoon with their little fist.

I shudder at how calculated Malak's fury could have been. "Other Blacksmiths were killed that night. All part of the supposed rebellion."

Erik gives a heavy sigh. "It wouldn't look real otherwise."

"The child would have died too. Another casualty of Malak's rage." I give a heavy exhale. "There's a part of me that hopes maybe it's alive somewhere. A Blacksmith child who escaped all this and lives in peace and safety. Somewhere."

I wonder if any such place exists. I shake it off and once again focus on the path ahead. "We need more information about why the fae are here and why they want Milena dead, but the sooner we leave, the better. My only goal before I go is making sure my family is safe."

"You won't ask Gallium and Tamra to come with you?"

Erik is studying me again. "Your brother is a strong fighter and Thaden could be an asset. Tamra's healing power could prove essential."

All of that is true. Having my family at my side would greatly increase my odds of succeeding against a Blacksmith of Milena's power and skill. Especially since Thaden's scales protect him from the effect of Blacksmith power, but...

"My sister needs time to heal. Asking her to come with me will only enflame the tension between us. Thaden knows these lands. It's my hope he can take her somewhere safe. As for my brother, I can't expose him to this fight. His heart is too good. I don't want him near this kind of darkness."

Erik doesn't argue. "I understand."

I swallow hard. "I want to give them the chance to live in peace. I will do whatever I need to do to make that happen. If I survive the fight ahead of me, then maybe I can join them and heal the rift between us."

Now, a growl hums deep in Erik's throat. "You *will* survive this, Asha. I will make sure of it."

I want to believe him, but already, the darkness is pushing in at the edges of my mind.

As if Erik senses it, he pulls me into his arms.

I bury my doubts in his kiss and welcome the heat in his hands as he leads me back to the bathroom, where the water is still running and still perfectly warm.

For the next hour, he takes his time washing me and I take my time washing him, and for that short time, I can believe that we will never break again.

CHAPTER 25

We've barely emerged from the bathroom, wrapped in clean towels, when Erik tenses and points at the door.

"Incoming," he murmurs, quickly tucking the cloth around his waist and freeing up his hands. "Five of them. All men, judging by the heaviness of their tread."

"The men take care of housekeeping," I say, relaxing a little, although my focus flies to my toolbox, where it has remained safely by the bed.

A moment later, a polite knock sounds at the door.

With a glance at Erik, I quickly pull the spare cloths from beneath the doorway—the ones that Erik had stuffed there to stifle sound—and step back from it.

"Enter!"

The door opens and the same five men who prepared the room file inside. The first one is carrying a plate of food. The next two are wheeling some sort of cart filled with linens, while the final two are pushing a larger cart covered in a black sheet so I can't see its contents.

The appearance of food makes my stomach growl. I'm starving. But I angle myself back toward my toolbox, intending to remain near it while they're here.

The first man, who has dark-green hair, greets me while the other four bow their heads briefly.

"Blacksmith Silverspun," the green-haired man says. "My name is Jerome. We've come to clean your room."

He deposits the plate of food onto the little table beside the wall. The plate is filled with what could be fruit, although I don't recognize any of it.

As the other men set about changing the sheets and wiping down surfaces, Jerome continues, speaking politely. "Queen Karasi has extended an invitation for you to dine with her tonight." He glances at Erik. "I'm sure she would have extended the invitation to your guest if she had known he was awake."

"I'll need something to wear," I say, eyeing Jerome as he scoops up the broken pieces of my armor—which Gliss had deposited beneath the table—and retrieves Erik's pants.

We *both* need clothing.

But I have other questions first. "How much time has passed since I first came to this room?"

"You've been here for two days."

Two days. I must have slept for the first one.

Jerome continues. "As for the dinner invitation, please don't worry about clothing. We've brought gifts from the Queen."

He pulls the cover off the second rack, which the final two men had pushed up against the opposite wall.

It's filled with sparkling gowns, all of them glittering.

I should be glad to see them, but the light catches them and suddenly...

I'm not in this room anymore.

I fight hard against it, but the memory pulls me back, a much older memory than of the last few days. It was ten years ago, but before the Vandawolf crushed my people. Before my parents were killed.

My mother had laid three dresses out on my bed and told me that I would go to one of Malak's parties. I didn't want to go. I was just an example of failure for them to mock. If I thought that the attendees would taunt me with words alone, it might have been bearable, but they didn't.

She made me pick a dress. She sat me on a chair at the back of the throne room, but it was positioned so that anyone looking at the throne would see me.

It was on Malak's left-hand-side, and now I wonder if it was *his* idea to sit me in the bright light near his throne.

My mother told me to stay there, but in the end, I didn't.

I couldn't.

Erik's touch on my shoulder brings me back to myself. "Asha?"

My focus falls to my hand where the two medallions rest. I haven't relived those memories for a very long time. But it seems that taking control of the light and the dark has made me vulnerable to all the things I've pushed away.

My voice is tight. "I can't wear those dresses."

Erik can't possibly know the memories those sparkling gowns have evoked, but he gives me a nod.

In contrast, the fae men are suddenly tense and pale.

"Blacksmith Silverspun, please forgive me," Jerome says.

"But if you send these gowns back, the Queen will be insulted."

"She'll punish you." I close my eyes briefly, preparing myself to acquiesce. "I suppose if I need to—"

"Wait." Erik's hand closes around my arm. "Will you let me try something?"

I nod, curious. "Yes."

Leaving my side, he quickly flips through the dresses and then pulls one from the rack. It's quite possibly the puffiest gown in the bunch, with an excessive number of overly large, material flowers sewn all over the skirt and bodice, even up under the arms, where they would force my limbs to stick outward.

Erik gives me a mysterious smile before he turns his back to me, the dress clutched in his arms.

The room fills with the sounds of threads snapping and material tearing while flowers fly free around him, landing on the floor and the bed.

Moments later, he turns back, now holding a simple, black gown with a few remaining colorful threads still caught in it.

The dress that was hiding beneath all the frippery is beautiful. It's sleeveless with a round neck, fitted through the bodice, and flowing from the hips. It appears to be made of multiple layers. While the bottommost layer is opaque, the top layer is gauzy with a very faint shimmer.

"Better?" he asks.

"Very."

I run my hand across the material. The dress looks a little small but has enough stretch that it should cling without restricting my breathing or my movements.

Refocusing on Erik, I ask, "What about you?"

Jerome reaches into the rack and pulls out a simple tunic and pants. Both black. "These were intended for when the Vandawolf woke up."

"Good enough," Erik says.

Soon enough, the men finish their work and leave us.

Half an hour later, we've taken bites of the fruit they brought, and we're dressed and ready to leave the room. I attempt to comb my hair, but it doesn't do me any favors, so I braid it instead.

Before we depart, I consider my tools carefully.

I don't want to leave them behind—or the mechanism I pulled from the Vandawolf—but I'm conscious that taking them with me could be inflammatory.

"You're a Blacksmith," Erik murmurs, his hand stroking my back. "Don't be afraid to show it. Not in this place."

He's right. My value to the Queen lies in my power. I shouldn't shun it.

Finding a dark-blue sash among the dresses, I wrap it around my hammer and then tie it to my waist, where it will be visible.

For the titanium device, the plain medallion, and the dragon-imprinted medallion, I reach for the thickest brocade I can find among the dresses, tear off a large strip, and fold it over and over to form a thick pouch that I tie to the front of my thigh.

This way, I can bring everything with me without appearing to carry so many weapons.

"Be careful of Queen Karasi," I say to Erik, hesitating at the door and daring to speak my mind despite the presence of the two warrior fae at the end of the corridor who are undoubtedly listening in now.

"Never trust a fae." Erik growls. "Not a single one."

At my surprised look, he shrugs. "My father told me that."

"Wise." I steel myself for the encounter ahead of us and forge ahead along the corridor, the dress swishing around my legs.

The two guards escort us without speaking—not that I attempt to engage them in conversation—but I don't miss the way they cast glances back at Erik. Aside from the fact that he wasn't expected to be awake so soon, his new appearance probably surprises them.

I take note of the path we take—and I'm much better able to orientate myself this time—so that I'm confident I'll know how to navigate the northern wing unassisted.

The dining room is smaller than the ballroom but no less grand.

Fresh air enters from a single arched opening on the far side, through which I can see part of a balcony that looks out into the vast, night sky. We must be very high up, because only the vague outline of far-off mountains is visible in the distance.

A large table dominates the space. It's covered in white crockery along with crystal goblets and is lit with candles, from which waft the scent of vanilla.

In the moment before our presence is announced, I quickly take note of the room's occupants.

My heart both lifts and then hurts to see my family.

My sister is once again seated directly beside the Queen.

My brother sits on my sister's left. Both of their backs are to me and their silver hair catches the light.

Thaden is seated on the Queen's right. Gliss is beside him. Like my siblings, they're dressed in evening attire—gowns for the women and dark pants and tops for the men.

The other seats near the Queen are occupied by fae I don't recognize, which makes me think that her 'chosen' companions might change daily.

It doesn't escape me that while the left-hand side of the table has chairs, it is empty except for a single dinner setting all the way at the other end. I'm sure that place is intended for me.

After all, I've proven myself to be dangerous.

Elowynn is the only one dressed in armor, the same black gear she seems to always wear. She's positioned exactly where I would expect the Queen's Champion to be—behind her monarch and slightly to her right, watching Karasi's back from a spot that allows her to keep the entire room and its entrance within view.

Because of that, she sees us first.

Her focus is immediately drawn to the Vandawolf, her violet eyes widening before tension settles into her shoulders and her brow furrows deeply.

A moment later, our two escorts step aside and the woman guarding the door announces our presence. "Asha Silverspun and the Vandawolf!"

Conversation within the room abruptly ceases. Chairs scrape as people turn in our direction.

We are suddenly the focus of everyone's attention.

"The Vandawolf?" The Queen rises to her feet, her

quick gaze flowing from Erik's head to his feet, her golden eyes narrowing before she wipes her expression clean.

He's relaxed beside me but has a far more formidable presence now that he isn't lying, near-dead, on a stretcher. He stands a full head taller than me, his dark hair slicked back, his muscular build clearly visible beneath the clothing he was given.

His focus sweeps around the room and I suspect he's able to take in far more than me—sounds, smells, heartbeats —but he gives nothing of his thoughts away.

There's a lot to take in, even for me, including the way both Thaden and Gallium have half-risen out of their seats while Tamra's face is like stone. I don't imagine she was expecting to see Erik, but his new appearance doesn't seem to have changed her feelings about him.

The Queen presses her hand to Tamra's shoulder, her fingers closing tightly around my sister's arm, while neither of them takes their eyes off Erik.

"Well," Karasi says, breaking into an overly bright smile. "I can't think of a more delightful surprise. Welcome, Vandawolf. Come, eat with us. There's plenty of food."

She gestures to the far end of the table with the empty seats and the single dinner setting.

With a glance at Erik, I head straight for that spot, needing this moment to be over, although... judging by the way the Queen watches us... I doubt we'll escape her attention at all tonight.

She remains on her feet as we take our seats. I'm now sitting directly opposite her with a space of twenty seats between me and her.

Her smile hasn't faded. "Now, we're just waiting for one

more guest before we can eat."

One more? There are no other dinner settings on the table, although there are plenty of empty chairs around me.

A second later, there's movement at the door and the guard calls out again. "Dusana of the Dusk."

I stiffen at the sight of the petite woman who tried to kill me and Erik in the mountains. I remember the way she declared that killing me was her ticket to fame and glory. She wanted to take Elowynn's place as the Queen's Champion.

I told Erik all about it. Where he now sits directly to my left, I can easily discern the tension in his features, the sudden ice in his eyes.

I reach for his hand under the table, only to find that he's already reaching for mine. His palm presses against the medallions, closing tightly, as if to urge me to cage my anger.

I'm not sure what kind of game the Queen might plan to play with me tonight, assuming she tells Dusana to sit with me.

At the other end of the table, Karasi is still speaking.

"Welcome, Dusana," she cries. "We were waiting for you."

Dusana sweeps into the room, her golden hair decorated with flowers, her long, pink gown trailing behind her. She's even more beautifully dressed than the other fae at the table. In fact, her dress looks nearly exactly like one of the dresses the Queen sent me, which means it could have been a gift.

Dusana seeks me across the distance, her brown eyes gleaming at me and a smirk on her lips.

Gliss assured me that Dusana would be punished for disobeying the Queen, but it seems not.

As Erik warned me: Never trust a fae.

CHAPTER 26

Queen Karasi takes a quick step away from the table, releasing my sister's shoulder to greet Dusana. "Darling, you look lovely in the dress I sent you."

Dusana gives a low curtsy. "Queen Karasi, I'm honored."

"Oh, dearest, please rise." Queen Karasi beams while Dusana returns to her feet. The Queen briefly takes both of Dusana's hands. "My dear, you are radiant."

Without waiting for Dusana to reply, Karasi swings to Elowynn, who has stayed a step behind the Queen. "Elowynn, doesn't Dusana look radiant?"

A faint smile rests on Elowynn's lips. "She does, my Queen."

Still speaking to Elowynn, Queen Karasi continues. "Dusana should have all the attention, yes? Elowynn, give Dusana all the attention she deserves."

"Yes, my Queen."

Karasi steps back while Elowynn strides forward.

Dusana gives Elowynn a triumphant smile, holding out her hand, as if she expects Elowynn to take it.

Elowynn's fist lashes out, so fast that I can barely follow it, smacking across Dusana's cheek with a *crack!*

I flinch at the sound of breaking bone, finding myself on my feet, as are my brother, Thaden, and also Erik.

Dusana lands hard on the floor, her scream echoing around us. Elowynn follows her down without respite and Dusana's reflexes aren't quick enough to avoid the second punch that smacks across her forehead and knocks her head into the floor.

I can't see her face and I'm glad for it.

Blood has sprayed across the marble.

Elowynn wrenches Dusana up by her hair, crushing the flowers in it as she snarls. "You struck the Blacksmith when you knew Queen Karasi had granted her amnesty. You disobeyed your Queen."

Dusana's jaw must still be working because she screams, "How was I supposed to know it was her? Her hair isn't silver like that of the rest of her family. I thought she was a dark witch."

A dangerously calm expression falls across Elowynn's face. Instead of countering Dusana's claim or refuting her defense, Elowynn whispers, "Did you just speak back to me?"

There's a pause, but in the silence that follows, I hear Dusana's gasped breath. "No, Commander, I would never—"

Elowynn's hand snaps across Dusana's face. Not a punch, but the sound is just as awful. *Crack!*

She drops Dusana an instant later and the blonde-haired fae falls back to the floor, clutching her head in both hands.

Elowynn remains crouched, blood dripping from her hand. "Be grateful that's the worst of your punishment," she says. "You laid hands on the Blacksmith, who has our Queen's protection. That is akin to laying hands on our Queen, a sin punishable by death."

Elowynn grabs Dusana's chin, forcing her to look up.

The champion's voice is dangerously soft as she asks, "Do you wish for death, Dusana of the Dusk?"

"No, Commander Dawn," Dusana replies, her voice slurring now. "I apologize, Commander."

"You will be removed from the Queen's Guard. You will not be recommended to challenge me at the Winter Ascending. As for your family..."

Elowynn looks to the Queen, who stands like stone for a long moment before she replies.

"Let it be known that I am merciful," Karasi says. "Dusana's family will not be shunned. In fact, I will do them an even greater mercy. I will excise Dusana from them. She is no longer their daughter. She is cut out, and therefore, they bear none of her shame."

On the floor, Dusana gasps. "Please... no..."

"Take her away."

At the Queen's command, Elowynn takes hold of Dusana's arm and drags her to the door, where the guards take over and Dusana disappears from sight.

Queen Karasi takes a deep breath and turns a bright smile on the rest of us.

"Well, now that's over," she says. "Let's eat."

At the clap of her hands, a stream of men carrying platters enters the room. The scent of vanilla is overtaken by the smell of roasted vegetables, several men stop to clean the floor, and the fae resume their conversation.

Moments later, Elowynn returns to her position at the Queen's back as if nothing happened.

I return to my seat, uncertain how I feel about what transpired. Ultimately, Gliss was right. Dusana was punished. But the way the punishment was meted out reminds me too much of how Malak used to operate.

Strike when they don't see it coming.

Ahead of us, Thaden and my brother are exchanging a rapid, but silent communication. I read wariness, uncertainty, worry, unease...

But it's Thaden whose eyes meet mine across the table.

Of course, I suddenly realize that my family may be unaware of what exactly happened back in the mountains. Gallium arrived after the fight. He didn't see what occurred between me and Dusana and Gliss beforehand. He could have been told anything.

It's also true that neither of them has attempted to come see me, although, judging by the way the Queen operates, that could be for any number of reasons, including by her design.

What's more, I'm now comprehending the paleness in Thaden's face when he looks at Erik.

Erik's new appearance will mean a lot to him. Erik looks human again, unlike Thaden, whose bronze scales are very much on display.

We're seated too far away from my family to talk with them, but I promise myself I'll find a way to speak with them without going near any of the other fae. Especially since the ones seated nearest to me and Erik have shrunk as far away from us as possible, even with the empty chairs already between us.

I smother my sigh.

I won't let their fear get between me and my family.

The next hour is filled with a stream of food and drink, much of which I don't recognize, but everything I try is delicious. Drinks flow freely, but a single sip tells me they have a high alcoholic content, so I keep a full glass in front of me, drinking no more of it. Erik does the same.

The more intoxicated the other fae become, the louder their conversations become until the room is filled with a raucous cacophony of sound.

On the positive side, I very much doubt a Frost fae could pick up anything we say. On the negative side, each time I glance at Erik, I find his jaw clenched, the tension around his eyes increasing when the noise peaks.

It can only be painful to his sensitive hearing.

I cast my eyes around the table, dismissing the pretty cloths and landing on the nearest candle. Pulling it toward me, I dig into the softer part near the top, wadding up two small blobs of wax.

Leaning toward him, I reach for his face, as if I'm about to whisper a secret into his ear. Which I sort of am. "For your ears."

With my other hand, I press the wax into his palm.

He glances down and seems to catch on quickly to my intent. "Thank you."

Within moments, he's pressed the plugs into his ears and the tension around his mouth and eyes eases.

When I look up, I'm conscious once again of Thaden's piercing gaze and I know I need to make a move to speak with him soon. I just need to find a way without causing a scene...

Directly opposite me, I suddenly find myself the focus of the Queen. She clicks her fingers at Elowynn, who seems to know exactly what her monarch wants.

Elowynn immediately heads toward me. The other fae don't seem to notice, they're so caught up their own conversations and apparently delirious with drink, which makes me even gladder I barely touched the liquid.

I tense as Elowynn approaches, aware of Erik also watching her carefully.

She lifts her hands a little, as if to show she comes in peace. "Come with me, please, Asha. Queen Karasi wishes to speak with you on the balcony." She glares at Erik when he begins to rise. "Alone."

When he ignores her command, continuing to stand, the furrow in her brow deepens. "Don't make me fight you, wolf-man."

"I'll be okay," I quickly reassure Erik. "The Queen has more to fear from me than I do from her."

When I rise from my chair, Queen Karasi does the same, slipping toward the arched opening leading outside.

My family watches her and then looks to me, but they remain seated and it's impossible to know what they're thinking.

Elowynn stays close on my heels until I step onto the balcony. The fresh air is a welcome relief from the cloying scent of vanilla. So is the quiet.

Queen Karasi's slender form is lit with moonlight, her bejeweled dress swishing as she reaches the balustrade.

I tense when she lifts her hand, snaps her fingers, and a

flame appears, licking at her fingertips. She quickly flicks it toward the lamp sitting against the wall beside the door.

"A little light for our conversation," she says.

Gliss described Karasi as a Solstice fae, having power over heat and fire. Given the amount of moonlight, I take the Queen's display as a demonstration of her power. Or rather, the tiniest hint of her power.

While keeping my distance from her, I step toward the balustrade. Beyond the railing, I can see for miles. It's a breathtaking view, but not unlike the one I had from my tower.

"You can leave us, Elowynn," Queen Karasi says to her champion. "Asha won't harm me."

Elowynn hesitates, then bows and disappears back into the room.

Karasi turns to me, her eyes twinkling. "Elowynn is fierce and unlikable, isn't she? Vicious when I ask her to be. But our culture values strength and ambition. We thrive on power and control."

Without waiting for my response, she cranes her neck to consider the revelers inside the room. "I've dulled their senses with vanilla candles and plied them with more food and drink than they've seen in months." She beams at me, her smile luminous. "It's a wonderful way to distract my people from the reality of their lives and encourage them to ignore the brutality of my decisions."

I narrow my eyes at her, wondering how quickly the fae in the room will forget the way Dusana's blood sprayed across the floor. "Why did you wish to speak with me?"

Her smile fades at my abrupt question, and all guile vanishes from her face. "You must think I'm heartless.

Luring my own people to punishment. Leaving your wolf-man to die in front of you. Keeping your family from you for the past two days. Forcing you into a deal that will once again separate you from the ones you love."

I incline my head. I can't disagree. At least she's confirmed she's the reason my family hasn't come to see me.

She tilts her head, her long, golden hair cascading to the side. "I learned very early on in my reign—as every leader learns—that keeping my people safe requires making harsh decisions."

She turns to the moonlit landscape beyond the balcony, sweeping her hand across the view. "What do you see when you look upon this land, Asha Silverspun?"

Cautiously, I take my eyes off the Queen to consider the landscape around us. Directly below me, spread out across the plain, are tiny dots of flame—probably campfires—and what appear to be many, many tents.

To my right, farther west, the sky is lit up with streaks of lightning. It's a struggle to stop the sight of the glittering energy from triggering my reflexes. For the last ten years, I've trained my body to react to lightning as a sign of another monster rising—the strongest and worst monsters.

To my far left, the landscape is darker. The contours of the land are harder to make out and it looks like a storm is brewing, the sky filled with clouds.

"I see an encampment," I say, pointing to the plain below us. "Which surely consists of an army of fae."

She nods. "A thousand fae warriors."

"A formidable army, then."

"What else do you see?" she asks.

"Thunderbirds protecting the sky on the encampment's

western perimeter. No doubt guarding it from your human enemies." I turn to face the other direction, where the clouds rest. "But in the east..."

My voice trails off as the back of my neck prickles and the medallions on my hand make my skin tingle.

I peer more closely into darkness that lies far off to my left, taking in the way the dark clouds roil in the east. An inky pall lies over that land.

My heart beats faster, but I don't have a logical reason for my body's reactions. "You came from there."

"We *escaped* from the east," Queen Karasi says quietly. "Or perhaps more accurately, we were driven from it by a darkness that kept growing and spreading, a blight that destroyed our crops and made our homes unlivable. Our Springtime fae fought valiantly against the spreading decay and we thought we could overcome it, but we soon discovered that the more we tried to fight it, the worse it got. It was as if our magic only fed it."

Her expression hardens. "Soon, crimson clouds formed in our sky, making the land beneath it appear tainted with blood. That's when monsters began rising from the sludge."

I stiffen with shock. "What?"

She nods. "Yes, Asha Silverspun. Your city is not the only one that is now cursed. What the Blacksmiths did in *Vadlig Odemark* has spread far beyond its origins. A vicious blight has caused our children to sicken and our animals to die and it drained the power from our strongest warriors. It poisoned our lakes and ponds so that anyone who drank from that water would die of thirst. We had no choice but to leave our once-beautiful country and push into the west."

Damn.

I never imagined that the wasteland—the Sunken Bog— had extended past the mountains and farther into the east. Or that lakes like the one the humans call the *Toxic Thirst* could form in other places.

Maybe I shouldn't be so shocked. Before I left, Genova warned that the Sunken Bog was encroaching into the city's food supply within the wall.

It certainly explains why the fae are so far west.

"What about Milena? Is your hatred of her born from her complicity in the blight that now plagues your home?"

"No, although whatever hand she had in creating it is certainly a cause for hatred." Queen Karasi twitches. "No, you see, Milena Ironmeld stands at the right hand of the human queen who opposes me. Milena has joined with the human army and uses her power to fashion weapons with which the humans attack my people."

It takes me by surprise that Milena would have aligned herself with humans here in the northwest when she sent a message with Thaden Kane threatening the human city in the wasteland. I suppose I imagined that her hatred of humans would have extended to their entire race, but maybe it's all about territory.

After all, her exact message was simple enough: She wants her city back.

It wasn't a message for the Vandawolf alone. It was for him *and* me. She told Thaden that the wolf who rules the city had killed her brother, and that the Blacksmith who serves that wolf is a traitor to her people.

I am a traitor to my people.

The fae may call the Cursed Wasteland *Vadlig*

Odemark, but Milena called it *Svikari Traidor*: Home of Traitors.

All of that indicates that her wish to reclaim the city is personal.

Still, the timing seems odd. If Milena is busy fighting a war in the north, I'm not sure why she would have sent Thaden Kane to threaten the Vandawolf now. Unless she believes that the war here will soon be over, freeing her up to attack the south.

I only have theories and no real answers.

Queen Karasi gives a heavy sigh as she turns to me, her golden eyes dull and her shoulders slumped. "Milena Ironmeld has emboldened her leader—nay, I would go so far as to say she has poisoned her Queen's mind. Together, they have rejected every peace treaty I have offered. Every plea for grace. We managed to make it to this open valley and here we have stayed, caught between humans in the west and the darkness in the east."

Her cheeks regain some of their color. "If you end Milena, so too will her malicious influence end. And then, we may have a chance for peace. Between fae, humans, *and* Blacksmiths."

She makes it sound as though I would become the fae's ally, as if I could somehow mend the rift that Malak created years ago. I suppose it depends on how she decides to spin it for her people. What story she might tell.

But something doesn't make sense.

I consider the encampment far below me, taking note of the countless tents and recalling all of the information Gliss gave me about fae power. I have no doubt that the small flame Karasi conjured to light the lamp on this balcony is nothing compared to the damage she could wreak with her fire—the damage a single Solstice fae could do, let alone many of them.

It puzzles me that an army like this could be challenged by any human force, regardless of Milena's support.

Carefully, I say, "Even with Milena's weapons, the human army is still only human. And Milena is only one Blacksmith." I turn to Karasi. "You have immeasurable power at your fingertips and a thousand warriors in your army, all of whom I assume have power of varying levels. You have fierce lightning-birds to carry your warriors across the sky and attack from above. How is it, with all that power, that humans have managed to repel you?"

She looks surprised. "But I thought you knew?"

When my forehead creases, she peers at me more closely.

Her voice lowers to a whisper. "Well. That would explain why you didn't hesitate when I asked you to kill Milena, as powerful as she is." Karasi presses her hand to her heart. "My dear child, I find myself suddenly filled with guilt and I don't like that feeling. Not at all."

A trickle of fear makes my blood run cold and my command for answers is sharp. "Explain."

She gives me a bitter smile. "Milena and her humans have crushed us at every turn because they have something we do not." Her golden eyes are cold as she says, "They have dragons."

CHAPTER 27

The humans in the north control dragons?

The blood drains from my face.

Of course, I know that dragons exist. There was a time when I thought their existence was a myth, but Milena killed one when she changed Thaden Kane. I felt its power in the imprinted medallion—an immense burn that could rip me apart—and it was a young dragon, not even fully developed.

But the idea that dragons are somehow allied with humans *and* with Milena is very unwelcome news.

Although... it's also somewhat puzzling... since Milena killed one of them and that seems counter to an alliance.

Unless that dragon offered itself to the task?

No. I'm sure it didn't. Its rage was too great. When I held the imprinted medallion, I experienced firsthand the pain and fury of its death. It was murdered. I may only have theories about many things, but *that*, I'm sure of.

My brow is deeply furrowed, confusion swirling within me. "Why would dragons align themselves with humans?"

Queen Karasi is suddenly wearing a wry smile. "You know... Malak asked the very same question when he first heard of their alliance."

"Malak?" Her statement cuts through the mire within my mind like an icy blade. "What are you talking about?"

"I met him," she says. "I was the previous Queen's Champion when he came to visit." Her face is an emotionless mask as she speaks. There is no regret, no sadness. Not a hint of failure even though she didn't protect her monarch. "Malak was charming." She shrugs. "Until he wasn't."

She clears her throat and continues. "But as for the dragons, I, too, didn't believe they could align with such fragile beings as humans until I saw it for myself. A human delegation from the northwest arrived soon after Malak did. They brought their beasts with them. Two fire dragons. Great, snarling creatures that could nip your head from your shoulders like a tasty, little treat."

Now, shadows form in her eyes, her expression once again haunted. "There aren't many dragons, but they are unbeatable."

Fuck. If I was uncertain about my family coming with me on the hunt for Milena, my mind is now made up. My interactions with Thaden have confirmed that Blacksmith magic has no effect on dragon scales. My siblings would be as powerless as humans against them. I have to keep Tamra and Gallium as far away from the northwest as I can.

I grip the balustrade, taking comfort in the press of the

medallions in my left hand, even though they won't help me in a fight with a dragon.

Something Gliss mentioned makes sense to me now. She said that Elowynn's dual powers make her particularly useful to the Queen. She also indicated that she herself can forcibly read the mind of an animal. Along with being able to heal the Queen if she's injured, it's very possible that Elowynn and Gliss could read the thoughts of an enemy dragon. It reminds me of the way Gliss tipped her head back when the dragon's voice roared from the imprinted medallion when I woke it. As if she'd been listening more intently than everyone else.

Regardless, my task is the same and the risk is mine to face.

"I've promised you Milena's dead body," I say.

"But now you must doubt your chances of success."

For a brief moment, I consider asking the Queen to send Gliss with us, but I immediately dismiss that option. As much as Gliss has proven herself helpful, her allegiance is wholly to her Queen. I don't need a potential traitor in my midst.

Karasi's voice lowers to a whisper. "Do not fear, Asha Silverspun. Your magic is the oldest of the old. It is wrung from the very fabric of this Earth. The very power of creation lives within you."

She edges closer to me. "Do you know that the bright elves, who live in the far south, call the magic of creation 'deep magic'? They can access it too, but only by an act of true sacrifice."

She holds up her hand and clicks her fingers. Another

bright flame bursts to life in her hands, causing me to take a step back until the flame fades.

"*My* power is elemental," she says. "I harness the energy in the world around me—the sun's energy—and concentrate it. At night, my power is weakest because the sun no longer shines. But you..." She gleams at me. "You hold the power of creation without having to draw on the environment or sacrifice any part of yourself."

My throat is tight. "That doesn't distinguish me from Milena. She, too, has this power."

"Does she, though?" Queen Karasi gives me a smile that chills me. "Your sister tells me that you hold the power of creation over both living and non-living matter. That is a truly frightening skill, indeed. If the gods still deigned to grace us with their presence, you would sit at their left hand, Asha Silverspun."

My heart is only colder at her words, the darkness in the titanium medallion burning beneath the silver one. "Malak had this power. He did terrible things with it."

I don't know for certain if Milena has this power too. Many Blacksmiths aspired to it. It was at the heart of their experiments, which Malak encouraged.

What I do know is that Milena is also a hammer-maker. I never had a reason to give much thought to what set apart hammer-makers from other Blacksmiths. Milena was the only one alive when I was little and too soon, she was 'dead.'

For all I know, she could be even more powerful than her brother. In fact, she must be, given that she captured and killed a dragon. Or possibly lured it to its death under the guise of being its friend.

Queen Karasi is once again peering at me as if I'm a

specimen she's trying to dissect. "You baffle me, Asha Silverspun."

"Why?" I ask, not certain I want her answer.

"Your sister betrayed you. Yet every time you looked at her during dinner, I sensed only your need to protect her, not punish her. This intrigues me."

My grip on the balustrade tightens. Then relaxes. "That is for me and my sister to discuss."

She lifts her hands. "Well, of course. I won't pry."

Now that the Queen has delivered her news about the dragons, and I have my answers about why the fae are in the west, I'm keen for this conversation to end.

"I'm leaving first thing tomorrow morning," I say. "The Vandawolf will come with me."

His old name doesn't come easily to my tongue, but I'm not sure if he wants his real name shared.

"Good," Karasi says. "I'll have armor and weapons delivered to your room in the morning." She clears her throat pointedly. "I ask that you take the shortest route from the castle and into the mountains to avoid encountering more of my people than necessary. They do not trust Blacksmiths. Elowynn can show you the way."

"That's fine with me." I pause. "However, I've made it clear that my family's safety is paramount to me. If you want me to succeed, I can't be distracted by concerns for them."

She lifts her hands. "I've granted them safety here."

"But by your own admission, your people don't trust Blacksmiths."

She shrugs.

"I will encourage them to leave this place," I say. "In

accordance with our deal, you will not try to stop them if that's what they choose to do."

She inclines her head. "Agreed."

"I would speak with them now. In private. Without listening ears."

"Of course." Again, Karasi nods. "I'll clear the room and instruct my Frost fae to restrict their power. But..." She purses her lips at me, as if she's a little puzzled. "At the risk of discussing personal matters again, you keep referring to your 'family,' yet Thaden Kane is no relation of yours, is he?"

"I consider Thaden Kane to be family, too," I say firmly.

She shrugs, as if she doesn't really care. "I simply wanted to clarify."

She turns and heads back toward the arched opening, but there, she pauses.

Within the room, Erik is visible. He's made his way to the other side of the space and is now speaking with my brother. They've taken themselves away from the table and appear to be in deep discussion.

"I wonder..." Karasi says, pressing a well-manicured finger to her lips. "Did the Vandawolf really hold you captive? Or was it the other way around?"

My forehead creases, but I remind myself that the Fae Queen is a master manipulator. Although I'm not sure what kind of seed she wants to plant in my mind with that comment.

She arches an eyebrow at me but doesn't wait for my response before she glides back into the room, claps her hands for attention, and begins crying orders. "Thank you, my darlings, for an excellent evening! You will all take yourselves off now and leave Asha Silverspun and her family in peace." She gives a light laugh. "No listening in, my dears. We don't want to make our guests uncomfortable."

It's a light order, but the look she gives Elowynn is steely.

Elowynn nods and quickly ushers the other fae from the room, including her sister. When the Queen follows, Elowynn shuts the door behind them, finally leaving me alone with my family.

I don't have much hope that every word we say *won't* be relayed back to the Queen, so I decide to guard my tongue where I can.

My sister has remained at the table and Thaden now sits beside her, both facing me. As are Erik and Gallium.

I tell myself to be factual, to keep my emotions out of it, but it's not so easy now that light and dark are finely balanced within my mind.

"I... Um..." I've barely opened my mouth when Gallium hurries across the room toward me and gathers me up in a hug. The strength in his embrace reminds me how much he's changed over the last ten years. Erik was right when he said that my brother would be an asset in the fight ahead of me, but I'm even more certain now that he can't come with me.

"The Vandawolf said it was safe to hug you," he explains before he clasps me tighter.

"It is." I exhale my tension and accept my brother's embrace. It feels like a lifetime since we parted in the Sunken Bog. But he has remained the same. Loyal and steadfast.

Gallium draws away a little, but now his features are tense. "The Vandawolf also told me you plan on leaving us behind."

"Yes." As I speak, I know that Tamra and Thaden are

listening. "I'm even more certain about it now that I'm aware the humans have dragons."

Gallium doesn't look surprised. "Gliss filled us in. Which is why I don't agree with your decision. You'll need all the help you can get."

My shoulders slump, but I quietly pull my hair forward, the tarnished strands resting in my left palm. "Humans did this to me. They're resourceful and cunning. They could do far worse with the help of dragons. Far, far worse with Milena's assistance. Judging by what she did to Thaden, she's a Blacksmith with a heart like Malak's—"

"A Blacksmith like you," Tamra says, her voice cold as she pushes back her chair and turns to face me fully.

The suddenness of her accusation cuts right into me.

Her chair scrapes the floor with a screech and the sharpness of her tone cleaves me as easily as a knife between my ribs. More hurtful because it carries an element of truth.

For as long as I use Malak's tools, I am like him.

"Yes," I whisper, trying to speak past the tightness in my throat. "Capable of great darkness."

She lifts her chin as she casts her glare on Erik. "When you kept our sister away from us, I believed it was because you hated us and wanted to hurt us. But now I wonder if you did it to protect us." Her focus flickers back to me, her green eyes hard. "Because she's so much like Malak."

I flinch and this time, I can't seem to breathe.

Erik's expression has hardened, all the beautiful angles of his face dark and tense, but he doesn't make a move toward her.

As much as I wish he would jump to my defense, I also recognize that he's a source of tension. The shadowed glance he casts my way, along with his stillness, tells me he knows nothing he could say would defuse her anger, only heighten it.

She takes a step toward me, even though it seems she's still speaking to Erik. "You tested her when you made her pick up Malak's hammer on that anvil. I wasn't there to see it, but I heard about it. The way she lit up, the strength she displayed, the awful power she suddenly controlled. You made sure she only ever used it against the monsters. You controlled her darkness."

I try to breathe through the stabbing ache in my chest that's growing worse with every word my sister speaks.

She isn't saying anything that I haven't said to myself.

There's nothing I haven't already acknowledged.

And yet, it hurts.

So painful that the dark medallion burns and the silver medallion heats, as if its light might fail in the face of my sudden need to harness the cold malice to protect my heart.

I finally manage to take a shaky breath as Tamra stops three paces from me, her silver head held high.

Nearby, both Gallium and Thaden are tense. Both of them have taken a step toward Tamra, and Gallium is shaking his head, as if he's going to jump in at any moment.

If she's aware of their reactions, she doesn't show it.

"We have a memory of you, Asha," she says to me, more quietly now. "Gallium and I. We were huddled behind Malak's throne while you fought for our lives, trying to protect us, and that's how we remembered you all through these years. But you aren't that person anymore. Now I wonder if you ever were."

She steps even closer as I fight the surge of ice in my hand.

"The humans didn't cover you in soot," she says. "They scratched off the shiny surface to reveal what was underneath."

She may as well have slapped me.

I take a sharp breath and a quick step away from her. I need to end this encounter before my grandmother's medallion loses its fight. Or my brother breaks his silence and creates a chasm between him and Tamra that doesn't need to exist. The anger he's directing at her back warns me he's seconds away from rebuking her.

"Thaden," I say, raising my voice to speak before my brother can utter a sound. "If you care about my family, please take them somewhere safe." Every word I speak is strained, my throat threatening to close up. "You don't have to tell me where. I don't have to be a part of their lives. But you know this land better than we do, and I trust you to keep them safe."

Thaden hesitates, his jaw clenching. He throws a glance at Tamra, his brow furrowed.

She's focused solely on me, her gorgeous, green eyes narrowed.

"Of course," he says. "I'll do as you ask."

"Thank you." I take another step back. "That's all I need. We're leaving at first light. I hope you'll do the same."

My voice is so tight that I don't trust it any longer.

Erik is like a statue a few steps behind me, but the moment I reach him, he snaps into action, pushing open the door and allowing me through.

The corridor is deserted. It's a small surprise to me that the Queen was true to her word.

"Fuck," I whisper when the door closes behind me. "*Fuck.*"

I need to move. I need action. If I could, I would run miles to release this awful energy within me, a fury without a target. My legs are moving and Erik pushes ahead of me like a shield against any fae who might get in our way. Hopefully none.

Mere seconds later, the door behind us opens once more.

I spin, my whole body tense.

Thaden hurries toward us, his muscular frame making the corridor seem small, especially with Erik on one side of me and him on the other.

"Wait, Asha." He speaks quickly, but his voice is low. "Tamra's hurting. She's vulnerable and Queen Karasi hasn't stopped whispering in her ear since we arrived."

I wish I could attribute all of my sister's hatred to manipulation, but I can't. She had ten years to dream and hope of a day when we could be a family. I was the one who brought her dreams crashing down.

I was the one who chose to bring the past with me.

"I'll take your family to my old village in *Myrkur Fjall*, where they can stay clear of the fight between fae and humans." Thaden's voice deepens, resembling a dragon's growl. "I'll do this because you asked me to. I won't deny what your family needs."

His hand closes around my arm, his dragon scales pressing into my skin, a hard grip that reminds me how immensely strong he is.

Behind me, Erik bristles, but his tension fades at

Thaden's next words.

"I need Milena dead more than anyone else," Thaden says. "I need her to pay for what she did to me." His focus flies to Erik. "You killed the Blacksmith who tried to control your fate. There is no peace for me until I do the same."

Erik gives a single nod.

Thaden turns back to me, but now there's a tone of desperation in his voice. "Once your family is safe in *Myrkur Fjall*, please don't deny me the option of finding you so I can fight beside you."

I'm hesitant, but only for his own safety. Ultimately, he could be my greatest weapon in the fight ahead.

"I need this, Asha," he says when I don't immediately respond. "I can't stay out of this fight."

His fury is palpable, and I feel it in my bones. The energy thrumming within him is as strong as a magnet. A constant pull. The same storm of power that writhes within me.

But it reminds me that he has more of a choice than he may realize.

I press my other hand—my right hand—to his chest. "I won't keep you from this fight. But you do have another option." I take a deep breath. "If Milena changed you using the same device that Malak used on the Vandawolf, then there's a chance I can remove it. You could have a life like you did before."

Of course, I'm not sure of the extent that his dragon traits will stay with him, the same way the wolf's strengths have remained with Erik.

Thaden's expression softens and so does his grip on my arm. "I saw you remove that device from the Vandawolf. I wondered if that's why his appearance has changed." Thaden's focus remains on me. "But if you do that—assuming it doesn't kill me—then these scales could also disappear, and with them, my greatest defense against Milena's magic."

"True. But you could walk away from all this."

He gives me a crooked smile. "There's no walking away, Asha. Not until Milena is dead. It simply gives me more reason to make sure you stay alive in the meantime. When this fight is over, maybe I'll be ready to take that chance."

"Okay," I whisper. "Come find us. But you should know, we'll do everything we can to conceal our tracks."

He gives me a confident smile. "That won't stop me." Then he continues. "You should head due west along the mountain range. The human army has an outpost about five days' walk from here on one of the highest peaks. That's where the dragons nest. I'm only guessing, but there's a good chance Milena will be where the dragons are."

"It's a starting point at least," I say.

He releases me and takes a step back. "I'll run night and day in the direction of danger if that's what it takes to reach you before the fight."

As my hand falls away from Thaden's chest, I'm aware, even more than ever, of Erik's presence at my back. The way the two men standing on opposite sides of me cast shadows across me.

A wolf and a dragon.

"I'll look after your family, Asha," Thaden says before he turns away. "I promise you."

I'm grateful, but I'm also facing the possibility that my family might never be mine again.

CHAPTER 28

I race along the corridor with Erik a step behind me.

My skin crawls with the need to escape my own body. My own nature. Even staying here one more night feels like too much stillness. Too much waiting.

"We need to leave." My declaration is quiet. Stifled. "*I* need to leave."

"Then let's leave," he says.

I'm startled by how quickly he agreed.

"The armory is that way," he says. "Gallium told me where to find it. Even if we can't get everything we need from within it, he's hidden packs of supplies outside the castle."

"My brother did that?"

"He may have been thwarted every time he tried to see you, but he wasn't idle. He was preparing in case you needed a quick escape."

I follow Erik's outstretched arm to the corridor on our right—apparently, the direction of the armory.

The relief I feel at taking control is immense. "First, I need my toolbox. I also want to bring the tusks I used for your stretcher. They're immune to Blacksmith magic and they'll make excellent spears. You pulled the first one free; I'm sure you can retrieve the second."

He gives me a small smile. "I can."

I hesitate only another moment. "Then let's go."

Ten minutes later, Erik stands in front of a wall of weapons and I consider the shelves on the other side of the armory, most of which hold neatly folded black suits like the ones Elowynn wears.

One shelf doesn't.

It contains multiple sets of tunics and pants, all in varying shades of brown and overlaid with what looks like leather plates.

It's an earthy sort of armor. Nothing like the finely crafted black suits on the shelf above it. At the end of the shelf containing the brown clothing are multiple packs of what look like rolled-up furs.

It's been a long time since I've seen furs like that. Only elite Blacksmiths ever wore them. Forest animals were nearly extinct when I was growing up. At least, they were extinct in the wasteland around the city, although from what Erik told me, there were wolf packs roaming these mountains.

I run my hand over the end of the wadded-up pelts. They're soft, but somehow, also *wrong*.

Erik appears beside me, holding a hunting knife, along with a bow and a quiver of arrows.

He also considers the furs. "Wolf. Or possibly bear."

"My mother had one of these," I murmur. "She was so proud of it." Then my jaw tightens. "But these garments are nothing like the fae clothing I've seen so far. Could these have belonged to humans?"

"Possibly," he says. "Regardless, we'll blend in to our surroundings better with clothing that color."

I scoop up a tunic and pants that look like they'll fit me well enough. It only takes Erik a moment to find a set that should fit him. In fact, there are multiple sets large enough.

All of the fae men we've encountered have been much slimmer in build. Not that we've met many, but it's another reason to believe the clothing was made by humans.

I prefer not to think about the possibility that these garments were taken from their dead bodies. Or that the fae may have kept them for the purpose of sending spies into human territory.

Their war is not mine.

I will do what I promised Queen Karasi and try to stay alive through it.

I strip off the black dress right there, conscious of Erik's glances, and even more conscious of his nearly naked body as he also switches his clothing. He pulls on a weapon harness to carry the hunting knife, as well as the bow and arrows, before he clips a pelt onto the harness as well.

Finally, we're dressed and my last task is to deposit my toolbox into a satchel, to which I also attach a pelt. I have no doubt the mountain range will get cold.

Then I hand Erik one of the onyx spears and keep the

other for myself. They're a little cumbersome, but we can walk with them like staffs.

At that moment, he tips his head to the side, a gesture I associate with him listening to our surroundings. "We need to move. The guards are coming after us."

When the fae guards waiting outside my room started to follow us to the armory, I threatened to end them if they took another step. They let us go, but I knew it wouldn't be long before their fear of their Queen exceeded their fear of me.

Erik earlier described a forest outside this castle and now he leads me through a series of short corridors toward the fresh air and the night birds he says he can hear outside.

Soon enough, I hear them too.

We exit into a cleared area, beyond which is thick forest, but a glance to my left tells me we're high up on the mountain. The vast, night sky washes across the horizon. It's a sky filled with stars that gives way to dark, roiling clouds in the east and, now that I peer toward the south, more dark clouds where the cursed wasteland lies.

I wonder if the humans who live there have had to fight any new monsters since I left.

I tell myself it isn't my problem anymore, but once... *if*... I succeed in ending Milena, I'll need to make a decision whether or not to leave that cursed city in my past, once and for all.

"Due west. Like Thaden said," I murmur before I head into the forest, orienting myself by the moon's position. It also helps that the encampment's western border is protected by thunderbirds, whose lightning bursts brightly across the sky. It's a clear warning to their enemy to stay away.

The ground underfoot is soft and mossy, vastly different from the sharp rocks of the mountain range to the south. It's a gentle incline for now.

We need to plan our path, but I want to get much farther away from the castle and any potentially listening ears before we stop to talk.

A few minutes later, Erik's hand presses to my shoulder and he gestures to our right. "Supplies."

We head in that direction, discovering four satchels containing food, water flasks, some spare clothing, and more pelts. The number of satchels indicates that Gallium thought I would leave with him. I guess he couldn't be sure what Erik would do.

"Let's take only one," I whisper, conscious that Thaden, Gallium, and Tamra need a pack of supplies each. "We can share a water flask—assuming you can find water sources with which to refill it?"

Erik gives me a wolfish grin. "Of course. I can also hunt for food if these supplies run out."

That's what I was hoping. "Then one pack will do."

Erik pulls the pack onto his back, and we set off again.

The air is fresh and the farther we travel from the castle, the quieter our surroundings become, the silence only broken by night birds and the distant cracks of lightning.

Suddenly, Erik halts me again, this time with a quick hand on my shoulder and a finger to his lips.

He points to our left, where the trees are thinner.

A moment later, the sound of quiet footfalls reaches me. I brace for an attack, holding the spear ready, aware of the way Erik's hand has fallen to his hunting knife.

A dark-haired female becomes visible through the trees.

I recognize Gliss a second later.

She freezes at the sight of my spear, then slowly raises her hands, palms up. It doesn't look like she's carrying a weapon, but she's wearing black armor and I know from experience that there could be blades concealed on it.

"I was hoping to speak with you before you left," she says, keeping her voice low as she glances around. "But here is better."

"How did you know we were out here?" I ask.

As far as Gliss knew, we were leaving in the morning, which means we should have still been in our room.

"I followed the wolf." She quickly adds, "I didn't listen to his thoughts, though. I only sought his presence."

Erik's brow furrows. I told him about Gliss's abilities, but I left out the part where she told me about his family, how losing them had broken him.

"So you can track us," I say, drawing conclusions from her answer.

If so, this is not welcome news.

"Only for a short distance. You were nearly out of range."

I narrow my eyes at her. She could be lying. It's hard to distrust her with her innocent, violet eyes and her open expression, but I remind myself to be wary. "You said here is better. Why?"

"Because the Frost fae aren't listening."

I glance at Erik and he gives me a nod. "There's nobody else nearby."

I relax a little, confident that Gliss doesn't currently pose a threat I can't overcome. "Speak."

"I heard what the dragon said."

My forehead creases. "Do you mean Thaden?"

She shakes her head and takes a step closer. "The dragon whose voice was trapped in that piece of metal."

"The imprinted medallion." I remember the way Gliss listened intently when I tapped the medallion with my hammer. The dragon's roar filled the ballroom and everyone else flinched. Not Gliss.

"I told the Queen I couldn't decipher its voice." She's tense and her face is suddenly pale. "She will punish me for this failure—and you know what her punishment looks like."

I do. It looks like cracked bones and public disgrace.

My jaw clenches. I may not completely trust Gliss, but she helped Erik and healed me without hesitation. "Why would interpreting the dragon's voice fall to you? Elowynn heard it, too."

Gliss edges even closer. "Dragons aren't like other creatures. Their thoughts are complex and concealed with magic: *light* magic. The purest kind. It's the opposite of the dark magic you carry in the palm of your hand, Asha Silverspun." She swallows visibly. "Elowynn has always protected me. Officially, she's the stronger one. But I'm the one who can slip into a dragon's mind and decipher its thoughts."

I'm alarmed. "What about Thaden's thoughts?"

"No," she quickly says. "His mind is locked down and I wouldn't invade—"

"Then why are you telling me this if not to threaten me in some way?"

She takes a sharp breath. "Dragons can speak the human tongue. They can converse as easily as you and I. But a dragon's death cry is something else entirely. It isn't spoken in words. It's..." She presses her lips together, as if she's trying to figure out how to explain it. "It's a wash of emotions, a blaze of sound filled with thoughts."

She looks up at me. "I don't blame you for not trusting me. But I'm here now because within the dragon's death cry, I deciphered a message." Her eyes are wide. "I think you need to hear it."

CHAPTER 29

I'm even warier now. "What message?"

"The dragon identified itself as Lysander Rex, the son of the great fire dragon, Graviter Rex. Graviter's name means *Solemn King*. He is the most powerful dragon. The one none of us wants to meet, let alone fight."

My jaw clenches. I knew the dead dragon was strong, but the son of a dragon king... It only reinforces how dangerous Milena must be.

Gliss continues. "Lysander was betrayed by someone he trusted."

That would fit with my theory: Milena used her alliance with the humans to lure the dragon to its death. I still don't understand why she would risk alienating such powerful allies, though.

I don't put voice to any of that, asking simply, "What does this have to do with me?"

Gliss shivers visibly and wraps her arms across her chest. "He cried out for vengeance, but his cry was... confusing.

Extremely difficult to decipher. What I can say for sure is that he wants *you* to avenge him. He said that you 'heard his heart.'"

There's a slight question in Gliss's voice.

"Heard his heart," I whisper, remembering the pain I felt when I came into contact with that medallion for the first time after it had been imprinted.

I felt grief and fear. I sensed a life cut short too soon.

I take a deep breath and set my intentions. "It's my oath to kill Milena Ironmeld, so the dragon will be avenged. At least it confirms that she betrayed him."

Gliss is reaching for me. "No, that's one of the confusing things. I'm certain that the dragon said: *He* betrayed me. Not *she.*"

"He?" I stare at Gliss in surprise. "Who was the dragon referring to?"

"I couldn't tell."

I narrow my eyes at her, but she looks to Erik. "If you can hear my heartbeat, then you'll know I'm not lying."

He nods. "She seems to be telling the truth."

"But that doesn't make sense." My brow is deeply furrowed now. "Thaden Kane said that Milena changed him."

"Maybe she wasn't the one who initially trapped the dragon," Erik suggests.

I don't like this possibility. "Do we have another powerful enemy we don't yet know about?"

"Maybe," he says. "Or it was simply a clever human the dragon trusted."

"Yes, it could have been." I exhale my sudden tension, even as my questions build.

Gliss casts glances around us. "I've stayed too long. I've delivered the message to you. I won't be able to withhold this information from the Queen for much longer." Her shoulders hunch. "I can't be sure that what the dragon said will make any difference to her. It might be for nothing, but my instinct is to conceal the dragon's meaning."

She steps back as she speaks. "I wish you well, Asha Silverspun. May the eventide light bless you and keep you safe."

With a brief press of her hand to her heart, she disappears back into the trees before I can reach out for her. "But—"

"You can't help her." Erik is solemn beside me, his face partly shadowed now. "The Fae Queen rules her life. You owe that queen a debt. You can't intervene."

He's right and I fucking hate it.

"What about my family?"

He gives me a sudden smile as his head tilts to the side. "They're already on the move. I can hear their voices. They've just picked up the remaining packs."

I rub my forehead with relief. "Okay, then. We have a lot of ground to cover."

I shake off my misgivings, needing once more to keep moving.

We travel cautiously for the rest of the night, but once the sun rises and visibility improves for me, we break into a jog, heading for a water supply that takes us only slightly off course.

We keep pace with each other, quickly navigating fallen branches and uneven undergrowth as we run through the thickening forest. I use the onyx spear to my advantage, vaulting over some of the larger fallen branches, and before long, I'm comfortable carrying it.

By the time I hear the flow of water ahead of us, the canopy overhead has become so thick that it's hard to believe we're weaving our way across a mountain range. The earth here appears richer than any I've ever seen, the tree trunks a deep reddish brown and the leaves are a bright green, even though the air is cold.

Finally, Erik indicates we should slow our pace and a few minutes later, we reach the edge of a shallow ravine with a narrow stream flowing through it.

The water runs clear and fresh, so we fill the flask and drink our fill.

We stop there for a few minutes, crouched at the water's edge.

The silence around us is more peaceful than I expected, the sounds of our breathing obscured by the gently bubbling stream.

Now that I'm not running to keep my body warm, I unroll the pelt and pull it over my shoulders. My breath frosts in the air in delicate, white wisps, but the fur keeps me warm enough.

"We can follow the stream and stay close to this water source," Erik says. "Or we can head farther inland, closer to the edge of the mountain range, and approach the western outpost more directly."

"Let's keep to the stream," I say. "I'd rather approach the outpost from the side than head-on."

It also staves off the inevitable battle for longer, which gives me more time to plan.

As we continue upstream, the minutes and hours blur together.

We avoid the deep, mossy edges of the ravine where we might leave footprints and stick to the rocks closer to the edge of the water. Despite the increasingly cold air, the trees around us are no less lush, although their leaves change color from green to a pale blue, a fascinating shade.

While the silence only seems to grow deeper, there's also a constant hum of energy around us, as if there's life everywhere.

Soft, scurrying sounds in the underbrush. Quiet bird calls.

Eventually, I choose to break the silence. "Did your wolf's pack ever roam this part of the mountain range?"

Erik shakes his head. "I don't think they ever came this far northwest."

I contemplate the trees and the stream. "It's far more peaceful here than I expected."

"There's peace, but also danger." He gestures off to our side. "Large animals are moving around over there on our right. There are also some to our left, but they're farther away."

"Bears? Wolves?" Then I ask more hopefully, "Deer?"

His forehead puckers. "I can't tell. Bigger than goats, not big enough to be dragons." He shrugs. "We'll know when we see them. On the positive side, I don't sense any fae or humans."

"Oh, okay. Only wolves or bears. No need to worry, then."

He gives me a smile. It's a full smile that shows his now-perfect teeth. His eyes are bright, his chest rising and falling rapidly from our quick pace, just as mine is.

The breath catches in my throat because I'm not sure he's ever looked so alive as he does right now.

I can't help my answering smile. Can't help but lean in, catch his hand, and draw him to a stop so I can kiss his lips.

In response, his hand tangles in my hair. I press my right palm to his jaw. He deepens the kiss with a groan that resonates through my body to my core.

Why shouldn't I have this?

"How far away are those bears or wolves or deer?" I ask, pressing kisses to the side of his mouth.

"Far enough." He growls, pulling me closer, his hands slipping beneath my pelt, tugging on my tunic and finding the bare skin across my lower back.

I carve a path with my fingertips to the top of his pants, tracing around the straps of his weapon harness and satchel to reach his stomach. "Good."

Somehow, we manage to dispense with our satchels, weapons, and pants without breaking our kiss for longer than seconds.

I want to be fully naked with him, but it's too damn cold, a fact he acknowledges when he pulls his larger pelt around us both.

Our body heat builds within it as he takes me to the soft moss at the side of the ravine and mutters something about worrying about our tracks later.

There, he kneels, drawing me down onto him so that I'm

straddling his hips. His hand rests between us, softly pressing against my core, a tantalizing pressure.

I rock against him, aware of his hard length beneath me, although his hand stops me from reaching it.

He kisses me, strokes me, his other hand moving under my shirt, his thumb pressing on my core until the needy impulses in my body become moans of want and my kisses become demanding.

Finally, he gives me access to his body and I sink onto him, taking him all the way in, a momentary relief that only grows into a more intense need.

He grips my hips as every strike of pleasure ripples through me, taking me beyond this place, shattering me and making me whole.

We may be headed for death, but right now, this feels like life.

CHAPTER 30

We stay for a long time kneeling on the moss, wrapped up in fur.

Erik's fingertips trace circles across my back under my tunic. I rest my head against his shoulder, listening to his thumping heart.

Too soon, we're forced to rise, but only because my legs are going numb.

"Silly legs," I grumble.

"Beautiful legs," he replies as I wobble upright while he stays kneeling, his gaze rising to follow the lines of my body from my rumpled shirt to my naked thighs and calves.

When I shiver, he swoops upward and wraps the pelt back around me, and then he does his best to keep me warm as we both get fully dressed again.

Once we're ready, he studies our surroundings and so do I, listening to the steady quiet, the gentle bubbling of water.

It's still peaceful.

He inclines his head upstream and we continue on our way.

When night begins to fall, the energy within the forest around us changes. The canopy overhead is so thick that only a few beams of moonlight filter through, but they trigger a change in the environment.

Everything seems to come awake, as if there are a far greater number of nocturnal creatures living in this place. We certainly can't be sure they're harmless.

The sounds of scuffling and scurrying and slithering grow louder. Small creatures can be just as dangerous as large ones.

The tension in Erik's shoulders has increased. "We need to find a safe place to make camp."

I agree, but I also put voice to a new worry. "Maybe we shouldn't sleep. Perhaps we should keep going and sleep tomorrow during the day when it's safer."

He rubs his temples. "You're right. We need to change our approach. But right now, it's been a long time since either of us slept. Even with our particular strengths, exhaustion is not our friend. We're more likely to make mistakes if our minds are less alert. We can make camp and take turns keeping watch."

I can't argue with that logic. The power in the medallions can keep me going beyond my normal endurance, but it's like a fire that consumes relentlessly. Eventually, there could be nothing left to burn.

"Up ahead," I say. "It looks like there's a clearing next to the riverbank."

He nods. "Let's try it."

The clearing is large enough for us to spread out the pelts and still have some clear space around us. We ration the food from the satchel Gallium prepared and then we have a standoff about who will take first watch.

"Me," I say firmly, noting the growing rings around his eyes. "The medallions will keep me awake." When he still insists, I growl at him. "It won't do either of us any good if you can't keep your eyes open while you're on watch."

He gives a soft exhale, nestles up against my side, and within moments, he's asleep.

I remain awake and on edge, but the scurrying sounds I hear don't amount to anything and a few hours later, it's my turn to rest.

For the next two days, we gradually adjust our sleep patterns until we're sleeping in the afternoons and halfway through the night, resuming our journey just before dawn.

I worry about my family, wondering how far they've made it away from the fae castle, hoping they're safe. I remind myself of Thaden's promise and how strong my brother is. And even though there's a rift between me and my sister, I tell myself that her survival instincts are strong.

By the fourth night, we've made good progress, but the stream has veered farther north, taking us off course, and we'll soon need to choose whether or not to continue following it. We need access to a water supply, and the trees growing beside the river bear fruit we can eat, but heading too far north won't do us any favors. Already, it's added another day to our journey.

That night, I sleep first, closing my eyes to soft, afternoon sunlight and waking to moonbeams.

I'm immediately aware that Erik isn't sitting beside me.

Next, I hear sharp snarls.

Startled, I jolt upright, quickly taking in the clearing and the growling animals gathered all around its edges.

I make out gleaming eyes and sharp teeth and the silhouettes of so many wolves that the hairs on my arms stand on end despite the warm fur wrapped around me.

Erik is crouched four paces away from me, his back to me, his large body hunched slightly forward while his right hand is stretched back in my direction. "Asha, don't move."

That's when I become aware of the snarls at my left shoulder, not more than an arm's length behind me.

Fuck!

I can practically feel the beast's breath across the back of my head.

I've fought creatures larger and more ferocious than this, but never so many. And I was always prepared and ready for them. I've woken with a fright, my heart is pounding, and my life is not the only one in danger.

Slowly, very slowly, I reach for my left hand, ready in case I need to wrench off the silver medallion so I can use the dark metal beneath it.

"Trust me," Erik says, his head tilted, his face barely visible to me. "Don't make a move. Trust me, Asha."

His request shakes me to my core, even more than the presence of these vicious animals.

Do I trust him?

I've shared my heart and thoughts and body with him but... trust?

At the edge of my view, the silver medallion gleams, a constant reminder of what lies beneath it.

It's impossible to trust someone else when I don't trust myself.

Even so, I stay frozen to the spot.

Erik's head turns back to the wolf that stands directly in front of him.

It's a large, black beast with eerie blue eyes. Its ears are flat to its head and its lips are drawn back from its teeth, revealing wickedly long canines. It gnashes at Erik and saliva drips from its mouth.

Erik's shoulders hunch further.

In the next second, he growls back at the wolf, a deep sound that sends a shock down my spine.

A dangerous sound.

It resonates through me as intensely as if he'd raked claws down my back.

The black wolf jolts as if it's startled.

The beasts on either side of it yelp loudly and several of them back away.

The first one quickly lowers its head, its body hunching down, crouching lower as Erik rises to his feet. His left arm must be bent at the elbow, maybe held to his chest, because I can't see his hand or if he's holding his hunting knife in it.

The bow and quiver of arrows rests on the ground next to me.

Another growl sounds, again from Erik, but this time, it turns into words. "Asha, stand up, but do it slowly."

It's the same voice he would use when he commanded me to do his bidding back in the city.

My instinct... is to disobey.

It's a liberating sensation. But possibly not the best time to experience it.

When I hesitate, his tension grows, but his voice is softer than before. "Asha, I need you to stand up. I need you to show dominance."

Slowly, I allow the fur to slide off my back so I can rise upward unhindered by the material.

I keep my hands together, ready to tear off the silver medallion if I need to.

The black wolf has stopped snarling and now it watches me with bright-blue eyes.

The animal at my back has also quietened, although that only makes me more nervous. I preferred it when I could hear it.

Erik edges toward me, still facing the black wolf, while giving another growl.

The wolf's ears lift, it tilts its head, and then it gives a loud *yip*!

There's a flurry of movement. My hand is on my medallion. I'm ready for anything, but in the next moment, the wolves disappear, fading quickly into our surroundings.

In the next second, they're gone.

I'm left staring at the dark shadows between the trees.

I resume breathing. "What was that?"

Erik turns back to me. For a second, I'm certain I catch a flash of black around his left hand, but then he too is in shadow, the moonlight behind him.

"Wolves," he says.

I let out a soft laugh and then stop, worried I'll draw the creatures back to us. "I got that. How did you make them leave?"

"I told them to fuck off." He studies our surroundings for a second. "They won't go far. They'll watch us now."

"Watch *over* us like friends? Or watch us like enemies?"

He grimaces. Shrugs. Makes a non-committal sound. But his focus falls to my left hand.

I haven't stopped gripping it.

Probably because I've been avoiding the conversation I know we need to have. I can't put it off any longer. I certainly can't go back to sleep after what just happened.

"We're only a day from reaching the outpost," I say. "Tomorrow, I need to take off my grandmother's medallion so I can sense Milena's presence when she's nearby."

Like sensing a rising monster in the wasteland, I can press my hand to the ground and detect the flow of energy from any Blacksmith who's wearing their medallions. I'm not sure, exactly, from how great a distance it will work, but I need to start trying.

I swallow. "I probably should have done it already, but... I didn't want to."

Over the last four days, I've experienced a peace I never have before. Taking off the silver medallion will mark an end to what feels like a dream.

At my words, Erik's smile fades, and it's like a little of the moonlight fades with it.

"Who's to say we'll get anywhere near the outpost tomorrow?" he says. "Maybe it'll take another week."

"Another week?" I ask gently.

"You didn't make any promises about how quickly you'd carry out your end of the deal. Another week won't make a difference. Or another one after that. Or a month—"

"Stop." My throat has constricted. "I can't escape from this."

When Erik sent me out of the cursed city to hunt Milena, it was a means to an end: to give me my freedom. Of course, I didn't know it at the time, but he wasn't actually sending me into danger. If I'd left with my family like he'd intended, I wouldn't be here now.

If he'd died like he intended... I wouldn't be here now.

He doesn't reach for me, but it feels like the distance between us lessens as he says, "You said your sister needs to heal. *You* need time to heal, too."

I wish I could. I've come close.

I finally release my left hand and hold it up. "There's no healing while this is part of me."

"Why not?"

I blink at him. "This is darkness. It's death. I carry it with me everywhere I go."

"It isn't who you are."

"Oh, I wish that were true," I whisper.

His brow furrows deeply and now he takes a step toward me, but his face is still in shadow.

"Do you believe what Tamra said?" His voice is hard. "Do you believe that you're like Malak?"

I answer his question with a question. "Did you keep me separated from my family because you thought I might hurt them?"

"*I* was the threat, Asha, not you."

My breathing is suddenly shaky. He asked me to trust him, but all my doubts are resurfacing. "I don't know if I should believe you."

He's always been two steps ahead of everyone else.

Always seeing more than everyone else. Always using that knowledge for his own purposes. Maneuvering pieces into place.

His voice is low as he says, "Tamra was right about one thing."

"What's that?" I ask, my throat tight.

"Refusing to heal me." He remains in shadow so I can't see his eyes, can't see into his heart. "Her healing power is Blacksmith power. It would have collided with the dark energy within the device in my heart. Fed its power. Made it stronger. She wouldn't have been able to control that dark energy like you did. It would have killed her."

I take a startled breath.

Did Tamra sense the danger? Did she wrestle with an unexplainable instinct that told her not to use her power on him?

Without knowledge of the existence of the device, she would have had no rationalization for any such instinct other than to focus on the choices Erik made in the past and her fears about the future.

"I knew about your sister's healing power long before you did," he continues. "I had time to think through the consequences of her trying to help me. I would never knowingly put her in harm's way, so I abandoned hope, and now..."

He turns slightly, half of his face now in the light, revealing the tension in his jaw.

It's the hollow in his eyes that strikes me the hardest.

"There's no clean slate for me, is there?" he asks.

I don't know how to answer him. I don't know if the answer is *yes* or *no*.

Before I can even begin to find the words, his eyes harden again.

"If you believe what your sister said about you, then give in," he says.

I stare at him, a cold shiver running down my spine. "...What?"

"If you truly believe you're like Malak, then take off your grandmother's medallion and give in to the darkness."

I jolt. "No."

He steps toward me. "I saw the way you looked at me every time you picked up your tools, Asha. The need to create is in your bones."

Even now, I'm aware of the impulses, although they feel distant thanks to the silver metal.

Mold the living to match your will.

Make him yours...

"So create!" he orders me.

I snarl back at him. "You don't command me anymore."

"Did I ever?" He continues to step toward me, but now I step back. "Did I make you fight monsters, or did I simply unleash you upon them? Because if you believe what Tamra said, then you were waiting for the chance to fight and kill. You *loved* it."

My voice is tight. "No."

"No, what?"

I shake my head at him. "I hate these tools. I hate how cruel they are."

"I don't believe you. *You* don't believe you." His brow draws down and so do the corners of his mouth.

Slowly, he starts removing his shirt, even though it's cold

and he must be freezing because his skin is covered in goosebumps.

"Let's settle this once and for all, Asha Silverspun," he says, dropping the material to the ground. "Then you'll know who you really are."

He darts forward in a flash, his hand closing around my left wrist, his speed breathtaking.

But so is my own.

My right hand shoots out, my weight carrying me forward, but he must have been counting on that, because in the next instant, he lets go of my left hand.

My forward momentum takes me toward him, both of my hands colliding with his chest.

It's only at the last moment that the *clang* of metal reaches my ears, and I register a flash of light as the silver medallion spirals away from me through the air.

With shocking speed, he removed it.

And now the titanium medallion has free rein.

Darkness washes through me and with it, rage.

Cold, malicious, deadly rage as my left hand presses to his bare skin.

CHAPTER 31

The sudden rush of power is overwhelming.

"Decide who you are, Asha," he says. "Make your move. I won't stop you."

My muscles flex as I fight my impulses.

Not to turn him to ash or dust, but to make him...

Furious, strong, kind, hard-hearted—make him forget all about me, make him think of nothing but me; make him more human, make him more wolf; make him love me, make him hate me; run from me, run *to* me; cover his skin with light, bathe him in darkness...

All the contradictions.

All the powerful possibilities.

His hand clamps around my left wrist, pressing the medallion to his chest. His eyes are no longer a deep night, but hard stone, sharp as flint, dark as titanium.

"Do it!" he roars. "Whatever the fuck you want to do, do it!"

My heart beats more slowly. A cold calm washes over me. My thoughts and impulses settle.

"Whatever I want?" I ask.

"Yes."

I lean in close to him, tipping my head back and allowing my instincts to take control.

I stop an inch away from his lips.

Make him yours.

He smells like earth. Water on stone. And beneath that, the honeyed scent of forge-fire. The power that was used to change him is in his bones.

This power is pain. There's no doubt in my mind about that.

But is that all it is?

It carries all of Malak's evil because it soaked up his emotions for years and years.

Surely, that means there could be a little of me in it now.

I close my eyes and seek the worst of it. An awful darkness filled with screams and torment, but I don't push it away.

I let it flow.

Through my mind and outward, then inward again. A cycle like water gently swirling around and around until it's a soft blur.

All the while, Erik stays very still.

When I open my eyes, I find him waiting.

I speak my wants.

"What I want... is your permission to kiss you."

The slightest crease forms in his forehead, the tiniest purse of his lips, as if my statement has surprised him.

"You have it," he says.

I reach up on my toes to brush my lips across his. Light at first. Then I follow the curve of his mouth, one corner to the next, nudging kisses as I go, deeper with each press until I fully capture his lips.

When I pull away, I'm breathless.

He's also breathing hard.

My right hand slips down his cold skin, across his stomach and to his waistband.

"What I want is your permission to undress you," I say.

Again, his brow creases a little. I sense his uncertainty.

Hell, he shouldn't trust me at all. I could lash out, hurt him, render terrible cruelty.

For him to say *yes* will require him to trust me, wholly and completely.

"You have it," he says, releasing my left hand at the same time.

Swiftly, I remove his pants before I step back and slip out of my own clothing, leaving myself naked and freezing just as he is. I continue to move fast, scooping up two pelts and dragging them with me as I prowl back to him.

That wrinkle in his forehead has smoothed out now, and there's a curious light in his eyes.

I spread one pelt onto the ground, still holding the other.

"Here," I say to him, patting the pelt beside where I kneel.

As soon as he crouches down, I push him onto his back and he doesn't resist. I slip my legs to either side of his waist and pull the second pelt over us, forming a den of my own making.

There he lies beneath me, even as I press my left hand to his chest, a constant threat.

Our body heat quickly builds and so does the need within me.

I drop my lips to his again, tasting his skin, an ache building between my legs where I rock against him.

My breathing speeds up, my body throbbing with an increasing heat I'm controlling with every heartbeat.

"What I want is your permission to fuck you."

"Asha," he groans. "You have it."

My body is ready, and I don't wait, drawing him inside me and driving myself down.

Pleasure shudders through me as I ride the waves, letting the darkness within me churn. Letting it burn within my hand. Letting it build within my core.

He gives me complete control, his hands resting on my thighs, the slight pressure of his fingers the only sign that he wants to do more. Until I snatch up one of them and pull it to my breast.

Then he rears up under me, his hand curved around me, his mouth playing havoc with my nipple for the two seconds I let him taste my skin before I push him onto his back again.

My left arm is once again extended, but I've caught his hand in mine. I draw it to my lips, running my tongue along his forefinger.

His breathing hitches when I pull his finger into my mouth, closing my lips around it.

As my tongue glides over his skin, he jolts and I sense him needing to take back control, to drive himself upward, his muscles tensing, his free hand gripping me hard.

That's when I lose myself, letting his hand, wet from my mouth, drop to my core.

Rocking against him with all the wild and dark in me.

Plunging so hard against him that I knock the pelt from my back and the cold rushes in.

I don't care.

Every intense thrust drives the darkness from my mind until I throw my head back and scream.

I let it all out. A release that drags all of my darkness to the surface, a storm of pleasure that breaks me apart. A taking and a giving that shatters my heart so I might mend.

I'm aware of him jolting and shuddering beneath me, aware of the way he growls my name as I come to rest on top of him.

The power in my left hand has calmed. Its rage has eased.

As I look down on him, a peace settles over me that I never expected to feel while this metal is part of me.

With the gentlest movement, he brushes the hair from my face. His thumb grazes my cheek, his gaze flowing across my skin, everywhere that the tarnish glistens in the dim light.

He studies me as if he's memorizing every tiny detail.

Over the last few days, I forgot about the tarnish.

I forgot that my hair used to be silver or that I ever looked any different than this.

My breathing slows, frosting in the air.

I can't help my shiver. "It's cold."

He breaks into a grin. "It's fucking freezing."

He pulls me back down to his chest while I'm still straddling him and wraps the pelt around us. His body is a mass of muscle beneath mine, pressing against my thighs.

I nestle my head in the crook of his neck and he clasps my left hand, medallion and all, entwining my fingers with his.

"You took an enormous risk," I whisper.

He's quiet for a moment. "When the wolves came, I asked you to trust me. Your heart pounded and that's when I realized what I'd said."

I tip my head back to see his face and press a kiss to the underside of his jaw.

He takes a deep breath and my body lifts and falls with it.

"I can't expect you to trust me if I don't trust you first," he says.

My heart warms as I take in the peace in his eyes. The trust I find there.

I give him a small smile. "I remember you once said to me that one day, you would find a way to free me from my magic. You said that if there was no other way, you would rip it from me like you cleaved the magic from the other Blacksmiths."

He cut off their hands, rendering them powerless.

"Fuck, Asha, I—"

"No," I whisper softly, pressing my fingertips to his jaw. "I need you to remember that vow." I take a shaky breath. "I need to know that if I ever hurt someone innocent, you will do what others can't."

He's shaking his head, but I persist. "You must cut this power from me. Promise me that."

He growls at me. "You don't command me, either."

I allow myself to smile. "True." I'm quiet for a moment. "But I know you will do what others won't. I know you won't shy away from something because it's hard or will make you hated."

When he gives me a reluctant nod, I take a deep breath

and acknowledge a painful truth. "Neither of us will ever really have a clean slate." I meet his eyes. "But we can start with each other."

"We can," he says, the tension leaving his body. "We already have."

I smile against his chest, but my smile fades.

I may have found a balance with the medallion, but soon I will need to use it.

To end Milena, I will need to call on all the darkness it gives me.

CHAPTER 32

At dawn, we gather up our things and resume our journey, but we stop following the stream and veer away from it to head west again.

If Thaden's estimate is accurate, then we should come upon the human outpost by the afternoon. Once we get there, we can decide whether or not to infiltrate it tonight or wait until tomorrow. We'll be able to make decisions when we have a sense of the layout of the place.

Thaden wanted to reach us before the fight, but I'm not sure how likely that will be. He has much farther to travel, and there could have been any number of delays on my family's journey to safety.

Midway through the morning, I stop and press my hand to the ground, waiting for the surge of power that will tell me if another Blacksmith is near. Of course, Milena could be only steps away, because if she isn't using her hammer or medallions, then I won't detect her presence.

I'm not surprised when nothing happens.

I'll just need to try again once we're farther along our path.

As the morning progresses, Erik also stops more frequently, tilting his head and listening.

"The wolves are following us," he says. "But they're agitated."

The fact that the wolves are tracking our movements isn't unexpected, but I don't like the idea of being followed by unsettled predators.

"For what reason?" I ask. "Are they nervous of the humans? Are they going to attack us?"

He shakes his head. "It's puzzling. They keep crossing our path up ahead and then circling back around on both sides. I don't recognize this behavior. I'd think they're trying to get in our way, except that they *aren't* getting in our way."

When his gaze remains far away, I ask, "What else?"

He wears a puzzled expression. "There's another creature in this forest with us, but I can't be sure what it is. I sense a sort of... *breathing*. But it's not much more than the breeze around us." He presses his fingers to his temples. "I don't know how to describe it."

"That's okay," I say. "Let's go carefully."

After that, we slow our pace, stopping regularly to check our surroundings.

Everything has become quieter and I understand what Erik was trying to describe.

If anything, it's *too* quiet.

Later, I bend for the fifth time that day, pressing my hand to the ground, fully expecting nothing to happen.

A streak of energy bursts through the undergrowth,

sizzling across fallen leaves and branches and snapping at my hand.

The force is so intense that it knocks me backward.

I land at a crouch, stifling my cry of alarm and attempting to channel it into a harsh whisper. "*Fuck.*"

"Asha." Erik rushes toward me, but I jolt back from him.

"Don't touch me. Not yet." The energy is still tingling through me like aftershocks of lightning and the power in my left hand is burning like an inferno.

He stops only inches from taking my hand.

I squeeze my eyes shut with a groan. "Fuck, that was strong."

He settles into a crouch beside me. "It has to be Milena."

I try to breathe out the hum of energy the shock left within me. Although the immediate streak of light has disappeared, it's left a bright line across my sight.

I point in that direction, slightly right of the path we were taking. "The power came from there."

His gaze narrows. "That's farther north than we were expecting."

I shake off the last of the aftershocks, making sure my palm has stopped burning before I take Erik's hand. Once I'm back on my feet, he becomes very still again.

"The wolves are gone," he says.

"Where?"

"Back into the forest. The energy must have startled them."

"It was stronger than any monster's energy I have ever felt." Stronger even than the energy I felt from my sister. "What about the other presence you sensed?"

"Silent," Erik replies. "Gone, maybe. I can't tell."

We make it another hundred paces before the trees begin to thin and the edge of the forest becomes visible in the distance.

Beyond it, all I can make out is that the landscape is a mass of white.

Fresh air filters toward us—freezing air that makes me grateful for the pelt.

The trees around us now have brown leaves and many in the distance seem to have lost their leaves altogether.

A white, powdery substance covers them and is sprinkled on the ground underneath. It immediately takes me back to the wasteland on the northern side of the city. A field of white ash where the earth burned for so long that even the dirt had been consumed.

White flecks float down in front of me and I find myself frozen to the spot. "White ash."

Erik is a step ahead of me. His boots make a soft, crunching sound in the underbrush that they didn't make before.

He crouches to the ground, gripping the onyx spear in one hand, his breath frosting in the air as he presses the fingertips of his other hand to the white dust.

He shakes his head. "Snow."

I'm equal parts relieved and surprised. Thaden said the outpost was high up, so snow would be likely, but it's a very sudden change from the lush forest environment so close behind us. Until now, not a single snowflake had drifted down through the canopy.

I wish I could see what lies beyond the trees ahead, but all I make out is a wash of white.

Erik has remained at a crouch and when I draw level

with him, I find his features pale and drawn and his gaze far away again.

"Erik?"

He gives himself a shake and rises to his feet. "Let's get a closer look."

Finally, we near the edge of the trees and the landscape becomes clear.

I pull up sharply and so does Erik, both of us crouching and staying close to the ground.

Ahead of us is a large, circular clearing. It's at least a hundred paces wide and deep, and then it simply drops away on all sides except the one we're standing on. There's nothing beyond the clearing but what must be sharp cliffs and blue sky. I could walk across the clearing and step right off the edge.

Snow covers the expanse, built up in drifts so that in places it looks like it could be knee-deep.

A lone tree sits in the middle of the clearing about fifty paces away from where we crouch.

Its trunk is easily the width of two adults standing side by side, but the bark is black and slimy-looking, appearing to consist of thick lengths of wood woven around each other.

Its branches are bare of leaves. Yet perfect, red apples hang from them.

"What is this?" I whisper. "Where is the outpost? The army? The dragons' nest?"

Erik is tense beside me, his gaze flashing across the snowy landscape.

He tilts his head slightly and, after waiting a moment, I ask, "What do you hear?"

"A single heartbeat. Very faint." His brow is furrowed. "I can't pinpoint its exact origin except that it's ahead of us."

He gestures to the snow and confusion thrums through me. "I felt powerful Blacksmith magic coming from this location, but I don't see anyone."

"I feel it, too," he says.

My focus is drawn to the fruit growing from the black tree.

Cold fear creeps down my spine. "Malak altered the nature of apple trees."

"Maybe his sister does the same." Erik appears to study the tree in the distance and the snow all around it. The strain around his eyes increases and he pulls back a little. "I don't like this, Asha. Something doesn't feel right."

"We could wait," I say. "But for how long? We have no guarantees that Thaden will reach us anytime soon. Whatever lies ahead, I'd rather approach it during daylight." I meet his eyes. "Doing nothing is not an option. Neither is turning back."

He hesitates, the tension in his features becoming more intense, but he finally gives me a nod. "If there's danger ahead, we'll face it together."

Slowly, I rise to my feet and slip my satchel from my back.

I pull out my toolbox but leave the silver medallion within it, along with the device I pulled from Erik's heart. I tap the plain, black band as softly as I can, awakening it. Rolling up my right sleeve, I press it to my bicep, where it wraps around me.

I consider the dragon-imprinted band. I can only use it overlaid over the band on my left hand. Otherwise, its power is too strong. But I can't ignore the possibility that I might need it.

I slip it into my pocket.

Erik, too, takes off his satchel, carrying only his weapons.

Taking a deep breath, I center myself. Then I hold my spear ready as we step out into the clearing.

Our footfalls crunch gently in the snow as we test the surface, sinking inches, but it's no worse than the depth of the ash in the wasteland, which I taught myself to navigate.

Carefully, we approach the center of the clearing. Erik scans the horizon while I focus on the tree and its closest surroundings, including the snow drifts that appear deeper on the right side.

I miss a step when I make out white objects sticking out from the drifts.

Another chill rides my spine.

"Those are bones," I whisper.

They're pure white with deep teeth marks, as if they were gnawed clean. There are too many bones to count, all scattered around the clearing, some poking out of the snow in neat rows that indicate they could be rib cages.

"These were four-legged creatures," Erik says with a low growl as he studies the nearest set of bones. His lips twist. "Wolves and deer. Judging by the size of the teeth marks, whatever killed them was larger than them."

"A dragon?"

He scans the horizon and then the bones again. "Smaller than a dragon."

I blow out an exhale, steadying my nerves, and we continue toward the tree.

As we near it, its ropey trunk becomes clearer. Each

thick strand is glistening and slimy, all knotted together and reaching up and outward into the shape of dark branches.

The crimson apples gleam where they hang, swaying from short stems when the breeze picks up.

Snowflakes blow across the clearing.

"The heartbeat is coming from the tree," Erik says, keeping his voice low, holding his spear ready. "From the other side."

My own heart beats faster as we take a wide path to the left, where the snow is shallower.

As we pass by, the boughs creak and sway, a groaning sound in the heavy silence.

The other side of the trunk comes into view.

I freeze, my breath stilling. "What...?"

"The fuck?" Erik snarls.

I struggle to comprehend what I'm seeing.

A dark-haired woman is encased in the ropey trunk, her black hair twined between the strands of the woody threads. Her legs are nearly completely concealed by the tree's trunk while parts of her torso are visible, along with her pale face.

Her eyes are closed, but I recognize her. I was only five when I last saw Milena Ironmeld, but I have no doubt.

"It's her," I whisper. "It's Milena."

My focus falls to her torso, where her arms are folded across her chest in the shape of an X.

Oh... fuck...

Her right hand is missing.

Her power has been cut from her body.

I struggle to voice what I'm seeing. "If she doesn't have her power, what did I sense? And what the hell happened to her?"

"Asha," Erik growls, his focus flying to our surroundings. "Something is very wrong here."

I couldn't agree more. But the way Milena's head is tilted to the side and the blue tinge in her lips, the way the tree sap oozes down her hair...

A certainty fills me and it's as strong as the conviction I felt when I made the choice to save Erik's life. "I can't leave her here."

I grit my teeth against the sheer contradiction between my need to help her and my vow to end her. A sharp and unavoidable conflict, and yet here it is.

"I'll deal with her when she's free."

Before I can take a step closer, Erik's hand wraps around my arm.

"Asha, no!" The sudden, deep growl in his voice, the stern command, snaps my focus to him.

His chest is rising and falling rapidly, and in his eyes, all I see is fear.

"I won't lose you here," he snarls. "Not in the snow. Not now. Not ever."

My lips part, a quick breath. I remember how still he became when he'd first stepped onto the snowy undergrowth at the edge of the trees. And then I remember back at the castle when he was dying and the way he gripped my hand and spoke of snow.

Now, he looks ready to scoop me up and carry me out of here if he has to.

"Okay," I whisper, wrapping my hand around his. "Let's go. We can come back—"

As I step toward him, I'm suddenly aware of movement to my left from within the snow drifts.

No, not from *within* them. An entire snow drift bursts upward, revealing an enormous body covered in pure, white fur, camouflaged against the icy backdrop.

I catch a flash of black claws and register a bear-like body with six powerful legs before a creature of nightmares knocks me down.

CHAPTER 33

I hit the ground, sending snow flying up around me, the bear's teeth descending to my neck, but my instincts have kicked in and my left hand is outstretched.

I make contact with the creature's chest in the heartbeats it takes for its jaws to descend and its claws to close around my shoulders, hips, and thighs.

Within my mind, I'm screaming. *Stone!*

My power's response is instant. Dark energy strikes through my body and into my palm, shooting into the bear's chest.

But in that very same instant, I'm aware of an even darker power rushing toward me from within the creature's heart, meeting the energy I'm streaming into it.

In that moment, I have a horrifying realization.

It *wants* my power.

I sense my energy rush through its limbs, sense the surge of strength and the coiling of muscles in all of its legs, as if it's feeding off my magic.

Growing stronger with every second that I press my palm against it.

I'm screaming, but Erik's roar is clear in my ears. His body is a blur as he rams into the beast, knocking it to the side.

Its claws were already descending into my flesh so it takes me with it for a second before it lets go. I don't have time to check, but I'm nearly certain the cuts are shallow.

I roll to the side, coming up at a crouch, my heart pounding.

Several paces away from me, Erik stands between me and the bear. His hunting knife is buried to the hilt in its neck, but the blade barely slows the creature down.

Erik has already nocked two arrows, letting them fly the moment the beast rears up on its hind legs. They meet the creature's chest, but once again, the beast doesn't slow. It charges forward, swiping at Erik.

Its claws slash across the air so fast that I can't follow them. Every cut could disembowel or dismember him, but Erik is fast, evading the strikes. As he leaps backward, he's nocking two more arrows and letting them loose.

It's only been seconds, but I prepare to launch myself back into the fight.

I can't use my raw power. It only made the bear stronger —although I have no idea how.

But I have plenty of weapons at my disposal.

My spear is three paces away, where the bear's initial strike forced me to drop it.

I leap toward it, intending to throw it through the bear's head, only to trip and fall, nearly impaling my hand on a jagged bone in the snow.

What the fuck?

I'm suddenly face down in the ice and trying to understand what I tripped on. I was aware of every bone, conscious of the uneven ground. I *don't* trip. Not even in the Sunken Bog with all its rotted vines.

Twisting, I seek the source of my downfall.

At the same moment, a shadow rises over me.

Oh, fuck, no.

Nearby, the tree is unwinding itself and one of its woody ropes is hooked around my ankle.

Nearer to its trunk, it holds Milena's unconscious body to the side, dangling her as if she were a doll, while other parts of its trunk strike toward me. Thick, slimy wood snakes around my feet, wrapping all the way to my thighs and yanking me toward it.

I manage to twist so I'm facing upward, using my stomach muscles to stretch toward the rope.

I slap my left hand against it. *Dust!*

But the moment my power streams through my palm, I sense it energize the tree, just like it did with the bear.

Dark power streams visibly toward the tree's trunk, which splits in countless places, and then my vision fills with woody stems and crimson apples that suddenly fully untwine in a mass of black and red threads.

The boughs above me thump down, smacking into the snow, as if they would crush me, while the woody stems from the trunk race across the ground, wrapping around my legs and toward my neck.

Once again abandoning my raw power, my thoughts fly to the weapons I can make with my medallion. Fuck it, I'll use the dragon-imprinted medallion if I have to.

As I twist as fast as I can, evading the crushing thumps from above, my left hand slaps across the medallion on my arm and a command flies through my mind.

Axe!

The weapon forms in an instant and I hack at the nearest woody rope, angling the blade so I don't cut myself in the process.

The thread snaps, but another takes its place, this one a bough from above me that splits into multiple strands, each one snapping at my limbs, attempting to wrap around them, the ooze coating them feeling like sticky tar.

I slice through each new woody thread as fast as I can, horribly aware that if they wrap around my arms and legs at the same time, they could tear my limbs from my torso.

The air around me is now filled with ribbons of darkness, all of them extending from the tree's trunk. All of them closing in around me.

Panic sets in.

Through the haze of fear, I'm conscious of Erik fighting the bear, aware of blood running down his face and chest. Conscious that he's shouting my name.

Black ooze drips down onto my hair and body, sticking to me as I thrash and reach for the dragon-imprinted medallion, preparing for the fury I'll feel in it. A spiraling, crimson ribbon smacks it out of my hand, propelling it through a closing gap between black threads.

In the next instant, my axe is wrenched from me. Then thrown beyond me.

Ropes are now wrapped around my torso, stomach, and legs, not pulling outward like I feared, but pressing inward.

It feels like they're forming a cocoon around me. A cage.

The same kind that enclosed Milena.

At the corner of my eye, I'm suddenly aware of a red apple morphing into the shape of a stinger. It darts from side to side, following my thrashing movements as if it's preparing to strike.

It dawns on me then that this tree isn't trying to rip me apart.

It's trying to spin a web of woody threads around me, the same way a spider binds its prey in a cocoon before it bites and injects its poison.

I scream and seek the fury in the medallion on my hand, my ears filled by my own pounding heartbeats.

I have to be able to use my power.

It *has* to work.

My left hand slides against the side of the cocoon already partially formed around me, but once again, the flow of power only sends more energy through the tree, the strength in the cage around me increasing.

The more anger and rage I feed into it, the angrier and more malicious it grows.

But if that's the case...

As the stinger strikes toward me, I close my eyes, exhale, and dig deep, seeking another emotion and letting it rise within me.

Peace.

Energy sparks within my palm, so strong that it's a burst of light behind my closed eyelids.

Beauty.

Like blue leaves and clear water and the color of Erik's eyes.

Calm.

Like slow footsteps and a gentle breeze and the soothing brush of fingertips across my back.

Happiness.

The hint of a smile, the warmth of a hug, a kind word.

I exhale, conscious of the lifting darkness around me and the continuing streams of light pulsing from my hand into the wooden surface I'm touching.

I push away the trickle of fear I feel before I open my eyes, worried that the peace I'm feeling could simply be because the stinger has done its work. It may have stabbed me and a cruel, euphoric poison is lulling me into a false sense of safety.

Beside me, a new tree has formed.

I find myself kneeling in the snow, my left hand pressed to the threads that are rapidly forming within its trunk. Strong branches grow across the air above me. The apples are gone and in their place are bright, blue leaves, each one glistening with droplets of dew that are quickly freezing into the shape of snowflakes.

A single, black rope remains directly in front of me, wrapped around Milena's waist, but it lowers her to the snowy ground, placing her so that her head rests in my lap, her body draped to my right.

She's breathing, but she's unconscious and horribly pale.

The last black rope retracts, lifting upward, healthy bark building along its length until it forms a new bough.

I take a deep, shuddering breath. I'll need time to process what I did and figure out *how*, but right now, I don't have that time.

Whatever relief I feel is broken by a nearby shout.

I wrench my palm from the newly formed tree.

Ten paces away, the snow is splattered with blood. The bear rears up on its hind legs again, and Erik rises from a crouch where he must have tumbled across the ground. His back is to me. I can't see his face or chest to know how badly he might be wounded.

My heart thuds with fear for his life.

I'm preparing to slide Milena to the ground and jump to my feet when Erik's roar freezes me to the spot.

His voice no longer sounds like his own.

Shivers cascade down my spine as the same guttural wolf's growl that he used last night echoes through my hearing.

But that's not all.

Shock fills me when claws as black and solid as titanium extend from the fingertips of both his hands.

He launches himself at the bear, his claws slicing right through its chest. The bear screams as Erik's fists drive deep into its torso before he wrenches his hands back, tearing the beast's chest apart.

The bear hits the ground and Erik leaps backward, clear of its flailing legs.

Finally, the creature lies still in the snow.

Silence falls, broken only by Erik's harsh breathing.

He rises to his feet, his back to me.

Blood and gore drip from his fingers, sliding down the black claws of his left hand, while his right fist is closed.

Slowly, he turns back to me and that's when I see that both of his eyes are amber. Both shaped like a wolf's eyes.

His lips are drawn back, revealing sharp teeth.

Gradually, his features change. His canines retract until they appear human again. His eyes shift back to their human shape and color. The hunch in his shoulders eases.

His breathing remains rapid and there's a new fear in his eyes as he says, "I didn't know how to tell you."

CHAPTER 34

My heart is in my throat.

It makes sense to me now that I saw a flash of black around Erik's hand last night when he confronted the wolves. He was facing away from me at the time and for all I know, he'd bared his teeth at those predators as well as showing them his claws.

I remain quiet and still in the face of this revelation. "When did it first happen?"

"Back at the fae castle. I woke up with these claws and then discovered I could put them away. I told myself I wouldn't use them." He looks away, his hair falling across his face the way he used to hide his wolf's features. "I don't want to be a beast anymore."

My heart hurts. "Did I do this to you when I removed the device?"

He nods. "You must have. I couldn't control my wolf's features before that."

I remember my thoughts in the moment before I pulled

the mechanism from his heart. I'd commanded the remaining metal to come away and leave him whole.

I could have ripped the wolf from him, but I didn't.

I'd asked for wholeness.

I consider the tree now standing to my left and all the branches and sapphire leaves, how strong and healthy they are.

Creation is in my bones.

Fight the old and find the new.

That impulse... Was it mine all along?

"I'm not afraid of what you can do," I say. "You have a choice now. Freedom to use your strengths when you want to. Or not."

"You gave me freedom," he says quietly. "What I wanted for you, you've given to me."

When he remains where he is, I hold out my hand to him. "Don't stay away from me, Erik."

He approaches slowly, dropping to a kneeling position beside me. His clothing is torn in places, but like me, his wounds appear shallow.

As he lowers himself down, he extends his right hand and unfurls his fist.

Another titanium device rests in it.

"I ripped this from the bear's heart," he says.

First, I press my hand to his cheek, reaffirming what I said. He closes his eyes briefly and accepts my touch.

Then I focus on the bloody mechanism in his palm.

It's like the one I pulled from his chest to the extent that it has many finely-crafted parts, but instead of wolf heads, it's in the shape of bear heads facing each other.

Like the device from Erik's heart, this one has become dull, its energy depleted. Lifeless metal now.

"Another device," he says. "Styled differently. More intricate. Certainly a different Blacksmith's work."

If I weren't so horrified at what the device achieved, I'd have to admire the skill it would have taken to create it.

"The bear absorbed my power and created more energy from it," I say. "It was like pouring water onto a thirsty plant."

I shiver a little. When Erik was dying, I avoided using my raw power on him, but now I wonder... Would he have reacted the same way the bear did? Would my magic have fed the darkness of the device embedded in his heart?

I'll never know.

Erik nods. "This particular design must have also allowed the bear to stifle its heartbeat and breathing. I didn't detect its presence until it rose up from the snow."

I nod. He would have warned me otherwise. "There must have been a device like this in the tree, too."

Judging by the design—a bear design for a monstrous bear, just as the device in Erik's heart was a wolf—I wonder if the device within the tree is in the shape of a spider.

I don't plan on digging it out to know for sure. All I know is that it must also be spent, its energy depleted.

Milena's head suddenly feels heavier in my lap. Her hair is draped across my leg and into the snow, her black pants and tunic are torn, and her lips have remained blue. She's shorter than I remember, but I was only a small child when I had interacted with her.

"I wonder if Milena designed these monsters," I say.

"If she did, her own creations turned on her."

Just as Erik destroyed Malak.

"Then there is some justice in that," I say quietly.

Erik considers the tree for a moment and I'm surprised when a hint of a smile lifts his lips. "You made something beautiful."

Happiness.

My heart lifts a little. "I fed it peace."

He reaches out his hand, palm up. I rest my free hand in it. A quiet touch as we kneel in the snow beneath this tree.

I know we need to get up, keep moving, figure out how to bind Milena before she wakes up. If she ever does. But there's something so fragile about this moment, so delicate that I don't want to move.

"Asha, I need to ask you something." Erik takes a deep breath and suddenly, that's all I hear. That single breath, as if whatever he's going to say could break him.

At my nod, he speaks, his voice low and soft. "Do you remember when we first met?"

I could never forget. "In the throne room."

He's very still. "Before that."

Before the throne room?

"Do you remember the snow?"

A sense of unease builds within me. My focus flies to our surroundings. Suddenly cold. Chilling. "We met in the throne room. You'd killed my parents. You broke down the door."

His eyes are deep amber for a moment, then gray again, their shifting shape taking my breath away. "That's when you first looked me in the eyes."

I remember that moment. Erik's gaze bored into me, as if he'd been trying to pull from me every fear and imperfection.

And then he says, "But that wasn't the first time we met."

"Erik, I don't—"

His hand closes more tightly around mine. "There are things I need to tell you and this is where I need to start."

The shakiness in his voice, the uncertainty, keeps me frozen to the spot. There's still so much I don't know about him. Some of it may be too painful to speak about. The loss of his family, the pain that was inflicted on him, the rage that must have driven him after he was changed.

"The first time we met, I didn't know who you were," he says. "I didn't know you were a Blacksmith. I wasn't your enemy. You weren't my enemy. You were just a girl in the snow. And I was—"

Milena stirs in my lap, giving a groan.

Erik is immediately focused on her, his claws snapping out and descending to her throat.

My left hand flies to her neck, pressing to her skin, but I restrain my power.

If Milena threatens us, she doesn't stand a chance.

But it's not the danger she poses that worries me most in this moment.

It's whatever truth Erik was about to tell me.

His focus is on her. His shoulders are hunched and a mask of resignation has slipped over his features.

The fragile moment is broken and all I can do is quietly vow that we will have it again.

I can't force truth and trust, but it's building between us, and all I can do is give it space to grow.

Milena's eyes open, an inky dark-blue as her lips move with the faintest sound. "Am I... free?"

"You are. But be warned, we are not your friends." I lift my left hand and hover it next to her face so she can see my medallion.

A faint crease appears in her forehead as her gaze passes across my hair and eyes and then to my palm. She seems to immediately recognize the medallion. "My brother's metal..."

Her gaze slips to the branches above us, her eyes widening as she focuses on the new boughs and blue leaves.

"So beautiful." She gives a soft exhale, seeming transfixed by the swaying branches and unworried about the threat of death. "You must be Asha Silverspun. Only you could do this. And with my brother's medallion, no less."

Her eyes suddenly glisten, a surprising rush of tears. "I was right about you." Her face falls. "But the pain I must have caused you, leaving you hammerless—"

My jaw clenches. *Pain and nearly irreparable damage.*

It's Erik who reacts, snarling at her, and once again, she startles, focusing on him and then on his claws, which have remained at her neck.

Strangely, she seems to only notice them now, but again, the threat doesn't seem so important as the fact that he has claws. "Erik," she rasps, her eyes filling with tears again. "I heard you had become a wolf. I hoped it wasn't so."

Erik stiffens. "How do you know my name?"

Milena's eyes are more alert with every passing second, but she hasn't moved a muscle of her body yet, and I'm starting to wonder if she can.

She looks past me, as if she expects to see something. "But where is...?"

Her voice fades off and her lips purse, then her brow furrows. Confusion filters through her expression. "Wait... I don't remember... How did I...?"

Her gaze flits between us, her expression growing increasingly confused. Then in the next instant, her expression clears.

She asks again, "Am I free?"

My lips purse and my brow furrows at her repetition and the way she seems unaware of the danger we pose to her.

Erik gives a heavy exhale. "Her mind might be damaged."

I can't disagree. I can only imagine what nightmares she might have experienced when she was encased in the tree and how her mind tried to cope with them.

On top of that, the loss of her power may well have shattered parts of her logic and reason and her ability to remain lucid.

But it doesn't erase her past actions.

I can't allow myself to feel pity for her, knowing what she did to Thaden and the dragon.

"Milena," I say, my voice hard. "I'm going to chain you now. I will feed you and make sure you're warm and then you're going to tell me about the dragon you killed—"

"Dragon?" Her arms twitch, the first sign of movement in her body, but her face has drained of blood. "Dragon!"

A shudder passes through her. "Oh, no." She gasps. "Lysander is dead!"

Her hand grabs mine, even though she comes very close to cutting her fingers on Erik's claws with the movement.

"He did this!" she hisses. "*He* killed Lysander. He betrayed me and caged me and—"

She's suddenly frozen. Abruptly silent. Her wide eyes become blank and she stares sightlessly upward.

A moment later, she mumbles, "I don't remember... Who was he?" She peers at me hopefully. "Do you know?"

I watch her carefully, once again wary of any sudden moves in case this whole thing is an act to catch us off guard.

In the next moment, her brow smooths out and she takes another penetrating look at me, as if she's seeing me for the first time. "Asha, you're all grown up. But, dear girl, what happened to your hair?"

I turn to Erik, register his wariness, and try to focus on the most important thing Milena said. "If she didn't kill the dragon, who did?"

"*He betrayed me*," Erik replies. "That's what the dragon itself said. That's what Milena said just now."

Cold is creeping through my bones. "There's someone else mixed up in this. There has to be. Someone hiding in the shadows."

"Possibly using Milena as a puppet," Erik says.

"Puppets! Dragons!" Milena jolts and gives such a sudden gasp that the air shrieks between her lips. "This is a trap!"

She shoves at me, even though she's too weak to move me an inch. "Run, Asha Silverspun. Run, *now*!"

I've barely registered her panic when screaming wind drowns out her voice, rushing from the direction of the forest.

Snow billows around us, spraying across my vision in thick streams. Our pelts fly across the clearing. Even the dropped spears wobble in the snow where they lie. Blue leaves rip from the branches above us and rush across the clearing, all the way past the cliff's edge and out into the sky.

In the distance, a ferocious roar sounds.

"*Go!*" Milena screams. "*Run!*"

CHAPTER 35

We don't have time to ask questions—even if I thought Milena could answer them.

Erik's arms wrap around us both, wrenching me to my feet and reaching for Milena, taking her from me.

I dart toward my medallions, scooping up the plain one, which is still in the form of an axe, and slipping the dragon-imprinted one into my pocket.

I seek the location of the onyx spears, but they're both too far away—it'll take too long to reach them.

The only way out of this clearing is back through the forest.

But that's the direction from which the new threat comes.

A bronze beast shoots toward us across the treetops. Its wings wide enough to block out the afternoon light. Its size and speed make my heart stop.

We've only made it three steps around the tree when a

beautiful dragon drops into the space at the edge of the forest, blocking our escape.

A beautiful, angry, *grieving* dragon.

Its head thrashes back and forth, its voice filled with pain. "Blacksmiths! Murderers! My son's blood is on your hands."

This has to be Graviter Rex, the dragon king himself. The one the fae never want to meet, let alone fight.

Sleek, bronze scales run from his snout to his tail, while his eyes are like brilliant gems, the horns on his head are as sharp-looking as daggers, and his teeth and talons are all larger than my arms.

I meet Erik's eyes for the briefest moment before he turns and places Milena onto the ground in front of the tree.

Her wide eyes are filled with fear and she's whimpering up at him. "Run... run..."

But there's nowhere to escape that the dragon's talons won't reach or his tail can't swipe. The clearing simply isn't large enough. In fact, it will only take him seconds to reach us if he decides to charge at us.

Erik straightens. His claws extend while his teeth sharpen.

I grip my axe and ready myself, preparing to change my weapon's form if I need to.

"Graviter Rex," I shout, standing firm as the dragon takes a thudding step toward us. "I didn't hurt your son, but I heard his voice. I felt his pain—"

"What do you know of pain?" Graviter's talons rake through the snow as he thrashes his head again. "You are a Blacksmith! There is nothing but betrayal and darkness in your heart."

For a short time, I believed that to be true. But not now.

"My name is Asha Silverspun," I say. "I'm not your enemy. I don't want to fight you or kill you—"

"My only child is dead!" he screams. With his breath comes heat, the burning light of dragon's fire glimmering around his snout.

The snow at his feet begins to melt. White bones swirl within the sludge.

"The light has been taken from my heart," he cries. "Do not try to reason with me, Blacksmith. I will not stop until your race is wiped from the face of this Earth. That is the only way this evil will come to an end."

I exhale a heavy breath. Beside me, Erik has lowered his fists. He, too, once wanted to annihilate all Blacksmiths.

This dragon doesn't know us, must surely know we had nothing to do with his son's death, but rage and pain are clearly driving him.

Heat continues to build around his mouth. "I promise I will kill you quickly, Asha Silverspun. The wolf, too. Even Milena. But when I find Malak's son, I will tear him apart, limb by cursed limb."

Malak's son?

I'm suddenly frozen to the spot. Erik has jolted backward.

I can barely form a whisper. "*Malak had a son?*"

Erik's shaking his head, his eyes wide. He keeps his voice low. "If he did, he didn't know."

I believe him. The shock radiating off Erik is palpable.

"The Betrayer!" Graviter snarls. "A child with eyes and hair as dark as night and all his father's cursed strength. Milena brought him to us. She thought he would undo the damage his father wrought on this land." Graviter Rex spits. "There is no *good* in pure darkness."

My mind is a storm of thoughts, all centered around a single fact: On the night she supposedly died, Milena went out to welcome a new Blacksmith baby into the world.

That baby wasn't in the city eleven years later when Erik ended Malak's reign.

"The baby," I whisper. "Milena must have taken him with her when she left."

"Not a baby anymore," Erik says. "A grown man."

I shiver. "He would be capable of... anything."

He would have the power to create monsters. To fashion dark devices like his father did—especially because he would have had the prototype that his father created, since Milena stole it and presumably took it with her.

If Malak's son is behind all of this, then it explains why Milena's actions seemed so contradictory—it answers the questions I had about why she would alienate the humans and the dragons.

She didn't. It was him.

And the message she sent, saying that she wants her city back... If she has merely been a puppet, then it's because *he* wants his city back. He wants the city that belonged to his father and would have belonged to him.

In response to that message, we came out to hunt Milena.

We found her on this cliff's edge, where he left monsters to kill us and, if they failed, well...

He could count on Graviter Rex to seek revenge and finish us off.

A trap, indeed.

All of the pieces come together within my mind while heat waves shimmer across the air between us and the dragon.

I don't know if Erik has come to the same conclusions that I have, and there isn't time to find out. Graviter Rex is prowling toward us, his head low and teeth bared. He'll reach us within seconds.

"Graviter Rex won't stop," Erik says quietly, and I'm shocked by the resignation now settling across his features. "I know the pain he's feeling. It only ends with death."

Sudden panic threatens to overwhelm me. Even with all the power in my hand, all the cruelty I've overcome, I'm weak compared to this dragon. "My power won't work on him," I say. "Dragon scales are a shield against Blacksmith power."

"Malak's son did it somehow," Erik says.

"Even if I knew how, his way can't be my way."

The corners of Erik's mouth hitch up. He reaches across to me as heat waves drift around us and cause the snowflakes on the leaves above us to drip onto our hair.

He pulls me close, his lips brushing mine.

"Fight until you can't fight anymore, Asha." His voice grows more intense. "But if you see a chance to run, take it. Don't look back."

With that, he turns toward the heat, launching himself across the melting snow, kicking up water as he sprints toward Graviter.

"Go," Milena whispers, her dark eyes wide as she looks up at me from where she slumps beneath the tree.

I don't hesitate another moment, breaking into a run, following Erik's path.

Ahead of me, he darts across the ground, feinting left and right, before he leaps at Graviter's neck, his claws outstretched.

Graviter is breathtakingly fast, following Erik's movements before his front paw snaps out, his talons cutting across the air right in front of Erik's chest.

Erik twists midair, narrowly evading being shredded into pieces.

I'm mere seconds behind him, taking advantage of the distraction to jump toward the exposed side of Graviter's neck.

As I leave the ground, I send a command to the axe to transform again.

Chain!

A black chain instantly extends from my hand, sailing up and over the back of Graviter's head.

Latch!

The far end of the chain forms a hook, swinging under the dragon's chin and back to the rest of the chain, forming a tight noose—the end of which I'm holding as I soar toward his head. I command it to shorten and, at the last moment before I would hit his neck, I kick out my feet, propelling myself backward.

I pull as hard as I can on the chain.

Graviter's focus whips to me, right before he would have closed his teeth around Erik's torso.

The new distraction allows Erik to land on Graviter's back, but now the dragon's attention is on me and—*damn*—I don't like being this close to his teeth. Or the flames I can now see licking around them.

Erik doesn't slow. Landing on Graviter's upper back, he drives his claws down against the dragon's neck.

He slices right through Graviter's scales.

Right across his spine.

Graviter screams, his legs buckle, and for a second, I think he's going to drop to the ground, but then he thrashes wildly.

I try to hold on, but it's impossible. I'm flung into the air.

Erik is poised to drive his claws once more into Graviter's neck, this time right at the base of his skull, but the dragon wrenches around so suddenly that Erik is knocked in the same direction as me, somersaulting to control his fall.

I hit the ground, rolling to my feet.

That's when I feel the fire.

Flames burst across the air behind me, as hot as forge-fire, blasting my surroundings with amber light and a heat that could melt the skin from my bones.

I'm one second ahead of Erik—one moment where I've regained my balance and my muscles can coil faster than his.

I throw myself into him as hard as I can, wrapping my arms around him and calling on all of my strength to propel us out of the flames.

Heat rages across me in a widening blast that follows our movement across the air, but then we're bursting beyond its edge.

The ground rushes up at us and I prepare to get my legs under me when I sense Erik's sharp breath against my cheek.

He gives a cry of warning. "Asha!"

Graviter's paw swipes through the blaze behind us, the speed with which he followed us filling me with fear.

His paw knocks into us, throwing us down into the ground.

Erik bounces against the hard stone that was, only minutes ago, covered in snow. I hit it side-on, my shoulder crunching and pain bursting through my head as I, too, bounce against the stone.

My vision flashes to darkness.

Then brightness again as I regain consciousness with Erik's name on my lips.

A weight presses down on my chest and Graviter's shadow looms over me. "Asha Silverspun. You look nothing like your silver-haired ancestors."

I can't reply. Can hardly breathe. His paw rests on me with a strength I'm powerless to fight against. The tips of his talons prick my sides. All it will take is a flex of his muscles and he will impale me where I lie.

At the edge of my vision, burning leaves waft through the air. I can't see or hear Milena. I don't know what's happened to her.

But I finally see Erik where he lies nearly ten paces away. He's facing away from me, his clothing charred, water sliding around him. I don't think he could have tumbled that far on his own and I'm filled with fear that in the seconds I was blacked out, Graviter has hurt him.

I will him to move. *Wake up. Get up, Erik.*

Graviter follows my focus to Erik, then moves his other leg and blocks Erik from my view.

I can't stop the rage and fear rushing through my mind, the barriers I've placed around the dark medallion breaking down.

Gasping for air, I force sound from my mouth. "If you want me dead, get on with it!"

Graviter lowers his face to mine, new heat wafting from his mouth. "First, you will tell me where to find Malak's son."

As he speaks, he eases up the pressure on my torso.

Dragging air into my chest, I stare up at him, a cold hatred building within me. "I don't know where he is. I've never met him."

"*Liar!*" Graviter roars, sending heat billowing around me, scorching my skin.

I scream back at him. "Why the fuck do you think I know where he is?"

"Because you *reek* of him." Graviter's nostrils flare and his lips twist.

"I... What?"

The weight on me lifts a little more as Graviter's paw moves down my body, the tip of his talon stopping at my hip and deftly slicing my pocket open.

The dragon-imprinted medallion drops to the ground.

It splashes into the shallow water, but Graviter stabs it with the tip of his talon, pinning it to the spot so it doesn't slip away.

"Here is my proof," he snarls.

I stare at the medallion in confusion, trying to understand what he thinks it proves.

And then... a horrifying possibility hits me.

No.

He has my family.

Graviter bares his teeth at me, the threat of flames only

seconds away. "Blacksmith, with your last breath, you will tell me: Where is Thaden Kane Ironmeld?"

Find out what happens next in
A Storm Like Iron.

Then complete the series with
A Soul Like Glass
the final book with no cliffhanger.

A STORM LIKE IRON
(KINGDOM OF BETRAYAL #3)

Betrayal is in my blood...

Coauthored with debut author Julian Madden!

Content information: A Storm Like Iron is fantasy romance, enemies to lovers, the third in the Kingdom of Betrayal series.

Recommended reading age is 17+ for sex scenes, mature themes, violence, and language. Ends on a cliffhanger.

*This is NOT a standalone. Contains the next instalment in Asha and the Vandawolf's story.

A SOUL LIKE GLASS
(KINGDOM OF BETRAYAL #4)

To save my family, I will become the betrayer...

Content information: *A Soul Like Glass is fantasy romance, enemies to lovers, the fourth and final book in the Kingdom of Betrayal series.*

Recommended reading age is 17+ for sex scenes, mature themes, violence, and language.

NO cliffhanger.

RECOMMENDED READING ORDER

Many of Everly Frost's books are set in the same world:
the Supernatural Legacy world.

They're written so that each series can be read in any order, with a
few exceptions highlighted below.

If you'd like a suggested reading order, here it is!

ASSASSIN'S MAGIC - COMPLETE

(Urban Fantasy Romance)

1. Assassin's Magic

2. Assassin's Mask

3. Assassin's Menace

4. Assassin's Maze

5. Assassin's Match

ASSASSIN'S ACADEMY - COMPLETE

(Dark Academy Romance)

*Best read after the Assassin's Magic series

1. Rebels

2. Revenge

SOUL BITTEN SHIFTER - COMPLETE

(Dark Urban Fantasy Romance)

1. This Dark Wolf

2. This Broken Wolf

3. This Caged Wolf

4. This Cruel Blood

DEMON PACK - COMPLETE

(Dark Paranormal Romance)

1. Demon Pack

2. Demon Pack: Elimination

3. Demon Pack: Eternal

STORM PRINCESS - COMPLETE

(High Fantasy Romance)

1. Book 1

2. Book 2

3. Book 3

BRIGHT WICKED - COMPLETE

(High Fantasy Romance)

1. Bright Wicked

2. Radiant Fierce

3. Infernal Dark

SUPERNATURAL LEGACY - COMPLETE

(Angels and Dragon Shifters)

1. Hunt the Night

2. Chase the Shadows

3. Slay the Dawn

4. Claim the Light

DARK MAGIC SHIFTERS

(Dark Urban Fantasy Romance)

*Best read after the Supernatural Legacy series

1. Wolf of Ashes

2. Bond of Flames

3. Crown of Fate

KINGDOM OF BETRAYAL

(High Fantasy Romance)

*This is the final series in this world and ties the world history together.

1. A Sky Like Blood

2. A Sin Like Fire

3. A Storm Like Iron

4. A Soul Like Glass

ABOUT THE AUTHOR

Everly Frost is the USA Today Bestselling author of YA and New Adult urban fantasy and paranormal romance novels. She spent her childhood dreaming of other worlds and scribbling stories on the leftover blank pages at the back of school notebooks. She lives in Brisbane, Australia with her husband and two children.

amazon.com/author/everlyfrost

facebook.com/everlyfrost

instagram.com/everlyfrost

bookbub.com/authors/everly-frost

goodreads.com/everlyfrost

Milton Keynes UK
Ingram Content Group UK Ltd.
UKHW010739080324
438959UK00004B/241